Power Struggle

When the lights go out...
where will you be?

A Novel by
Linda J. Pedley

Look for this novel in ebook and paperback.

Power Struggle
ISBN #978-0-9866981-6-3

I dedicate this book to my dad, Henry J. Pedley.

The first draft of this novel was started in a small notebook at his bedside while he recovered in hospital from a near fatal accident. National Novel Writing Month (NaNoWriMo) in 2010 proved to be a crazy time but produced a work born of overwhelming emotional and physical stress. Its completion and publication are a tribute to the power of healing and how we deal with life's challenges.

The story relates to the bigger world around us – and both of us having worked in the electrical industry, realize the growth required while appreciating the roots from where we came. It is also a salute to the strength and endurance within our own hearts as we face struggles along our journey.

The mercury on the gauge reflected a mid-day heat at 5:00 am – unheard of in the Alberta countryside even during the hottest summer months. July brought its share of moisture to a weary land – much needed moisture – necessary to boost a late spring planting and save a pitiful growth of ailing crops. Much of the livestock fared well in the wet, cool weather, able to sustain itself on the cache of Timothy hay farmers stored over the winter. There was a cooperative sharing reminiscent of days long gone and those farmers, still hanging on to their livelihood, lived by that code, though, unspoken. But August was a different story.

The heat wave brought with it new issues and concerns that could not be relieved no matter how much cooperative spirit existed among the rural tradesman. They required the help of modern conveniences and interdependence was the only way they would get through above average heat.

The coolers in the hog barns worked overtime; boosted by rapid interflow connectors running from the ranch's own generators and the hill top turbines. A combination of self-generation and metered power provided the farm its electrical services. During a heat spell, there was no excess to sell back to the grid for extra income – it was consumed to keep the livestock cooled and alive in the soaring temperatures.

The sky was a red blaze over the horizon as the sun stretched its rays to the heavens. Unearthly blood red cloud formations streaked across a hazy morning sky – no almanac predicted such a turn in temperature, especially within a two week span in a province that tended to not see such extremes. It was either wet and cold or dry and moderately hot; the almanac would not proclaim a wealthy year for farmers in 2017.

Martin Wells Senior tested the input valves for the tenth time that morning. It was a process he administered day after day since the hot weather descended upon them in late July. His sunrise check of the Wells ranch confirmed all functioned as required but he took nothing for granted – he just couldn't take the chance. The five hundred head of hogs were his lifeline to clearing a long running debt. The livestock had to make it to market – all five hundred of them. Friday past, the bank called in the ranch loan.

Alberta Rancher's Corporation was insistent, in fact, they were downright demanding. They would not reconsider due to a bad start to the year with an early spring flood that wiped out the newly planted Canola crop. They would not talk about rewriting the loan or reconsidering any of the terms. They had been rather hard to deal with and their reasons involved their perception of dismal farming futures, and the agricultural industry, in general. They had other clients to protect and lending to farmers had not proved to be in their best interests. Following the obligatory "Dear Sir" their letter opened with *"considering the early problems of the year, our risk assessment analysis will not allow us to carry further losses to an unforeseen close. We regret to inform you we are no longer convinced of the ability of the agricultural market to respond to natural disasters."*

"Unforgiving" had been Martin Sr.'s word of choice in the spring – at least in public. In fact, that whole year seemed rather unforgiving – the weather, the bank, and even his son's attitude toward him – all stacked against him. Martin Jr. called him stubborn for holding onto a dying legacy. He couldn't argue with the weather or do anything about it. He couldn't argue with the bank and they were unwilling to give. He wouldn't even argue with his only son. He could do something about that and it came in the form of avoidance. Their conversations escalated to verbal debates over the probability of farmers and farms going the way of the dinosaur.

"Not if there is still a breath of life in me." Martin Sr.'s stance would always end with that statement. He was unwavering in his commitment to the way of life despite the growing hardships.

The introduction of new electrical legislation challenged many to reconsider their chosen livelihoods despite their past and the pathway they thought was theirs, for the long run. The Provincial Electrical Plan (PEP) and the changing government cabinet forced the passing of controversial rulings without the usual public forums. Likened to the Bill 50 Transmission regulations of 2009, the new government chose to make all power decisions "critical" and many plans, once thought innovative, became intrusive and mandatory. The shift in the political climate mirrored the current year's weather – a cool session stormed through the early spring sitting leaving in its wake an ousted premier and an uprooted cabinet.

The vote of non-confidence took many by surprise but the overly cautious Conservatives were blindsided in the movement. A government leader who refused to act quickly on necessary reform yet green lighted billions for big business initiatives was not who a cutting edge province needed at the helm. With worry about the province's global image, an international electrical exchange deal was almost signed – that was, until the truth revealed kickbacks for local companies who signed behind the door distribution contracts – *exclusive* distribution contracts.

This lack of transparency was what closed the current government's term with a proclamation that all energy would again fall into the hands of government control under the newly developed AB Power Corporation. Small companies and electrification units still in existence would be legislated to voluntarily turn over their power company rights to the "powers that be" or they would be mandated under the Corp Phase-out Project.

With the project in place, the new government's updated smart grid plan would be all-consuming. Negotiations began with working out zone deals. Pilot projects were already implemented in the fall of the previous year.

Martin Sr. pulled the switch transfer which allowed a temperature controlled water flow to fill the troughs for his beloved animals. The constant movement of the water not only provided a source of sustenance to the hogs but the continuous flow maintained a cooling effect on the barn through the large pipes running along the perimeter of the buildings. The over precautious farmer didn't need the extra boost the generator and wind turbines provided, as long as the grid supplied the pre-arranged power he needed to the farm. He didn't need the extra but he couldn't take chances, either. His own generators guaranteed a constant power source and it was like a personal insurance policy to Martin – something else eliminated in the farming industry due to the uncertainty of hog futures and canola trading prices.

As support for farmers and the traditional rural life fell away, layer by layer, it pushed the generation farmer into obscurity. Most of the families fled to the urban centers with very little to show for their blood, sweat, and tears.

In the cities they could be guaranteed a living and a home that still had an abundance of modern conveniences, unlike the farm that was fading into history as fast as they could pull the plug on the power lines to them. Many of the older farmers and ranchers, who sold out, took what they could get by accepting the one-time offers meant to coerce them into selling before they really had a chance to reconsider the value and the payout. *That is,* of course, all except those stubborn and tenacious enough to stick it out until what they thought was the end. Someone like Martin Wells Sr.

"No one is going to take what's mine without giving me my worth."

And, so it came to be that he stayed on alone – without his son's help – as one of Alberta's remaining natural hog meat producers. There was still a market demand, albeit a small one, and that was what kept the old man's hopes alive.

"Anyone with a lick of sense will appreciate meat from hogs raised the old fashioned way – not in a controlled, artificial environment where they are inseminated in one end of the processing plant, force fed, and then ground out at the other end. It's not right. It's not natural – ways or times. Anyone with a lick of sense could see the injustice in that."

Martin Wells Jr. tried to see the sense but, although he agreed with his father in principle, he refused to outwardly support his father in a business that would be his eventual death, financially and, God forbid, physically. Without insurance, without financial backing from the bank, and with a continued stress over available and necessary power sources, Martin refused to encourage his father when he could see no positive way out. He would never agree there was worth in the long days starting at 4:00 am to milk a government cash cow. He would, however, do what he thought was best to help even if it wasn't as obvious or relevant to his father. He knew at some time in the future they may see eye to eye but, until then, Martin Jr. was prepared to go his own way and use the business devices he knew would work in today's world.

His father and other hangers-on were determined to pioneer a new rural niche despite the lack of supporting evidence by any government or big business entity that it would succeed.

Nothing would exist as it was by the end of the year. In the year ahead, the 2018 initiative would force a buyout of all remaining farming operations for pennies on the dollar, in an effort to transfer agricultural control, soon to be "agri-manufacturing," to the hands of the government in power at that time.

2017. It was supposed to be a time of rejuvenation and re-energization, but instead, power issues became power struggles that not only encompassed the control of the electrical industry in the province, but also consumed a leadership that lacked control. The dynamic Smart Party took control with promises of a brighter future replacing an aging government regime.

"Martin?"

A feminine voice cut through the drone of the motorized noise in the large barn. Its soft sound was out of place but it soothed the rough edges of the farm life Martin embraced.

Faith was more than just her name. It was a wife's undying support and devotion for a husband and his chosen way of life, one that became hers when she said "I do" many years before. Faith came into Martin's life during his early farm years. Soon after their marriage, his father transferred the reins to the family farm to his capable hands. He took a vow then, to the land and with Faith, never to leave either one, no matter what. She was the one person he could always count on in a land that was fast fading of old family values. She would support him to the end in his endeavors because it was the farm that kept him alive and healthy for a man of his years. At seventy, no one even thirty years his junior, could keep up and no one dared try, for to do so meant to challenge a confidence so deep that failure was inevitable. No one dared – not even Martin Jr.

"I'm over here." His voice was clear and it rose above the whir of the cooling engines. "I'll be in right away, Faith. Is all okay?"

"Just checking on you – it's nice in here. No wonder you spend your time in the barns." Faith's curly white-blond hair stuck to her forehead, wet with perspiration. The mid-morning sun was already ravaging the outside world. "Martin, we should go to town for an early dinner today."

"Hmmm..." Martin was concentrating on the gauges and dials connected to the generator and wind power sources. They were wired to the barn's distributing outlet and recorded usage data that ran in LED precision across the digital display monitor. The biggest benefit "they said" – "they" being the backers of the PEP implementation – was the ability for consumers to view their power consumption and, with a little education and a lot of intimidation, change their usage patterns based on the data received to the meters installed on every customer's property.

"Two-way intrusion," Martin had called it, until he became familiar with reading the data – only then, did he agree to at least review it and make what changes he could, personally. He argued staunchly, though, alongside advocates for rural electrification associations as far back as 2008, his animals would not be able to change their usage patterns.

The farm consumers were not the culprits in the power consumption wars, but the political activists of the time needed a scapegoat. No special allowances would be made to anyone because of the precedent setting nature of such an arrangement. Despite only comprising a small percentage of the actual load in the whole province, farmers were lumped in with everyone else.

Alberta electricity was painted with one powerful brush stroke. The wide sweep advocated a change for all but Martin, and others in similar situations, maintained that their PEP slogan should have been "change or pay through the nose."

The politically diluted ploy pulled all under its blanket policy and even those loyal supporters who blindly thought the smart plan was the best thing "since sliced bread" realized the fallout too late. The white wash covered dirty signatures.

"Marty, did you even hear me?" Her hand touched him softly on the shoulder and he looked her way with a loving smile, one that never left his face, while he was with her. Faith was his hope and he'd do *almost* anything for her ...except leave the farm.

"You've been working so hard and it's so hot. Why don't we go to town for an early dinner?"

"Monitors are accurate and everything seems to be running well. The turbines lack input generation with no wind in this heat." He never meant his comments to ignore or exclude her but rather to confirm to her his prime concern was their future. He had everything riding on the animals he groomed for market.

"The generators are running at capacity though?" Although Faith didn't visit the barns often to employ the inner workings of the farm, she was still aware of the life lines to her husband's livelihood. She understood more than anyone the importance he placed in diligence and the necessity to monitor constantly all power supplies.

"Yes, it's been good so far – green lights."

"So? We can leave them for a bit then?" Her voice was never demanding although, at times, she could be firm. She decided a long time ago, whatever Martin decided, was what she wanted, too.

He would never do anything to cause her distress or concern, and this acceptance was what worked well in her favor. He would do almost anything to please her except entertain conversation destined to be about considering a change in lifestyle. She would love to see him slow down and relax although, secretly, it was her hidden desire to spend more time together. He just wouldn't go... so she quietly did what she needed to do, in hopes that it might happen someday.

"I guess a couple of hours away can't do any harm. As they say, 'a change is as good as a holiday'."

"Good." Faith just smiled, knowing a holiday was a luxury she would never see.

"Back by peak, honey – you know, it's just something I have to do – no one else to depend on these days."

"A couple of hours will do you good, dear. And yes, of course, we can be back at whatever time you decide. Perhaps you can get a well-deserved sleep tonight if the heat doesn't keep us awake."

"Give me a few minutes and I'll be in to change." Martin gave Faith a quick kiss on the cheek but a lingering touch to the side of her face. His smile never faded in her presence because he loved her even more than the first day they met, if that was at all possible.

They dined late afternoon and into the early evening. In the comfort of an air conditioned restaurant they relaxed that August 11th day. It was like an oasis away from the stress and strain of the sixteen hour days and it embraced Martin and Faith in a pleasure to which they did not often indulge. He laughed with her during the meal and their conversation led them from the daily grind. They sat side by side in the booth engaged in each other, thoroughly enjoying their meal. Martin teased the young waitress, who was enthralled with their loving relationship.

"She is much too pretty to have just one man." Martin laughed at Faith's expression of surprise.

"And perhaps, I should be looking for another, too?"

He laughed and drew his wife closer, hugging her lovingly around the shoulders while he kissed her cheek.

"Just teasing, my darling. You are much too pretty, too – but one true love is all anyone needs."

"You are both so sweet. You give me something to look forward to," the young waitress surmised. "A long lasting love is a dream for me… with the right person." She exclaimed her jealousy and expressed a longing to discover something similar for herself. The senior couple, evidently, was still very much in love.

With a generosity unfamiliar to a struggling farmer, Martin left their amicable waitress, Tessa, a large tip and a warm thank you. The meal was a memorable one that both Martin and Faith deserved yet rarely enjoyed. By the time they left the restaurant, their stay extended hours longer than they had originally intended. The sky was clear but darkening as the sun slipped behind the foothills. Traffic was heavy as they maneuvered their way to the connector lanes leading to the highway and the secondary road to the Wells Ranch.

"What is with this damn traffic?"

"Maybe there's an accident?" Faith strained to see over the traffic ahead of them to the next intersection.

"Not sure but it better clear soon – move it, dammit!"

With a blast from the horn, Martin's aggravation with the bumper to bumper traffic escalated. His anger soon chipped away at whatever relaxed feelings were acquired over the afternoon's casual meal. The situation quickly dissolved the cool, collected Martin to a perspiring pool of sweat and swear words.

"Dammit!" His hand hit the steering wheel.

"Marty, calm down. We'll get there." Faith placed a reassuring hand on his knee and he forced a weak smile admitting his overreaction. "Thing's will be fine, Marty. Don't worry."

As if to contradict to her positive assurances, street lights along the West Side Hills Causeway blinked off and on in succession, and then blacked out. In a chain reaction, up the entire Hills district, lights in windows went dark.

Office towers, that usually glowed all night long, were black. It was still light enough outside that all the street lights had not been triggered by the automatic sensory cells. Those already triggered on were now off.

Martin looked over at Faith as she watched the traffic below them on the south exit turn pike come to a screeching halt with a series of hard impact rear end crashes. The traffic lights overseeing the main road no longer demanded stop or go and, for as far as they could see from their vantage point on the overpass, no traffic lights anywhere signaled such control.

"What is going on?" Martin's hands gripped the wheel.

When Martin realized most of the traffic in front of him was backed up with intent to leave via the next exit, he pulled carefully into the left hand lane.

Traffic then inched forward until it passed the last crossroad considered to be within the town's limits. No longer hampered by the stop and go traffic, Martin urged the Escalade to a speed he knew was beyond the limit but within his own abilities to handle. Even with his concern for Faith forefront in his mind, his thoughts were on his farm, and the eminent danger a power outage could cause. He trusted the generator would hold at maximum capacity with the input needed to handle the stress of the heat on that August 11th day.

"Why did we stay so long?"

"We both needed the break, Marty."

"I knew it was a bad idea."

Faith let it go. She knew that arguing with her husband would only aggravate the situation. He would blame himself for letting his guard down no matter what she said.

It never occurred to Martin that the drive from town was as far as it was. At that moment, they could have been hours away instead of only forty minutes. The countryside began to fall into shadows as the sun dipped lower behind the western foothills. The sky was clear and the temperature felt as if it still hovered around the mid-thirties. Martin's hand reached absentmindedly to hold Faith's in his; she squeezed his fingers, knowing he was reciting to himself an underused prayer. She didn't dare look at him – the anger, the worry, the panic – she knew there was nothing she could say to change the course of his thoughts.

Each remaining farm they passed was in twilight shadows. Familiar, odd shapes loomed eerily without the familiar orange glow of yard lights. There was no comforting stream of yellow reflections stretching across the grass from the windows of illuminated barns. As they rounded the top rise near the back quarter of their property, Martin gasped.

From the road they could see there were no green lights along the meters that lined the power grid markers. There were no telltale red warning lights on the panel he mounted outside the barn. There were no pumps running to the feeders drawing water into the pipes that cooled the hog barns. There were no lights, there was no power, and there were no signals. *Just blackness.*

"The barns..." Martin's voice trailed off as he threw the vehicle into park in the middle of the farmyard. He first checked the I-Meter on the grid feeder coming into the farm property. There was no life in the device but the time/date stamp that marked a voluntary shut off or a forced shut down indicated the meter recorded out at 15:21:04 – at 8:18 pm that was almost five hours without power input from the grid.

His only hope lay with the farm's generators. They always managed to kick in and pick up the output needed when the transmission grid reduced power input to end of the line customers or when rolling black outs occurred.

"Martin?" Faith's voice carried with her concern a touch of fear; the silence of night was eerie and she tried to shut out all the horrible scenarios playing in her mind.

"Go inside, Faith, I need to check the barn generators. The grid shut down five hours ago – damn government!"

Martin headed for the barns in running strides and Faith knew when he reached out to touch a water pipe and pulled his hand away quickly that the situation was not going to turn out as they hoped.

All she would remember in the years to come would be the sound of repeated shots. Her eyes closed and she cringed with each pop that broke the night. The first one made her jump and she almost ran outside into the night to the barn and Martin's rescue. But she could not save him from the fate that took the last hope he held in farming.

The next one sent her to the phone and when she could not get a dial tone – the handheld cordless was useless in a power outage – she grabbed her cell phone. So rarely used, it caused her anguish as she fumbled with the multitude of buttons and screens. The third shot accompanied the fast dial for her son's number and she held her breath as she held it to her ear.

"Son – Martin – please come home. Your father needs you."

Martin did not have to ask why. The pleading in his mother's voice, and the use of a cell phone she vowed she'd never need, confirmed there was something beyond what his more than capable mother could handle.

"Mom – I'm on my way – I'm right in town. So, you know forty minutes tops once I get past the traffic."

"Careful, Martin, the lights are out."

"I know, Mom, they're out all over."

"Martin – hurry..."

Another string of gun shots echoed from the direction of the barn and Faith began to sob.

"Your father needs you, now."

She placed the phone on the counter and sat down in a chair near the window, in the dark, to watch for her son. He would approach from town and she was unsure of what he would find. Another round popped and she covered her ears as she hunched over in her chair, eyes closed.

She would not hear the last shot or the silence that followed. She would not hear Martin Jr.'s car screech to a stop in the yard. She would not hear her son scream for his father over the raging flames that consumed the barn and its contents.

Martin sat bolt upright in his bed. The orange glow from the street lights laid broken patterns across the cotton sheet covering his sweat drenched body. The room was heavy with stagnant air and without an open window there was no air movement to cool him. Although winter, it was reminiscent of a not so long ago August night, one that haunted his dreams, one that once in a while crept up on him and assaulted him at times when things were unusually stressful at work. He would sometimes forego sleep on those nights in expectation of the horrible memories. Martin wiped a soaked edge of bedding across his forehead and threw it aside.

He knew without a doubt the hour of the early morning awakening without glancing at the clock. The premise had become an eerie game as he tried to avoid looking at it just to confirm his already knowing suspicions. The dream always woke him exactly at 4:00 am.

He surmised it was a reminder of how he had admonished his father for the ungodly early mornings all those years working a bleak land. As a self-proclaimed punishment, he would rise even before a sliver of light cracked the horizon – that being the point when he finally gave in and turned to stare at the red LED display. He always did despite his attempts not to.

The episodes were so vivid after the death of his father that Martin resigned himself to the services of the company health plan and the council of a well-meaning shrink.

His need for multiple visits was kept a secret but as the events slowly faded to a once in awhile occurrence he let the counseling slide. He chose to avoid the continued professional help although he was not quite sure he would be able to control the constant reminders. In that regard, he became diligent in keeping his own prescription of sleeping pills on hand, just in case.

As he moved past the tragic event and tried to get on with his life, he shrugged it off thinking things had come to pass, and for a couple of months the dreams did not occur. In the back of his mind, triggers remained, and there was always that "once in awhile" occurrence. It was for that reason, he kept the liquor cabinet and the medicine chest well stocked.

Although he could understand the reason for his stress, he did not understand the reason for the recent reoccurrence of the nightmares.

Disturbing images of bullet riddled carcasses burning to ash filled his nights and he woke in such a heated panic that he was sure he himself would succumb to flames. Despite his valiant attempts to ignore what he knew he had to do, the dreams began to manifest themselves again almost every night and with a painful message. It was with reluctance he would concede.

December 31st, 2017 was the firm deadline for intervening on the 2018 Farm and Ranch Assumption Initiative. It had changed names and hands and governments but it was all the same in the end. Any remaining agricultural operations not owned by the government were to be assumed upon the expiry of an agreement signed back in 2012. The Wells Ranch stood dormant since the passing of his father, yet Martin refused to sell.

Martin and his mother lost touch in the months after the tragedy, not because he did not love her enough to care, but because she did not care enough to love. No one would ever replace Martin Sr. and she felt a cemented guilt that would not let go despite the assurances from friends that *she was not to blame*. It weighed her down; bitterness replaced the hope she once felt toward the prospects of a happy future and she could not face the days alone. Without Martin, she would not stay on the farm. With wisps of steam still rising and the blackened ashes barely cooled, Faith packed her bags and took the Escalade, their savings, and faded into the great darkness.

The land passed hands to the son yet it was without applause that he accepted the transfer. He didn't want to be a farmer after all his attempts to convince his father to move to the city and take his mother away from the worry; yet he could not find it in his heart to sell the only thing that meant the world to his own father. In keeping the land, he felt he was at least preserving some kind of memory and in the back of his mind he knew his mother would return. At least, that's what he told himself.

The dreams made him question the real reason behind paying the outstanding loan and clearing a land title he knew no longer held value. It gave him small comfort to know that no one would be able to take what his father had worked so hard to obtain "without paying him what it was worth." It was doubtful the true worth his father alluded to would be offered in the course of any deal, especially with the current government's drive to assume all single rural lines with or without collateral damage.

As December dwindled closer to Assumption day, Martin decided there needed to be more research into the proposed legislated move. Armed with his knowledge of the electrical industry – at least from a new innovation standpoint – Martin Wells (he dropped the use of Jr. soon after the death of his father) filed and registered his *intent to participate* with the Utility Corporation Commission as intervener on behalf of all remaining farmers. The email accompanying his return registration confirmation was not what one would consider standard business protocol. He had to read it more than once to convince himself that the apparent threats contained within the wording were unintentional and perhaps, even common, given the circumstances of the filing.

The email read:

"If it is your intent to oppose the government recommendations on the 2018 Farm and Ranch Assumption Initiative filed by the Smart Party, it would be well advised for parties to seek legal consultation.

"It is also recommended that financial affairs are in order and of a substantive nature due to the cost of regulatory interventions without cause."

He reminded himself that an issue such as this was not going to be an easy one to argue. To gain the upper hand, at this point in the game, a presenter would have to have quite a magic trick up his sleeve. He felt he owed the farmer at least an attempt to oppose even though his prowess at regulatory intervention was severely lacking. He had to take a serious look at how he was going to approach this because he wasn't sure he'd hold up through a whole commission inquiry given his emotional state. To protect whatever evidence he might need, he copied the notice and filed it in his personal papers, just in case.

Determined to present the best case he possibly could, Martin decided it would be prudent to record the details from that fateful night as best he could remember even if they were difficult to visualize. Daytime had a way of erasing the terrors that were so easy to appear at night. Through work he could focus on the details of the matter because it was not only a personal loss he suffered but a professional one, too. Working in such close proximity to the groups responsible for the radical power changes offered Martin a front row seat to the upcoming struggles and the impact they would have on the way things were always done. In his past endeavors, he prided himself on his ability to analyze the speculative nature of a manufactured invention and when a device or plan or project came to fruition successfully, it was a well-received report. He came to realize very quickly, however, that the government had direction and focus but it did not always have the support from the very people it represented. Often the largest support ended up coming from organizations such as Alternative Energy who had their own agenda.

Martin's notations indicated the forced black out had continued well into the night with most of the Wells' neighbors experiencing a tragedy in one way or another. The heat wave brought many of them to the edge of the proverbial cliff sooner than expected. It gave them the needed incentive to bail; otherwise, they'd be buried in the inevitable landslide of governmental control and big business deceit.

Most speculated that the black out that August night was deliberate but no one could prove it. No matter the reason for the outage, it was as if the planned attack solidified the progression to the agricultural Assumption. Farms were too few and far between making the continued service of power to singular lines unproductive and uneconomical.

Areas abandoned by the agricultural process were to be better utilized for the mainstay of the province as a whole. The nuclear power industry would provide a guaranteed future. The government mandate proclaimed the redirection of power transmission to a high level focus, and the construction of the necessary upgrades must service more than just one dead end consumption outlet.

A farm at the end of a single three phase line would no longer be supplied with power. In a proclamation that made world news headlines, the mandated Assumption also warned that the configuration of private generators rewired back to the grid would trigger an immediate seizure order for the property *and equipment* along with an evacuation order. In essence the pre-warnings meant – take what was being offered now or risk receiving an eviction notice. The inevitable reality would happen, sooner rather than later.

Sitting on the edge of the bed, the new day sun just clearing the horizon, Martin stared at the clock. He did not want to rise like a farmer or be reminded of the loss of one in such a tragic manner. *Why, on God's green earth, was he delving into matters that might end his resurrected career? Some felt he didn't deserve the second chance, but he worked long and hard to get it back and the government was not going to force his hand, this time.*

He knew one reason for the dreams was that his destiny lay in gaining compensation, not just for his parents' sake, but for all farmers who were being forced to choose a life they did not want. He knew the real reason behind the dream was that it was a constant reminder to reaffirm his resolve to fight the companies that coerced him to make the decisions he, in all good conscience, wouldn't normally make. An all-consuming guilt drove him to make things right before it was too late.

Chapter 3 – Faith

Faith May Anderson became Mrs. Wells not long after she met Martin and with that promise came life as a farmer's wife. She was seventeen when she said her vows and her new husband was thirteen years her senior. The older man always appealed to Faith, despite the warnings of her friends, for she felt they took a more caring attitude toward their mates, looking out for them and putting them number one, and most of the time that was true. The difference lay in the fact that Martin made the same lifelong promise to the land he made to her when he asked her father for her hand in marriage.

To her it did not matter; she loved Martin with all her heart and, in return, she promised to stand by him "until death do us part." She did not have to make sacrifices as Martin appeared to be the type of man to dote upon those he loved, whether human or animal. She accepted from the beginning that his tie to the land was as strong, if not stronger, than the tie to her as his wife. Over the years, Faith could fault him in no more times than she could count on one hand, and it usually included an extreme of habit rather than the absence of one.

Too many hours in the fields, too much time in the barns, long days with harvest, with weaning, and when the years turned profits from farming too low to cover much needed improvements and purchases, Faith stood by her husband when he signed the deed to the farm over to the bank in order to secure a large loan. She knew it was a matter of survival and would stand by him even if he refused to leave, give up, or succumb to the conditions of the market although most of their friends and neighbors eventually did.

They warned him that "holding out" would be as good as foreclosure because the value of his property would drop due to less interest generated by farming.

He did not fault them for their decisions but took pride in the fact that he maintained the farming life like his father and his father's father. This land would not pass from a Wells' hand to someone else who might not have the respect he held for the natural world around him.

Faith came into Martin's life at a time when farming still reaped a feasible living if you were frugal and if you considered things on a smaller scale. One had to be diligent in raising market animals to produce healthy, abundant meat products. Martin received the reins to solitary control of the farm soon after he and Faith returned from their honeymoon. His devotion to the land convinced his father of his commitment and his long days confirmed his ability to uphold the Wells family tradition. His father could see that Martin took his marriage vows seriously and weighed in with that the maturity he had offered over the years prior to that event. As a young boy, he did not need prompting or prodding to get his chores done or even verbal request to lend extra help when needed. Martin's father didn't need too much convincing to sign the papers and officially retire. He was well into his eighties and ready to enjoy some well-deserved time off. Martin knew longevity ran in his family and was content in the assumption that he would farm for the rest of his life, however long that might be.

As a farm wife, Faith found her days to be just as busy but alone for sixteen hour days; she began to assume her own identity. She cultivated private interests and hobbies even though she maintained publicly that Martin's chosen way of life was hers, too. She would proclaim they shared happiness in whatever made him happy.

It was that misplaced satisfaction that soon revealed a void and the desire for a child hit early in their marriage. Faith welcomed the change thinking she might be better able to deal with the long days alone if she had a baby to keep her occupied.

So, with early passion in the marriage to keep them intimate, it was without much trying they were able to make the happy announcement before their first anniversary. She was pleased to tell her husband they would have another little Wells to fill with the love of farming.

Martin was overjoyed and couldn't profess his love loud enough. She knew by his reaction he would make a wonderful father and they began planning for the happy event. When Faith miscarried before the end of the first trimester, Martin became despondent and was withdrawn for weeks, even going so far as to push Faith away. Depression hit both of them and although she didn't blame him for the way he felt, she couldn't deal with the silent treatment which left her alone with her thoughts.

At that time, she seriously questioned if the farm was truly where she should be. At only eighteen, her whole life spread before her and the late seventies made promises to independent women not freely available during previous decades. Faith explored other options as she tried to erase the erroneous feelings that the unfortunate event was somehow her fault. In some odd way, the long winter to come seemed like it would be more intense than the short-lived pregnancy she'd just endured.

When Martin realized he might lose his wife to a world beyond the fences of the farm, he warmed up quickly. Both were reluctant to try again but the desire to have a baby consumed them both, but for different reasons. Faith feared making a change. It involved something that would be so far removed from what she thought was the journey she was supposed to take. A baby would solidify the family life she chose.

Martin, on the other hand, feared the worst by selfishly thinking only of the need to have an heir – a son – to pass down the name and bequeath the farm for another generation. To kill the legacy built before him would not happen. They continued to try although they did not lose themselves to hope.

When Faith announced she was again carrying the Wells' namesake, Martin broke from his daily grind to attend to Faith whenever he possibly could – mid morning, afternoon, early evening – allowing her to safely rest in bed with all the daily household chores done. Martin would then finish his own work and the sixteen hour days still consumed him but they were sufficiently rearranged so that Faith was his number one concern, at least, until the baby was born.

Martin Wells Jr. arrived in the world to the happy couple in 1979 after a relatively easy pregnancy. So much so, that it led Faith to believe the previous effort was not meant to be, no matter how difficult. She finally let go of the guilty feelings regarding the miscarriage even though she secretly harbored a woman's intuition that her first child might have been a girl. The birth of a son sent Martin into a high that pushed him to work even longer hours.

He was determined to hand over something he could take pride in; something that would be the envy of his friends and neighbors; something that proclaimed his success. The legacy propelled his hard work – his dad did it for him and he, in turn, would do it for his son.

Growing up on a farm with doting parents provided the young Martin with a life he could never say lacked love or luster. A young boy's natural curiosity provided Martin Sr. with ample opportunity to share and spend time with his son. It was all he could do each day to contain his excitement until the school bus pulled up at 3:00 pm and young Martin Jr. descended to his outstretched arms for a hug and then a race to the barn to do chores until supper time.

About the time Martin Jr. turned thirteen, it was obvious that being a farmer was not in his future. The split between father and son began soon after that with Martin relying on his mother for most of the guidance during his early teen years.

It was hard for Faith to sit back and watch as her husband abandoned his own son and left all the issues of raising a boy to her, despite her pleading for him to be a part of his life again. She warned him that if he continued in the manner he had chosen, it would be a rift he would not be able to repair.

Martin Jr. excelled in school, thanks to the support of his mother, and he decided to go on to university. Although his father did not outwardly accept this decision, inwardly he was proud that his boy had the courage to stand up to him and go his own way. With her son away in Calgary attending his first year of university, Faith was again alone despite Martin's renewed devotion.

It was a time in farming when diversification was the only way to survive. Faith realized there were concessions to be made and she accepted her husband's absence. But even with her husband's proclaimed loyalty, she no longer wanted to be just a farm wife, strapped to the successes or failures of the family farm based on what he alone accomplished.

She decided she would invest her time in raising horses. Quality quarter horses would bring in a sizable contribution to the Wells Ranch bottom line and give her a useful and fulfilling mission of her own. She could help make the farm operation the success it needed to be to survive, thrive, and provide for their intended future together.

Martin was impressed with the investment of time Faith put into the business venture. She grew attached to the animals and realized her love for them was soul deep. At one time, she could claim only one true love in her life – now, she wasn't so sure. The ponies challenged her and unconditionally showed how much they depended upon her; she could not say that of Martin, even if she thought so long ago.

There was a respect for the animal and what they could accomplish as a team. Again, it was something she once felt of her spouse and would argue it was still there, *somewhere*. In the long run, it did not matter as long as Martin was happy and he was, as long as the farm was thriving. She could honestly admit she was truly happy, too. The horses brought not only a life altering pleasure to her life but also a lifesaving investment to Martin and Faith Wells.

When Martin Jr. married in 2006, to a woman he claimed to have met in university, Faith was disappointed. She could not determine why her only son would not have trusted her with the knowledge of his love all those years. It upset her if they were as close as he claimed why the relationship was kept secret. It was clear he intended, someday, to perhaps have their two-point-one children to contribute to the overpopulation of the earth and he would follow that up with a forced laugh when she would admonish his flippant attitude. Her son's avoidance to the things she found so fulfilling throughout her life left her wondering but she tried to be understanding and was wise enough to realize it was a new age – things were not always done the same way as they had been.

During his final year of his studies, Martin Jr. and Erin moved to Edmonton. His chosen line of work required him to be closer to the centre of the power industry and the controlling government offices. He worked long hours and despite their claims to be career-oriented first, family driven second, they proudly announced the expectant arrival of a grandchild by the end of the following year.

Faith kept in touch with her son and his wife, interested in his venture into the electrical industry, and was surprised that he even entertained working as an adviser for the provincial government. She wanted him to move closer to them so she could see her grandson once in awhile because leaving the farm was impossible, for the most part.

He would promise to make the trip and then would have to re-promise the next time they had a conversation. Moving back did not come up. Work kept him away from his own home right in the same city, so much so, that he couldn't justify making time to travel any farther away on a regular basis even if it was to see his own mother. Their phone discussions would start with Mickey gibbering into the phone, Erin rambling out a quick hello, and a summarized catch up with Martin on what was new on the electrical front.

He warned his mother that new initiatives were being considered that might make life on the farm less than desirable. He even asked her to consider investing in a condo in town – just in case they decided to move at some time in the future. Faith did not involve herself in politics and didn't feel the changes her son spoke of would make that much difference, *if* they were even implemented. The government she was used to often took too long to legislate changes and would often spend billions of tax payer's dollars just to employ a consultant from an expensive firm to review a plan or project, that might or might not, make it to the approval process.

She also confided in him that his father would never consider moving and he felt that at this point government initiatives were just idle threats, however ill-conceived they sounded.

She joked that the initiatives he spoke of might come to fruition sooner than a visit from her own son. He would laugh, and "oh, Mom" but his promises lacked conviction and he would soon be talking about something else in an effort to avoid any further confrontation.

Her son was involved in government, though – it was hard to accept given they were so much alike in so many other ways. Faith tried to convince him to work with her raising horses; he could bring his family and live in the guest house right on the property. Although Martin loved the horses and felt comfortable with them, and he loved his mother dearly, he refused to succumb to the inevitable – his father's wish that he come home to the farm and work side by side together toward the future legacy.

He refused and was pleased to let his mother have the recognition of bringing fame to the farm and its quarter horse operation. Southern Alberta cattle ranchers drove hundreds of miles, even if her son wouldn't.

With the prospect of the sale of horse stock going so well, Martin Sr. decided it was time to upgrade the farm equipment and he had his eye on the newest, most expensive Massey combine. His work could be accomplished so much more efficiently and with the upgrade, in a timely manner. The bank approved his loan based on the performance of the crops and using the backing the guarantee of the quarter horse breeding operation brought to the books, it was an easy deal to arrange. Martin reported one hundred and sixty acres in canola, one hundred and sixty in Timothy alfalfa, and another smaller section in grain. Faith co-signed the guarantee on the loan using her breeding stock and the growing herd as collateral. She felt accomplished in her ability to help Martin, considering all he did for her over the years.

Despite the hardships and hard times, Faith loved Martin and he could still steal her heart, making it beat faster with just the whisper of her name. As they grew older, they grew closer and their interdependence was more than just the mutual contribution they were now making to the farm as a business. It was an easy assumption based on the current state of affairs that they would see a healthy future together. Faith knew that Martin still harbored hope their son would come to his senses and move home to take over the business in the same manner he did from his father. If he did, it would then allow the two of them to enjoy retirement, when the time came. Faith just smiled and accepted her husband's hopes, knowing in her heart that it would never happen.

Chapter 4 – Martin Jr.

About the time things were going well for his parents in 2009 – the addition of the quarter horse operation and the investment in more modern farming equipment – Martin had long secured his own future by building a reputation within the electrical industry. He would not only be announcing to his parents his move up in the Energy Department to be involved more directly with innovation and technical design, but also the expectation of a second grandchild.

He felt uncomfortable to some degree that he never found the time to bring his family to visit his parents, but it was like an avoidance he couldn't explain. He rationalized it to himself by thinking that going there he'd lose the control he had when he wasn't there – that lead to a fear, founded or not, that he would be talked into moving back to help his father. Recently, Erin had confided to his mother she was unhappy in the big city and would do her best to try to persuade Martin to reconsider moving at least closer to the Wells farm. Grandparents were an important part of growing up and she felt Mickey needed the chance to see and learn about rural life.

Martin was used to the less than desirable tactics within the realm of his job, but felt betrayed by the woman he loved. He felt pressure from all sides and this planned attempt only forced him to dive further into his work causing a bigger rift between him and Erin. There was just too much to have to deal with and too many things were of extreme importance within the industry that he began to stay away overnight, often taking up residence right in his own office, days on end. Anything to do with the family or the kids or the house, he left to Erin, who soon got the message that her husband wasn't interested in being involved, so she took care of it.

Along with the letters from pissed off consumers, he soon received divorce papers and he treated them almost the same. They were received, date stamped, and processed with a dictated letter to his administrative assistant, who inserted his scanned signature and ran them through the postage machine for interns to drop at the mailbox on their way home. It was with not more than an extra rye and water that Martin signed off his family responsibilities and turned to concentrate on the heated power debate.

There was pressure building from rural electrification units who were at odds with the government over new smart grid proposals and the power companies were involved in more than their fair share of litigations. His time was spent trying to douse rapidly spreading flames, because the coals that burned beneath were not going to be extinguished easily. He had to focus directly on what was happening, and what would be happening, depending upon the route the government took with its renewed energy strategy. He needed to focus all his energies and family life issues could not distract him.

Back at home on the Wells ranch, his parents were enjoying a productive season and Martin was pleased to hear of their joy in personal and business success. Although he was reluctant to agree with his mother's decision to sign the guarantee on such a large farm loan, he knew she would support his father "no matter what" as she always said, and respected that despite his own reservations. There was a suicidal feeling about depending on the viability of things you couldn't really control. Crops were bound to the weather conditions; animals by their health; and even your own productivity could not be guaranteed one hundred percent of the time.

As he reflected upon his lack of enthusiasm for their necessary actions, he took another drink and a revelation hit him. *He was no more in control than they were.* Working in the provincial department, he was driven by politicians who washed their hands of public deals even after a handshake and then secretly appeased the private corporations that lined their pockets with dirty money.

Was it any wonder he didn't have a family to go home to? What right did he have to call them on their dealings when he was just as much to blame?

Another drink would let him forget about the things to come for another night. The problem was that it would all be there again in the morning. It was at that time that Martin's indecision led him to believe that private consultation was the route to go and he formulated his resignation letter to the department stating "... although I appreciate the opportunities I was given to work within the government, I find there are other areas where my expertise is required at this time. My decision is in no way a reflection on my employer, but rather, a realization on my own direction in life."

"Mr. Chairman, I find the presentation submitted by EnCorp to be erroneous in their claims that the consumer would not be held responsible in any way for the implementation of the smart grid application – who is responsible, if not the end user? Is that not the reason for considering such a drastic change to the way we market power and power options?"

"Mr. Chairman – if I may..." EnCorp's rattled representative arose quickly from this seat in the first row gallery, his hand raised as if to receive welcome to his desired explanation.

"Mr. Brown – EnCorp had their chance to present their stand on the issue at hand here today and we cannot accept interjections at this point. Mr. Wells, please continue. I am assuming that your questions are for emphasis and clearly ones that don't expect an answer right here and now? Am I correct in stating this, Mr. Wells?"

"Yes, for the time being, although all questions in this matter must, at some point in time, receive appropriate responses. I am content in raising them with that future consideration in mind. To continue... it is purely supposition to argue that a project proposal the magnitude of PEP would not have some kind of ramifications for all consumers. If, in fact, we are to implement something on this grand scale, the province is going to look at billions of dollars to invest not only in the pilot projects that are being suggested, but also in the form of grants to those companies and entities that do not have the capacity to convert to the necessary technical equipment – both hardware and software – required to mesh with the rest of the grid."

From his podium to one side of the presentation floor, Martin could see the representatives from other organizations sitting just beyond the circle of light illuminating the staging area, the big screen on the middle wall and the panel of speakers who wore official name tags etched in gold from the Power Commission. He knew his comments to support the government were not going to win him friends among the smaller groups who came to argue their stand during the intervention, but he had to be honest when presenting his findings. The end consumer was going to pay for whatever upgrades, implementations – project or pilot – were introduced in the name of "the good of the whole."

"Mr. Wells, from your perspective, and based on the findings in your report, do you find any one group or organization adversely affected by the implementation of smart grid?" The chairman in charge of delivering the Commission's questions, prompted by behind the hand whispers and scribbled notes ushered from the other men flanking him at the long table, was known to everyone in the industry. For quite some time and for almost as long as most of the newcomers could remember, Raymond Knorr, led the helm of the Commission, bringing the power regulators full circle in the change from non-private, to private and back to a resumption of power control by the government, in all aspects of the meaning. The hearing before the council that day would bring to light arguments about the implementation of a province wide project that would assume everyone was the same, big or small, and that everyone would be charged alike, big or small. Those registered to argue their position were mostly those smaller companies and associations who stood to take the brunt of the charges because of their size and it would be the rural consumer paying in the end for the good of everyone in the province.

Martin had warned his mother, yet again, about the initiatives on the horizon.

"Honored Commission, yes... there are those who will not benefit in the same capacity as everyone else. There are those smaller companies who are not in a position to fully realize the economic benefits that will be realized by larger corporations. It has come to my attention during my research as well, there are those consumers who will not benefit by the proposed changes because they cannot change their consumption habits to reap the rewards offered to those who can."

"What percentage are we talking about?" The question was handed to the Commission chairman by Earl Witten, a known advocate for the large commercial operations who were well represented at the hearing and who often showed their support of the Commission with large sponsorships and endorsements.

"A small, but measurable percentage..." Martin was loath to answer such a question. Numbers could misrepresent the actual effects and there were those who would argue he worked for something just as reprehensible to some as big business, he was, after all, defending the government even if he was an independent consultant.

"Can you be more specific, as in a number, perhaps?" Earl just smirked as Knorr proceeded to pull the required answer from the presenter. It was his job to do so even as reproachful as it was.

"Two per cent..." Martin said the number louder than he wanted to, almost as if he didn't want to admit that rural consumers didn't really make a big difference in the scheme of the whole plan. Most of the talk about rural consumers involved transmission and the availability to large corridors of cropland needed to construct unhindered towers that would export even more power than the province could ever use. Even with the big commercial applications drawing their necessary consumption there would be an overabundance of power. He knew in his heart this was not right but the way of the future had to consider everyone and the benefit that would be derived for the most gain.

Preserving rural history yet blocking the way to the future on a mere two percent was not production, even if it wasn't right, morally or ethically. Prompted by what he thought was a low, collective groan, he started again and continued before there could be any interjection on the part of the Commission.

"Two percent of the consumers in the province are not able to change their consumption or use patterns to fit the plan of the proposed smart grid application." He paused to flip through some papers stacked on the presentation table beside him. "In fact, it is not only cost that prohibits this change but the nature of the agricultural business that prevents this consumer group from cashing in on the benefits perceived to be the encouraging point in the conversion."

"Are you saying they can't or won't change their habits?"

"Not habits, Mr. Commissioner. There is a big difference between something that is chosen and can be freely changed and something that is required and cannot be changed due to that need. This special demographic utilizes power at specific times in order to produce for the rest of us and has done so for generations. Perhaps, a special consideration might be in order but that recommendation would, of course, be up to the Commission when it analyses the findings of this hearing." Martin felt an inner personal success to defend his own family history despite his past attempts to ignore it. It was something he struggled with but didn't reveal to anyone.

"Thank you, Mr. Wells. If you have nothing further at this time we will continue with our next presenter. Your reports have been posted as public documentation and we thank you for the information you have provided to us today."

Martin returned to his seat wary of the glances from opposing and confirming sides of the issue. He realized how dry his mouth was and remembered he should have paused just a bit, if not for affect, at least to quench his thirst and ease a dry throat. The room was almost oppressive with its directional lighting and shaded high mounted windows.

The number of people in attendance crammed to capacity the presentation theatre, and if it weren't for the necessity of his job to hear the offerings of the next presenter, he would have made his way casually out the door, down the hall, and kept on going until he reached some fresh air.

"Good job up there." The whispered compliment came from over his shoulder and he turned to reply, face to face with a woman he recognized from past power intervention hearings. His confused smile relayed a too obvious question. "Suzanne. Suzanne Peters. We met, unofficially, at the March hearing."

"Yes, hello, I remember. Thanks." Martin turned his attention back to the speaker now standing at the presentation table. Marshall Winslow was unmistakably corporate and obviously a well-paid lawyer who represented the interests of a controversial stakeholder in the electrical industry registered as Alternative Energy Corporation. They were a cutting edge private company which sparked debate from its inception. Innovation would be an understatement for this company because everything it produced was over the top in not only application but also in the amount of investment and the type of investors involved.

Martin was familiar with their type of business and it was disconcerting to even think the government would entertain their recommendations or suggestions. It was, however, an open hearing so he had to at least have an open, albeit, wary mind.

"Mr. Winslow – the smart grid application for the province will consider interties to existing and newly developed structures throughout the province and beyond. Where does Alternative Energy Corporation figure into this scenario and in what manner do you propose to fit into the grid?"

"Honored Commission, I appreciate this opportunity to speak on behalf of Alternative Energy Corporation and, as legal counsel for the company, I would like to refer to the presentation submitted for consideration at these hearings. The Innovation and Design Department of an associate company, TechnoCorp, is proud to be a leader in technological design and configuration in the IT capacity. On behalf of that company, I have been instructed to report to the Commission that implementation of such a project, the magnitude and extent of smart grid, will require an system of communication and computer based knowledge unmatched and virtually unknown to most of those in the power industry today. We are extremely proud to be able to report to the Commission, at this time, we have been undergoing extensive testing on new technologies capable of interconnecting with existing and proposed transmission, distribution, and generation power components. As you know, there are few companies worldwide that can make this claim, despite the global domination of smart grid pilot projects."

Lawyer Winslow paused for the necessary effect that Martin wished he offered with his presentation, and he even took time for a drink of water before he continued. There was no interjection to his presentation or questions, just directed interest and a lot of frantic pen scratching.

"I have also been authorized to present to the Commission our proposal to the government with our endorsed support letter signed by the executive officers of both associated companies. We are in a position to begin work whenever the Commission offers its report to the government regarding their findings through this hearing. It would be irresponsible of us to propose a product that we were unsure of, considering the nature of the smart grid and its wide spread, wide reaching effects. We also can promise that all consumer applications have been considered and we are able to address each with the uniqueness they possess."

For a short time, Martin believed that the Commission would not interject any of its own questions given the silence in the room once Winslow completed his presentation. Copies were made available for participants and Martin would be sure to pick one up as he had some questions of his own and would like to review the document. The offerings of the company seemed extreme, and almost impossible.

Despite the air of confidence and poise of the presenter, Martin wouldn't believe everything he heard, and working as a consultant for the government and now on his own, allowed him that prerogative. He questioned their capacity to 'address each with the uniqueness they possess.'

"Just one question…" Commission chairman Knorr leaned forward with a smile on his face. "When can you start?"

There was a collective laugh that circulated the room knowing he was joking considering that the position and duty of the Commission was to review all options, presentations, and concerns which included a review so thorough that everything presented was given its due, without prejudice.

"Just joking, of course… but thank you, Mr. Winslow. That will conclude today's hearing and the Commission would like to thank all of the participants for their input. Please review the documents you have received today and forward any comments and concerns via your coded entry to our web site. If there are any questions that might not have been answered to your full understanding or you feel there was a lack of completeness in any way, the Commission welcomes that input, as well, for consideration. We will provide all participants with today's transcripts if you remembered to request them in advance. You can expect the Commission's report by the end of the year." Raymond Knorr stood and straightened a creased jacket.

"Thank you everyone. Drive safe."

Martin collected the necessary paperwork and made his way to the door, eager to take that first breath of fresh air. He felt a light touch on his arm as he slipped into the crowed hallway and turned to find Suzanne, again, smiling face to face.

"Hey. Are you in a hurry to get somewhere? Maybe we could grab a drink?" She was about five foot seven and had long blond hair. He knew she was probably about two or three years older than he was because he recalled their conversation at the past Commission intervention involved a discussion about courses, graduation, university, and the City of Calgary. At least, he assumed she was. Sometimes you could never really tell for sure. He was about to answer and was uncertain of why a "no" answer played upon his tongue, when they were approached by Marshall Winslow, the extravagant Alternative Energy Corporation lawyer.

"Mr. Wells?"

"That'd be me."

"Can we talk for a moment?"

"We were just going to grab a drink – would you like to join us?" He was surprised and unsure of why it became a "yes" all of a sudden but knew that he'd like to find out what Winslow had to say, perhaps even more than what Suzanne had to say. His indifference to her could only be explained by his attraction, knowing there was bound to be trouble if he just let things go as they usually did. It had been awhile since he left Erin and he knew that it wouldn't take much coaxing to get into more hot water.

"I would prefer alone. I would prefer without the accompaniment of drink. Let me just say, I am in a position to say something that might be of great interest to you if you feel our mutual company is worthy of this conversation." He paused, like he was presenting again, and looked from Martin to Suzanne, then back to Martin.

"Well, I'm going to share a drink with this beautiful woman so if you don't want to join us, please, speak freely." Martin smiled, encouraging Winslow to continue.

"My employers would like to invite you to work for Alternative Energy Corporation." It was brief, to the point, and with little ceremony Winslow handed Martin a sealed envelope. "If you choose to consider their offer, I would open it." He was gone with a wave and he proceeded to Blackberry his way down the hall to the exit door.

Martin didn't really know what else to say.

"How about that drink?"

His mind wandered from the moment, in and out of questions and wonderment, despite the company he kept. Or to others, it looked as if he kept, to anyone watching the handsome couple. Over drinks, Suzanne managed to distract him off and on, even using her feminine wiles to tease and draw his attention, and in a last ditch effort, eventually resorted to a little bit of annoyance.

Martin was more intrigued, arguably so, with the offer presented to him via Marshall Winslow, the overly astute lawyer "representing his client, Alternative Energy Corporation" as he expressed repeatedly to the Commission. It would seem despite his numerous years of legal training and council, his overt attempts were to immediately separate himself personally in any way from the task at hand, distancing the outcome he was certainly highly paid to deliver, considering the source of the offer.

A quick, secretive peek into the package, once they found a quiet corner in the nearby lounge, evidenced an official letter of offer and a cheque for encouragement as a signing bonus. *A ten thousand dollar encouragement.* Martin's mind veered away from his usual logical thinking to a place where "why not" reigned supreme over "why". He would think on the consequences later and measurably weigh all his options, but for the time being, he basked in the glory of cashing that bonus cheque to do with it just about anything he cared.

For now, he only had to put it aside and enjoy the evening in what would most likely culminate in an even more profitable finish, if he didn't screw it up. The tendency to be "not involved" ruled over his life lately, especially since his falling out with Erin. Not involved was a distance from commitment, however, and he still had needs. Suzanne looked more than capable to sufficiently meet them.

He pulled his attention back to her conversation, albeit, too late to recover even an ounce of respect. Apologizing would have to be fast and furious if he intended to mend what would soon end up to be a very big insult.

Despite feeble attempts to make idle chit chat, Martin's attention wavered as thoughts strayed to the reason, or reasons, for Alternative Energy Corporation's request for his services.

He was certain their dealings with the government and industry stakeholders included following the same regulatory processes and best business practices that he himself counseled power companies on. Nuclear power companies, however, were new and the wave of the future. His innovative design training and industry experience taught him at least that much. It did make him wonder, though, why a consultant in primarily transmission and distribution facilities would be of interest to production and alternative methods of manufacturing such as that offered by AEC. He wouldn't yet go so far as to say he'd steer clear of the offer or outright refuse it; he knew all too well that reservations were a good accompanying companion to good sense. Even if there were ten thousand reasons to just say yes.

"Martin?" There was a slight sound of annoyance in Suzanne's voice as it intruded upon his wandering thoughts, blocking them from proceeding on to who knows where without her. The situation was as if it wasn't real, a huge sum of money, a lucrative job offer *and* female companionship – on the same night? It was almost an unlikely event with Martin. In fact, he couldn't...

"Martin!"

"What?"

"Would you like me to leave?"

"Now why would I like that..." he was a bit abrupt, perturbed almost, as he tried to hide his embarrassment. "I mean, do you want to leave?" He'd leave it up to her – he guessed – he couldn't do any more harm than already accomplished in such a short span of time.

"I wouldn't have suggested the drink, if I weren't interested, you dolt..." Suzanne stood suddenly, grabbing her jacket and pulling one arm up over one shoulder. Martin was on his feet, placing a hand on her arm to keep her from finishing the task.

"Suzanne – so sorry..." he leaned over to slide a hand up the soft leather to her collar and pulled it down over her shoulder again. He placed the coat over the chair next to hers. The faint smell of lilacs hit him and he blinked, as if for the first time actually realizing the situation surrounding him, and the tempting company within arm's reach. It stunned him into realizing a conclusion that he almost screwed it up – "it" being an assumption on his part, at this point in the evening, especially now.

"Suzanne, I am truly sorry. My mind has been preoccupied lately and this new revelation kind of got the better of me. Will you forgive this dolt and give him one more chance?" He smiled with the charm of little boy innocence that had little trouble in the past tempting and soliciting the company of women. His recent state of mind prevented him from acting upon many of the offers. "Please, just one more chance. Here..." Martin slipped the envelope into the inside breast pocket of his blazer and buttoned down the flap closure. He motioned for the waitress to bring them another round. "There all put away and I promise, forgotten... for now." He touched the side of her face in a gesture that made her smile and she sat back down.

"Okay, one more chance." She patted his knee as he sat down close beside her. "But one more distraction and I'm gone."

No more distractions pulled him away from the conversation with her as he realized her genuine interest included much of the same things involving his every day work that surrounded him on a regular basis, in and out of the office. They strayed finally from topics involving power and talked of other interests. Martin did not bring up the ex-wife or the two young children; he did not bring up the fact that his greatest companion other than his computer was Jack Daniels on a lonely night. He did not reveal the frequent indulgence in drink once he left the auspices of the work place and prying eyes. Contrary to what most would think – he did not have the cliché hidden bottle in the bottom drawer of his desk. The out of sight liquor cabinet at home gave him the same forbidden feelings.

Hobbies were not something he afforded time or attention; his work was his hobby and if he found time or made an attempt to find time, he picked up his kids for a short outing. But he did not reveal that. His thoughts as they talked now only confirmed the lack of things in his life, that was, the lack of important things that meant something in any life. His thoughts did not let him focus on the things he did have, like an expensive car, a stylish loft apartment, and all the other amenities availed to him. They provided his immediate happiness but they *were* only possessions.

"So what are you thinking about now?"

"How lucky I am to be sitting here with you, right at this moment." He lied, but she pretended otherwise with a quick smile. She was smart enough to know he'd almost wandered away again and *she was just kind enough to ignore it* – he thought.

"Wow, good answer. I thought I lost you to that all-consuming thought magnet that seems to pull you out of reality really quick right in the middle of something. You do that all the time?" The husky whisper to her voice implied she was hinting at more than just conversation with a teasing, passing fancy.

"No. I'm here. I promise."

The conversation shifted to Suzanne. She worked as a marketing and media consultant for a local power company association that Martin didn't readily recognize – Power Innovations – but then again, with the number of new technological corporations springing up, it wasn't any wonder he didn't know it and he barely tried to keep up with the registrations any more.

With the growing demand for IT products and the implementation of new metering technologies over the last few years, it was just a matter of time before improved services, quality state of the art products, and the means to sell them in profitable ways, were required.

"How long have you been with them?"

"They're a fairly new company but I like their processes – just under a year."

"There's a need I would imagine for new ways to market these new products."

"Oh, yes – and more so than just locally, too. We've secured numerous international media contracts that share information with global consumers on alternative markets that start right here at home."

"That works fine for tangible products – you can ship, like, let's say – computer programming software or the AMI digital display meters."

"Services, too," she replied with intriguing confidence.

"How is that beneficial in the power industry? There is literally a chain of transmission that flows – literally, again – from one breaker to another, first one – then the next..." Martin's interest was piqued even if somewhat skeptical.

"Oh, I'm sure it's nothing new to you, being in new product design – so how do you suppose it would work?"

"There would have to be an extreme abundance of over power production, something that we are currently upgrading towers to manage, and then extensive lines dedicated only to that flow. They couldn't have any off lines, or end feeders. It would have to be continuous to be used as we produce it. Now this is a stretch even for today but the farthest possible reach would be the southernmost tip of South America for an extensive continental grid." Martin shook his head. "But storage capacity does not exist nor is it available to handle capacity requirements in this type of scenario. The corridors would have to be twice as wide to allow for the upgraded tower construction."

"Oooo, that sounds intriguing." Suzanne played the coy junior card as if enticed by a new idea never before heard of, then switched just as quickly back to the serious business of the conversation. "But, no. Think nuclear, Martin. You really have to up your inventiveness to encompass this kind of process, especially if you plan to take that offer. You do realize, Alternative Energy Corporation is not just about intertying wind turbines and bio mass generators to the grid, don't you? They are about nuclear energy and they plan to take over major control of the power supply on the grid with nuclear production. It's not just the wave of the future; it's what's necessary to produce the required demand."

She was direct and informed. *Almost too informed for just a marketing and media specialist*, Martin thought. From what she said, it would appear that Alternative Energy Corporation was not just considering new power alternatives, they were new alternatives with nuclear power high on their list of sources.

"You know your stuff." Martin took a long drink from a now watered down rye, eyeing her over the rim of his glass.

She smiled and raised her glass to him in thank you. He continued before she could speak.

"Everyone knows that's what AEC is about. The government is open to options but I wouldn't go so far as to say that nuclear energy will be the major player in the upcoming plans. The consultations did not come back with enough favorable responses to warrant wide spread plant construction, just yet anyway. People aren't going to just step aside and let it go. I don't doubt it could be the wave of the future, but that future, my dear, is a long ways off yet."

"Keep in mind where you heard it first, then when it happens, I'll try not to say I told you so."

Martin pulled the sleek BMW into the spot marked "M. Wells" in the underground parkade at his south side office building just before 7:00 am. The busy traffic filled the morning commute along the Henday but it was clear and crisp as most mornings in November tended to be by mid-month; a warning of things inevitable. He let the engine idle then turned the key and sat for a moment. He made a quick Blackberry entry to call the garage – he hadn't taken the time to get the dark blue machine in for the seasonal oil change but knew he must. There were soon to be trips out on the highway to his parent's place and that commitment was already fast approaching in the next few weeks. His mom had been persistent in their last phone conversation about seeing the kids – soon – *it will be close enough to incorporate the annual Christmas run, anyway,* he thought.

In his office, Martin sat back in the oversized executive leather chair and spun around away from the desk and the blinking lights of messages waiting. There was a stack of "called while you were out" notes left by his administrative assistant from the previous day while he was at the Commission hearings. There was usually the same share every time he stepped out of the office for any length of time. His consulting business was at its best and increased at least two fold over the past year alone. The new innovations required by all power companies due to the provincial energy plan and their inevitable need were causing a big stir. Many of the calls and requests for research came from the rural sector, the hardest hit demographic by the proposed changes. Most were changes that proved to be detrimental to the most basic operations of a farm or ranch.

As he gazed out the window, the tenth floor allowed for a clear view of the south side city roof tops and to the distant south, transmission lines broke the horizon with the hazy morning sun fanning the eastern sky with a reddish glow. Martin thought of his father.

Not specifically, his father – but rather, the whole idea of the farm and how hard it was in the present day world to make a decent living, especially with all the roadblocks to an affective agricultural business. He checked his thoughts quickly and regretted his use of the word "decent."

He hadn't meant in quite the condescending manner it sounded, even if it was only in his head. He hadn't meant it wasn't a respectable job. He had the utmost respect for the time and effort his father put in to give him a good life while he was growing up. He just didn't like thinking of how hard his mother had to work, too, just to supplement a touch and go success.

Each year was different; each year had new challenges; each year had its own share of ups and downs. All meant there were annual reservations of some kind or another or cutbacks or compromises. And now, the province was introducing changes that would adversely affect them even more. *Them. His parents* – he wondered as he watched the ant-like traffic below, stop and start, proceeding as directed, *how did he become so distant and detached?* He knew it didn't have to be this way, although at one time he felt forced to take a stand and although the distance between them grew he did not regret it, *usually.* They were going to need his support more than ever, if the proposed government changes implemented all the smart grid components.

Farmers would suffer the brunt of it and his parents would have to choose. Hopefully they would change, and then take a chance on a life with even more challenges or try something completely new altogether.

Let go of the legacy already – there was no need to hang on to it for his sake and with no siblings to offer it to, he definitely did not want it left for his kids. He didn't want them involved in the farm life past the obvious joy filled weekend of visiting their grandparents, once in awhile, especially while it was still fun to do so.

Fun. The word made him smile, suddenly, remembering the previous night. *Wow, he didn't screw it up this time, he just screwed it.* His groin grew warm thinking of her nakedness next to him, on him, under him and then he inside her with an explosive coordinated culmination of pent up energy. He did not realize how overwrought with passion he was and how just plain orgasmic the lust had become.

"Whew!" He let out a long breath as if reliving it over again. She left her number and told him to call her but he wasn't sure if it would be much more than just a really great fuck. He didn't need more right now – *well, perhaps more of that...*

But he didn't need the complications that came along with any kind of expectations. Right now, he had none – not even for himself. In truth, he just went along doing what was necessary for his job and the basic necessities for living. He certainly didn't live up to other's expectations – his dad, his ex-wife, his kids, or even his own good sense most times.

He touched the breast pocket on his blazer and felt slightly relieved. *Why,* he had no idea, but he was. He pulled out the contents of the envelope and spread the papers on the window height credenza. He sat back, cheque in hand; he gazed upon it as if it were a thing of worship – *ten thousand dollars* – he repeated it to himself like some sort of indulgent mantra. That kind of money would mean a new theatre style game system for the kids so as to impress their little friends on sleepovers, even though they were only in day care and he didn't really agree with the concept of sleepovers anyway.

It was more, perhaps, for Erin and her new boyfriend. He shuddered and moved on to his next thought. *It could mean a really nice bonus for my overworked and underappreciated assistant, Jessica. Or, it could mean a nice Christmas vacation for me on a beach somewhere with no other pressing decisions other than that of "mai tai or pina colada?"*

He exchanged the cheque for the letter and began to read:

> *"Attention: Mr. Martin Wells:*
>
> *Dear Sir..."*

"Sir? Okay, sure."

"Please find enclosed our signing bonus in anticipation of your agreement to join us as a valued member of the employment team at Alternative Energy Corporation in the position of Director of Innovation & Design Research. As you are well aware, the industry is in transitional mode and we intend to be the best in the industry, therefore, we also require on staff the best in the industry. We want you on our side."

"Best in the industry, huh?" He continued, with a somewhat inflated ego.

"We understand that employment for Alternative Energy Corporation will be all inclusive; meaning it will restrict your professional private consultation practice, but your expertise is valued and, therefore, sought by our company.

"You will be well compensated. We guarantee it will be well worth the consideration.

"Please accept the enclosed token of our appreciation and call our offices to arrange a meeting, at your earliest convenience. We look forward to hearing from you in the very near future."

The official letter was on embossed Alternative Energy Corporation letterhead and was signed by the Chief Executive Officer – *Rowan J. Cott.* A notation at the bottom of the letter indicated a copy was cc'd to Arthur Brand, President of Unified Nuclear Corporation, tagged as an 'associate to' Alternative Energy Corporation.

"Unified Nuclear Corporation? Seems it's more than just a coincidence that nuclear energy is the talk of the day." He spun back around to the desk as the phone rang. He let it ring twice until he realized it was still early and Jessica would not be at her desk for another half hour. He grabbed the receiver.

"Martin Wells."

"Hey. Hi." It was the voice of lost reason, back to haunt him and he felt a betraying shiver run up his spine.

"Hi, Suzanne." He quelled the urge.

"You left kind of early."

"Ya, sorry, business to tend to..."

"Too bad... I would have loved to tend to more business myself this morning, too." She followed it up with a teasing laugh and he felt the urge return.

"Hmmm.... sounds good, listen, Suzanne. I had a great time..."

"But..."

"But..." Martin decided quickly in mid thought that it was best to choose his words carefully, not knowing where things might go and if he might need an ally in the nuclear field. "But... I'm really sorry now that I left so soon..." He let his voice trail off filled with enough sincerity that he knew he'd hooked her when he heard her catch a shallow breath. He knew he had that ally now whenever he wanted her.

The dark glass office tower of Alternative Energy Corporation stood mid downtown proudly thrust up between the Alberta Government offices and the Media Trade towers. Martin sat patiently awaiting his call into the dark recesses of another world, beyond that of his own familiarity and what was common place to him. That situation usually meant involvement in his minding his own business. He hadn't closed his office permanently, but rather, paid Jessica the handsome well-deserved bonus to keep her there until he was sure he was where he wanted to be. He wrestled with the change and decision, not able to come up with a clean yes or no. It was a definitive and indecisive maybe. It was the best he could do.

The decision was not made any easier by a night spent again in Suzanne's bed; in fact, it had been really hard to concentrate on anything at all, other than the task at hand, or mouth. So the decision he left with was the same as what he went there with – still, just a maybe. *Perhaps? Why not? Why?* For the most part, it didn't much matter.

"Mr. Wells?"

Martin looked up and nodded as he rose.

"Mr. Cott will see you now." The assistant smiled, a pleasant smile – *superficial,* he thought, but at least pleasant in any case even for a male assistant. Martin thought it odd but reserved his comments for another time and kept his opinion to himself. "Can I get you something – coffee, tea?"

"No, I'm fine, thanks." He followed him into the stylish office. Polished brass and walnut décor throughout; luxurious Persian carpets adorned the floor in front of the large desk, and on the wall off to the far right.

There was a grouping of dark brown leather furniture arranged around an ornately carved coffee table. The large picture window had a breathtaking view for anyone with a penchant for urban landscapes. The neighboring buildings protruded from the mass of cement and glass and the view wasn't really of anything natural except for the odd sliver of sky in between. It was impressive, but Martin already longed for the familiarity of his own. *This was going to take some getting used to,* he thought.

"Ah, Martin Wells – what a pleasure."

Rowan Jasper Cott was an older man with a young look, one he probably worked hard and paid thousands to maintain. He was fit and hadn't begun to show any grey yet, or at least had taken all preventive measures not to. For his sixty two years, he was well preserved.

"Mr. Cott." Martin extended his hand for a firm handshake.

"Rowan, please. We are colleagues – none of this employer employee crap. That wouldn't work right for me when I have such respect for you and your work."

"Thank you. I appreciate that but I'm afraid you have me at a slight disadvantage in that respect." Martin was reluctant to disclose he hadn't heard of Rowan J. Cott before a few days ago, but truth be told, he hadn't. He wasn't even able to find much information on him despite his research ability and Internet prowess. Google proved only that he was current chief executive officer of Alternative Energy Corporation.

"On purpose, Martin – I keep a low profile, on purpose. Until there is a bit more acceptance from the public stand point for nuclear energy, development of such is kept as a behind the scenes production. Most media and communications issued hold only the seal of this company and they are not endorsed publicly – *yet* – by our directors or executive management."

"But other alternatives are widely accepted, and I'm sure they have legitimate offerings to end users of the grid."

"Yes, definitely. But nuclear power input into the grid is what's going to be able to satisfy and sustain the growing transmission demands. Increased requirements are going to necessitate its implementation and that's where you come in."

"Research and development?"

"More like research and convince." He stopped for a moment to take a drink of water from a crystal glass on the desk. "Look, we need someone like you to review our methods, report and analyze any findings, hold public consultations and provide hearing proceedings similar to the Energy Commission.

"With your input and, of course, once you hold public information sessions, the confirmation your signature has on a project shows it's one that's been given the Wells' approval. Convincing is not really the word I wanted to use – or meant – it's more like creating a trust based on the proven facts and the stamp of approval from Martin Wells.

"You realize, I hope, the respect for your knowledge, your integrity and honesty, your experience and industry track record are second to none."

"Whoa! That's a big set of industry boots to fill, Rowan."

"True – that's why we hired you."

"Alternative Energy still falls under the Energy Commission regulatory process." It was more of a statement than a question, because Martin knew all companies except those small rural electrification units fell under the Commission's scrutiny.

"Of course, it does."

"So your own hearings are precursors to the Energy Commission applications."

"Absolutely."

Martin felt a little more at ease knowing Rowan was aware of his knowledge of the required processes and the CEO's confirmation, however brief, confirmed his own decision. The red flags he raised for himself from the onset were not quite as bright. The nature of the job meant he had to be wary and consider all the facts – it was something he had to have control over from the start.

He'd take the job.

The affirmation was more for his own peace of mind, as he followed Rowan to his new office just down the hall and across from the AEC Corporate Board meeting room. Rowan handed him some files and left him to his own devices while he familiarized himself with his new surroundings.

Martin made a quick call to his own office to retrieve any necessary messages. Jessica informed him that all was quiet, "not to worry" and she'd call his cell phone if there was anything she felt he should know right away. Satisfied he'd made the right decision, he settled into the expensive leather executive chair and opened the first file in front of him on the desk.

"Daddy, Daddy." Three year old Mickey was the quintessential rambunctious toddler – driven by pure hyped up energy. Martin often wished he could package and sell the power within his son; *he'd make a mint selling that to the grid.* He smiled thoughtfully as he watched as tousle haired innocence bore down on him, a handful of mud or dirt or scaly animal thrust upward for him to see.

"Hey Sport, slow down there." Martin grabbed the running boy and carried him upward where giggles let loose as he was twirled about in the air. "What've you got there?"

"A slamader."

"A sal-a-man-der, you ninny. You best not be showing that one to your mom or your grandma, my dear boy. Scare them all to squealing." He saw the curious look of George cross his son's slightly grimy face and he thought, *perhaps, best to let him find out for himself the bit of ruckus he could innocently produce by showing them his farm treasures, especially slimy ones.* "You want to try and maybe you'll believe, me, boy are they frightened of slimy little scaly things."

He barely placed Mickey on the ground before the boy was off running, calling out again. Martin heard the screams and chuckled to himself. *Serves Erin right for wanting to tag along with him* – he really couldn't fault her totally because his mom had insisted he bring her along knowing full well he probably wasn't capable of looking out for Mickey and taking care of baby Essie, too.

The weather held nicely into the beginning of December and the trip finally materialized as something he'd been promising for some time; his only regret in going so early was that he'd have to return for Christmas because no one was even considering this would be a trip that combined everything into one.

Faith almost exploded on him when he even suggested it and his mom didn't raise her voice to him many times that he could recall. He conceded for the kids, after all, he did love them and wanted what was best. He just wished his mom would move into the city nearby – *it would solve a lot of problems... selfish,* he thought to himself, but he couldn't help but think in any other way. The farm was sucking the life out of her and his father was still working the sixteen hours that left her on her own a lot.

Thank god, she was doing so well with the quarter horses. He had to admit they were a beautiful bunch of animals.

He stood at the fence watching as she worked a frisky little bay colored mare through her paces in the riding ring. *Stop. Proceed.* It reminded him of the traffic he watched from his office tower. He thought of all the processes and procedures with anything. Everything followed suit and he shook his head quickly – *geez, can't even get away for a weekend without my mind wondering back to work.* He caught his mom watching him and he smiled, trying to convince not only her but himself that he was in the moment and actually trying to enjoy it.

Somewhere in the back forty he heard the distant drone of the machine that kept his dad busy into the late hours of the evening and even into the late months of the year. Nothing was ever completely finished on the farm. It was always a race to do more than you humanly could so you were one step ahead after the winter subsided and spring brought renewed attention to the land. The animals kept Martin Sr. busy during the winter because their very survival depended upon his constant unquestioned care and attention.

Martin felt guilt slide into his thoughts and appreciated they were private. Someone might take the guilt as caring and then push that to reconsidering his harsh stand against his dad's chosen life. *No. Stop. No. Don't proceed here.*

"Martin."

"Ya, Mom."

"You want to take her out – I'd like to see how she handles with someone other than me at the rein."

"You want to see me thrown to my death."

"Don't be so dramatic – she's gentle, for God's sake, Mickey could ride her."

"Me. Me. Ya. Ya."

"Mom!" Neither one of them saw the boy hanging over the bottom rail of the fence, arms through, chin mounted on a forearm, thoughtfully watching the horse and rider. He looked like his dad, all quiet and serious, pensive and thoughtful. Faith laughed.

"Get up here and show your son you're not a big 'fraidy cat." She held the reins out to him, almost daring him to actually enjoy something other than a seat at the power commission hearings or his executive leather high back chair.

"Daddy. Daddy. Cowboy Daddy." Mickey's prompting wasn't helping his case any because if he didn't get up there he'd not live that disappointment down.

"Okay. Okay. Two against one, how fair is that?"

Martin hooked a toe in the left stirrup and swung effortlessly into the western gear on the horse's back. He pulled up on the reins, turning the mare's head away from the fence, and to the cheers of his son and admiring smile of this mother, he broke her into a trot around the training corral. He stopped her short with a tug on the reins and reversed directions. Feeling like he was born in the saddle, he put her through paces matching the training he watched his mother do just moments before – *okay, this feels too natural.*

He walked her back over to the fence; confident he proved a point not only to his mother but to himself. There was a natural streak that he could not deny lived down inside – one he would continue to deny publicly. He took a stand and must support it even though it felt good to be on the horse; it felt good to see the look his mother gave him; it felt good to be somewhat of a hero in his little boy's eyes. He lifted a leg and slid off the horse, smacking the dust from his designer jeans, as he handed the reins back to his mother.

"You looked good up there."

"Daddy." Mickey's arms were outstretched waiting to be picked up. He grew tired, rubbing little eyes with dirty fists.

"Thanks, Mom. That's all I'm saying because you'll pull it every which way from reality you can if you knew how good I actually felt to be up there." He kissed her cheek and smiled. "Come on partner – let's go wash the entire farm off your face. Man, what were you doing, digging for that salamander with your mouth?" Mickey giggled and then yawned again.

Martin knew his mother watched as he took Mickey toward the farmhouse. He realized he could be a very good father if he was just present and accountable. He also knew Erin watched as he approached the back deck. *He wasn't going to go back there;* in his mind they were finished. She smiled, cautiously, allowing Martin to pass with Mickey hoisted up over his shoulder.

"Thanks," she almost whispered when he was beside her, "thanks for all this."

Dammit. He knew it was in there; the kind of man he was meant to be as a son, as a father, as a husband.

He couldn't continue to fault his father for things he repeated for himself. The constant work and just getting all caught up in what you considered to be important, took its toll whether it was what you planned or not. He knew things could never go back to what they were with Erin – *they couldn't* – but only because he wasn't in a position to change what it was he did and what it was that came between them.

He was married to the career he took and putting his best effort forward in that took so much out of him he didn't have anything more to contribute anywhere else. It was a lame excuse but the only one Martin could come up with that made any sense. Being there, on the damned farm, away from the pressures of work allowed him to focus on the other things that were supposed to matter more, not just to him, but to anyone who takes a wife, cares about his parents, and loves his children. He wanted the best for them and felt his contribution to that best was something he didn't have to give.

It concerned him even more that his father was not around for most of their visit and, although it bothered and hurt him, he could not fault the man. Martin was a mirror image of him despite his denial. The stand he took against his father was one he should have discussed honestly with himself – he was selfish. *Driven, but selfish, because being away wasn't what the family you were supporting really wanted.* They wanted you near and it was a hard argument for a man to accept. *It was like he had to be away and constantly providing in order to prove his worth.* No wonder he pushed away any internal feelings lately, to accept and deal with them would admit his ways were wrong and that would mean he was much more like his father than he cared to admit. *They weren't wrong to so many others, then why were they so wrong for him?*

He watched his mother deal with his dad's ways and still hadn't learned from indications that he did the very same thing to Erin despite their love and initial longing for one another. He resented the fact that his father would force him to make a choice between what was right and what was expected and yet he wouldn't make a choice that was right for Mickey – *his own son would grow up feeling the same as he did – if – he didn't change his ways.*

The dilemma was in that accepting and changing them for him, he would be displaying acceptance for his father as well. *Why couldn't he do that?*

He wanted them to get out of the business while they could and he didn't want the burden of the legacy even though generations of hard work were going to be for nothing just because it wouldn't go any further in the family. *Why couldn't it just be accepted for what it was – a means to an end for whomever was in charge?* The farm served its purpose, now it was time to be done. *Give it away, for all I care.*

He felt a surge of bile churning from his stomach and knew the stress was going to get to him if he didn't slow down and take into consideration what was most important.

Could he convince his father otherwise while on this trip – did he chance ruining everything that was going well by approaching the subject? The other option was to avoid it, like everything else.

Dinner time table talk was light and laughter surrounded recollection of the day's events. Martin Sr. came in from the fields and barns, quiet and reserved – even more than usual.

"Hey Dad, what's wrong?"

"Nothing."

"Are you sure? You're kind of quiet since you came in."

Martin didn't want to push it but he was concerned. He noticed the concern on his mother's face soon after Martin Sr. washed up and sat down at the table.

"Nothing to concern you, Son."

"Anything I can do to help? Sorry... I know, kind of late to offer help after a day's chores have gone by..." He looked to his mother, apologetic, and she smiled weakly, with a slight nod of her head. He knew she appreciated any effort he made toward his father and accepted what needed to be done.

"I guess I can always hope that my only son would want to help me."

"You know I would – in whatever way I can – Dad."

"Sure." Martin Sr. let it go without an argument, slightly out of character for him. There was a pause but not the usual awkward silent moment, but rather a Wells' pensive thought filled pause. "Perhaps, you can do some checking for me – would you do that, Son?"

"Sure, Dad. What kind of checking?"

"Well, there was a crew out on the right of way today, working, but not the regular power crew I usually come across along the corridor."

Martin Sr. stopped for a moment, perplexed, then continued. "I think the truck was marked with lettering but couldn't quite see what it was – like a surveying crew of some type. Usually, the local electrification unit is out there or the transmission line company. But this wasn't either of them."

He paused again, this time taking a mouthful of water first before he continued. "Don't like strangers out on my land even if they pay me to access it."

Martin took out a small note paper pad from his pocket and scribbled a couple of notations. "I understand that, for sure. What time were they there, Dad?"

"It was late morning, early afternoon. They were only there an hour or so. Light beige trucks – guys had grey on their jackets."

"Sure, Dad, don't worry about it. I'll check it Monday when I'm back in the city. I'm sure there's nothing to worry about but I'll give you a call one way or another."

"Thanks, Son."

"So how's the hogs doing?" Martin didn't really care about how the hogs were doing except to be nice and flat and crispy on his plate at breakfast. He felt bad thinking that way about the animal but it was all the feeling he had for them. *Now, the horses were another story.* There was a connection there Martin couldn't deny, just like the one his mother felt for them. In all honesty, if – *and a big if, at that* – he had to farm or ranch, it would be working with horses, not hogs or cattle or sheep or...

"Fine as far as hogs go."

"That's good. Did the fields come off profitable this year for you?"

"Fine as far as fields go."

"I know, Dad, it's just small talk but at least it's a conversation. I'm happy things are going good this year. Really."

Martin inserted a sincerity he knew worked in other areas of his life, hoping his dad would take it for what it was – genuine interest in his well-being even if it wasn't true interest in what the farm had to offer.

"They're good. Could be better, but thankfully your Mother's horses are a booming business. They brought us to the best year yet."

"Honestly, Dad, I'm happy to hear that."

"Daddy?"

"Hey, Mick. You finished eating?"

"Yup."

"Time for bed?"

"Nope."

Everyone laughed. There was a way a child could break the tension just by being honest – at least, a young child. Martin knew it was not the case for him now and, often, being honest just hurt everyone around him.

Those expectations dwelling inside lay claim to bitterness and rejection and the best thing he could do was just stay in the moment and remember how small things only needed to be in order to create a basic happiness. If he left things as they were right then, he could go away happy and continue to do his job. But there were changes he knew coming on the winds of the future and he didn't like the way things might go around there. He would leave things as they were and he made a silent promise to himself to do so unless the right opportunity presented itself later that evening for opening such a conversation.

After the kids were sleeping, the four adults took an evening drink out onto the large wrap around deck and, although the evening was beginning to cool off quickly, warm sweaters and hot toddies kept them comfortable enough to sit for a quiet moment. A chair positioned at the window to the kid's room allowed Erin to watch closely, especially for Mickey who had a tendency to get up and wander about during the night. Essie was in her crib and contentedly sleeping through the night.

"Mom, you're doing a fantastic job with the horses."

Martin sat alongside his mother a casual arm draped over her shoulder; she turned her face up to him and smiled. The soft light from the porch lanterns caught her eyes and he could see the questioning glance, and he hoped she wouldn't go there – to the spot where he did not want to go.

Home was in Edmonton and he just couldn't bring himself to move back despite her need to be near him and the kids and Erin. He kissed the top of her head and continued quickly.

"So you have how many clients now?"

"There are about a dozen ranches calling for your mother's stock, Son; quite impressive they tell me." Martin Sr. spoke up. There was pride in his voice even as he gave reserved credit to her – most of the time it was a Wells Ranch group accomplishment. Martin knew his dad meant well but also knew that pride kept him from admitting any differently.

"There's another bunch being shipped Tuesday. The guys from the Long Bar from down south are coming up to pick up a dozen including the little mare you rode today." There was almost regret in her voice. "I get attached to them and almost hate shipping them out. I just can't be right there when it happens. Stupid emotions."

"Mom, that's not stupid... it shows how much you care. They are getting good stock and I sure hope you're charging them for it."

"You looked like you were born in that saddle today, Martin; I didn't even know you knew how to ride." Erin interjected and took a slow sip of the steaming liquid from her mug, watching her ex-husband as she drank.

"Something we just never did, Erin; just didn't even think of it."

"You never rode before, son, in fact... growing up – don't you remember when your grandfather came by to visit and we went to Heritage Park? You screamed so loud you spooked the ponies and they're used to crying babies and fussing kids not wanting to ride 'em..." Martin Sr. grunted as he continued. "You were scared of 'em."

"Marty. He was not. Quit your storytelling right now. Martin was on that horse today like he was born in the saddle." Faith came to her son's rescue not wanting her husband to start something she knew her son wouldn't overlook. Every time the conversation started out by innocently poking fun, it veered very quickly into something tragic.

"It's okay, Mom. I was afraid at one point in my life. I guess more so because I was actually afraid of getting stuck out somewhere I didn't want to be..."

Martin was sorry it came from his mouth before he had a chance to consider the consequences. One would think that honesty was always the best policy but his thoughts of earlier did not come to his rescue and the intent to make peace quickly left.

When he hit the defensive mode he took it and ran with it, especially when he didn't have to worry about justifying rudeness to his own little son.

"You always were a might rude."

"Dad, it has nothing to do with being rude – give it up – it's about being truthful."

"Truth is, Son, I gave up on you a long time ago. I accepted the fact that you'd never come around to seeing it my way. Too bad 'cuz that's the Wells' way."

"I could say the same. Why do think I moved out of here and refused to waste my life on the farm? It's not going anywhere but down, Dad. Can't you see the changes I've been trying to tell you about? They're happening and they'll be happening fast and furious once the current legislation goes through. Don't you think I know? You are not the only one who works knee deep in shit every day. And I think about you and Mom every day. I didn't abandon you. I made a choice and went away and I still can't get rid of the dirt from under my nails and the fear in my heart that something awful has to happen before you'll see the light."

Martin Sr. stood, slowly, and turned to leave them. "Is that so, Son?" He went out toward the barns and Martin was immediately sorry.

"Mom. I'm sorry but he gets me so upset about this. I hate to see you stuck out here, too, refusing to hear the information I have to share with you both."

"I hear you, Martin. I believe you, Martin. But I choose to be here with your dad and I intend to stay until he decides otherwise. He's been good to me so I don't have any reason to leave him or abandon him."

"Well, I didn't abandon him, either."

"I know, Martin, but pride is an awful big thing. It's like an impenetrable road block that's impossible to see around, especially when it's someone as stubborn as your father. I keep in mind the things you say and take to heart your warnings, for I know in my heart you truly love us both and would do anything to save us."

She smiled and got up, pulling the loose knit shawl closer to her body.

"That is, if we need saving." She paused looking off into the night after her husband.

"And, just so you know, I do listen to what you have to say. I invested like you said in that little condo in town. Good idea. Good night, Erin. Good night, Son." She patted his arm as she walked by him on her way into the house.

He felt Erin's eyes on him even in the low light of the night on the deck. His mom and dad had left in their own ways and he wished she'd say good-night and leave him to wallow in his own self-pity. He didn't want to start something with her again, meaning, a conversational defense as he knew that's where it would go. He did not regret the things he said but perhaps the manner in which it came out – *and timing. Shit.* Timing was always a problem for him in the general manner of speaking. Put him in front of a power commission hearing and he was as cool and collected as anyone up there, more so than most.

Argumentative debates were his specialty with the assuredness of logic and informative research backing his corner. Put him in the emotional arena, though, and he came out the blithering idiot a good percentage of the time. His hands were cold on his face but felt refreshing on the heated blush of his anger. He sat, head in hands, contemplating making his own move. It startled him out of his reverie to feel her hand lightly upon his shoulder.

"You want me to leave you to your thoughts?"

Did she really expect him to be honest here, too? Why ask me, of all people, such direct, honest answer questions? He could feel another disagreement coming on; perhaps, he should just take the farm truck and head into town for the night. It might be safer being out of the range from family, farm, and foe. Thoughts of running filled him.

"Erin..."

"It's okay. Honestly, I wish you'd have been so forthright with me."

"Wasn't I? I let you leave."

"I can't guarantee that anything would have been any different."

"I know. Sit." He patted the cushion next to him on the wooden bench. "Stay, please, even if we don't talk. Nice, quiet company is always welcome."

"Oh, are you suggesting I talk too much..." There was softness and teasing to her voice that quelled the urge to take up the defensive stance. He laughed.

"Yes."

She slapped him playfully on the knee and her hand stayed a little longer than both expected. She pulled away but not without the awkwardness of that first date feeling. Martin took the cue and leaned back on the wood posts of the surrounding enclosure and stared up into the dark sky.

"There's a million of 'em out there, Erin."

"Just like excuses."

"And reasons..."

"And wishes... and if they were horses..."

"Beggars would ride... but I'm through begging them to change and move. They gotta do it for themselves, Erin. I'm tired of trying to convince them there's something better."

"But what's wrong with what they have? To them there might not be anything better."

"And believe me, I'd let them alone if I didn't have the knowledge I do. It's not immediate, but it's happening. Changes are in the works and the farmer and the rancher are the ones going to pay for it."

"Is it really all that bad?" Erin sat back, close enough to him to feel the heat from his body but not close enough to touch.

"It could be. The costs are detrimental. The changes are something they argue over and over without resolve. They cannot implement the things they're talking about without major changes to how they do things. And, in some instances, it's just not possible to change at all." His frustration came through in the words he said but it was like tossing them out into a wind storm – they tended to blow away before anyone had a chance to really hear them and process their meaning.

"If you don't want the farm, does it mean that they have to leave it, too?"

He sat up and faced her; he grabbed her shoulders gently and spoke in a voice that she knew he was trying to keep from trembling. "I don't want the farm. I don't want them to leave it for our kids. I just don't want them to get hurt. If they don't leave they might – perhaps, not physically but financially and emotionally. I can't make him see that it's not worth it."

She was looking directly at him, her eyes watching his, listening intently – no tears, no fear, just a concentrated effort focused directly on him. His emotions boiled and he shook his head slightly.

"There's got to be a way to make them understand. I just haven't figured out the best way to ensure they hear me."

"I hear you and I believe you, too."

She did then what he'd hoped she wouldn't ever do again. The confusion of all their troubles stirred around inside his head; he thought of the possibilities of being close to his children every day then realized it wasn't possible with his job. It was a new job that would pull him away from home even more hours than before. He thought of the ease of how things would go without having to guess and to just know and keep in touch and be close to someone again, and not just in the physical sense when the need hits, but in a supportive, emotional way. *That's what was missing right now.* He thought of the reasons she left and the excuses he made and the way it became once he accepted the separation. He weighed the options and like so many decisions he had to consider, nothing he considered made any sense at all. Indecision was his best friend and it went hand in hand with avoidance and a noncommittal attitude. He didn't know what good would come of it, *if anything.*

She did what he hoped she'd not do again.

She kissed him softly on the lips and he kissed her back.

Chapter 9 – Orientation

Back in the office Monday morning, Martin had the luxury of time to himself in the quiet solitude of his new Alternative Energy corporate surroundings. His assigned assistant, he was surprised to find out, was a young man by the name of Adam Winters. Although at first he was confused by the assignment, and it was by no means that he questioned the capability of the man, it was with some thought he came to realize not long into the morning and into his thoughts, that perhaps this was the best thing that could happen for, and to, him. He already had too many distractions and if there was one thing Martin knew for certain about himself, it was that he didn't swing that way. With that in mind, he knew he could concentrate on work while at work.

Before reviewing the files and research he needed to have compiled for the upcoming board meeting, just hours away, Martin pulled the small piece of paper from the note pad he kept in his pocket and, remembering the promise to his father, despite all else, hit the search bar for Google. On his lap top he punched in "local power company trucks." He was hoping that by some stretch of good luck there might just be an image of the logo or the vehicle his father described out on the corridor right of way over the weekend.

He wished his father would have had the where with all to call him out to the field during the time they were there, but Martin Sr. didn't do things the way his son might have expected. He would always weather whatever storm and then make a report afterwards without a needed s.o.s. call when it might have made the difference.

He let out a long breath as he realized he was holding it in with the stressed thoughts of the weekend and his father and all that had happened. He was also avoiding the replay of pleasantries he hadn't expected to happen again in his lifetime and it wasn't even anything of major issue. It was just a kiss...

"Mr. Wells?"

Adam's voice pulled him from that place and plunked him squarely into Monday morning reality.

"Yes?"

"There's a visitor here to see you."

"I'm not expecting anyone – who is it?"

Before Adam could answer, she moved into view and politely excused herself around and past the surprised assistant.

"Suzanne. How nice. Come on in." Martin motioned to a chair and he motioned to Adam. "Thanks, Adam, that's all for now. Hold all my calls." *He always wanted to say that...* but being in charge of your own office and dependent upon the calls that come in, you don't always have the luxury of fending them off. In his new position, he got paid no matter what and he just decided to take that into consideration.

"You've moved right in."

She waited until the door closed, then approached him, throwing her fur coat to the floor. As she reached out for him, he backed into the desk and she pressed her body against him.

"Did you miss me?"

Her voice was a whisper, husky and suggestive, that took him from the board room to the bedroom in one fast thought. He blinked. *What the hell?* He caught her up in an embrace that pressed her breasts to him and his lips to hers and he felt himself grow responsive.

The deep kiss lasted minutes and he knew it had to break now or it wouldn't and he had to right now or it wouldn't look good to be on the new job, fucking right there in the middle of the floor on the expensive carpets – *the Persian kind* – in the offices of Alternative Energy Corporation. He wanted to lose something right now but it wasn't his job. *What the hell,* he repeated to himself – *meaning whoa. Stop.*

"Hey, babe, save it for tonight. Whew, you are so hot." He didn't have to interject the usual contrived truism into his voice. He missed her and he wanted her but it would have to wait until a respectable time and place.

"You didn't call this weekend."

"I left you a message. I took... I went to my parent's place. You know – the farm." He just about spilled it. He had been meaning to tell her about the kids but how could he just keep going on and on and then one day just break it to her... *like, oh by the way I have an ex and two young kids that will always be there because they live just a neighborhood over and she goes with me to the farm and we were just sitting there and she unexpectedly got all understanding with me and in the heat of a moment of connection, she kissed me...*

"Martin... where are you now? You know I know when you go somewhere in your mind and leave me standing here awaiting your return." She laughed. "I find it weirdly reassuring that you always tend to come back but who knows where you go in that intelligent wandering mind of yours."

"You don't want to know."

Martin buzzed his assistant and then picked up Suzanne's coat and draped it across the chair in front of the desk. She took a seat on the plush sofa in the little alcove to one side of the large office. That was something Martin noticed about all the offices in the building – they tended to be on the large size and if you considered staying overnight because of the amount of work you had to do or for some other less work related reasons, there were a myriad of niches in which to make yourself comfortable.

A careful employee would go almost undetected. Martin thought he'd have to test out that theory sometime... his thoughts were interrupted when Adam came in to the room.

"Yes, Mr. Wells?"

"Can you do me a favor?"

"That's my job..."

"Um, I mean, can you check out this information for me and just make a notation of it and email me any findings. I have a call to make later and need to find out something about this for that call." He handed the folded note to Adam with the scrawled information his father had given him. He smiled and dismissed his assistant.

"And hold all his calls..." Suzanne playfully called after him.

"Now, to what do I owe this pleasure? I thought we'd get together later in the week." Martin sat down across from Suzanne ignoring her obvious attempt for him to sit next to her. He really didn't need these distractions. He'd barely got started on the files he'd received before taking the atypical weekend off. He wasn't sorry he did even though some things didn't quite turn out as hoped and others were totally unexpected.

"Come over here and I'll show you what pleasure."

"Keep it business – you want me to get fired."

"No... rather, get you fired up. But okay, suit yourself."

"I should really get back to work. You want to go for dinner later?"

"Hmmm... sure. What time does the board meeting start?"

"Starts at 1:00 – why?"

"I'm the guest speaker."

She said it so matter of fact it caught Martin off guard as to why she might be speaking at the meeting; then he recalled the big media campaign that would launch public information on nuclear energy production in preparation for its implementation to the grid. It seemed to him to be moving a slight bit faster than expected since he really didn't have much more done than distant public hearings booked for the New Year.

His paper wasn't anywhere near complete or the findings anywhere near conclusive and there they were already talking promotion.

"Oh. Promotion already?"

"Just a few preliminaries, Mr. Wells. I don't want to lose this account to some other fame and fortune hungry firm, so I get in when the talks start and work the campaign from introduction to end. Is there a problem?"

"No, not at all. Besides that's not my call. I'm just the research guy."

"Oh, you're so much more than that, don't sell yourself short. I've heard what they say down at the Commission, you know. I hear you really know your industry stuff and if it's signed off with the Martin Wells' signature of approval, it's as good as implemented."

"Well, I appreciate your confidence. I'm sure you do a fine job doing what you do as well..." He caught her sly smile and wink and couldn't help the slip from polished presenter to flustered flounder. "You know what I mean!"

He outstretched a hand to pull her to her feet and to him and kissed her urgently. "Now, go. I've got to prepare for my first meeting or I'll be fired before I even get my first pay cheque."

"See you there."

She left the office slowly, with a deliberate coyness knowing he was watching her walk away. He made sure she knew he was, and he also knew he'd call her later if they managed to get out of the company board meeting at a decent hour. *If not, perhaps holed up in that little niche with locked doors would suit just fine.*

The rest of the morning Martin kept his head down and pen to paper figuring furiously over the projections for the nuclear interception. It wasn't like there wasn't already talk and procedures in place for companies looking at plant construction in northern Alberta.

And it most certainly was not a new concept given that there were already seven nuclear power plants in Canada and, worldwide by 2007, already fifteen per cent of the world's power was supplied by nuclear generation. It was, however, new territory for Alberta and it concerned Martin that there seemed to be a rush to "play catch up" with the global energy market place. He was proud to claim his home province was a leader in many cutting edge innovations, but power development and upgrade was not one of them. Almost last to jump on the smart grid band wagon, there was a growing concern by all involved that proper procedures were being ignored or slighted over, including a missing business case that involved the analysis of the implementation of things that couldn't possibly derive benefit for all end users. Even if there were some kind of implied benefits, there was no statistical proof the costs justified the end.

Perhaps, he could be of some assistance in getting them to slow down to realize the necessity for involved study. A slow and deliberate, informed implementation would be the best thing for all Albertans. He had little time to prepare for his presentation that day, but plants were nowhere near completion and no one had completed their public reviews, let alone made application to the Energy Commission. *A trip up to the construction sites might be well worth his time,* he thought, as he scrawled a projected time line on the page in front of him.

Construction would most likely start by the end of the coming year, 2011, but completion was something he wouldn't foresee for one plant until at least 2017. That schedule gave Alternative Energy and all its subsidiaries six years of planning, testing, plant construction, and then preparation time before start up could even be considered. Even with that, it gave them a very tight schedule that wouldn't compensate for market fluctuations or allow for much deviation. Martin readjusted the line to include contingency plans taking up to two more years in the construction stage with his final projection aimed for late 2019.

Pleased with the schedule he produced, he proceeded to review the vast amounts of research he was able to pull together regarding reports from the existing plants and the effects, if any, they had on neighboring communities, the marketplace in general, and what benefits might be evidenced in support of this type of energy production.

The seven Canadian plants were his best reference points as they would closely mimic the type of market conditions Alberta faced.

Martin realized something most industry professionals didn't stop to take into consideration, something that his public consultations provided him access to – the public. Just say "nuclear" and the red flags go up and warning bells sound, loud and clear. It was a common reaction and given the potential for irreparable damage if there ever was a failure or incident, the reaction was a natural one. The public was not yet ready to see the Three Mile Island or Chernobyl catastrophes in their own back yard. It would even be his educated guess that most consumers in this province lacked the knowledge that plants already exist and, in some countries like France, account for a whopping seventy seven percent of the country's power supply. He would bet that not many would guess or assume it was already upon us like an apocalyptic movie.

As Martin finished up his initial report he copied the document to the handy jump drive he kept in his pocket and then saved the file to the desk top of his computer. As he sent it to the printer located on the side counter along the wall behind his desk, the "you've got mail" icon lit up on the bottom task bar on the 20" desk top screen. He glanced quickly at the time – twelve fifty five – no time for email now; he would have to leave it until after and, as it was, he was close to being late. *Good thing his office was just across the hall from the AEC board room,* he thought, as he grabbed his lap top, Blackberry, and the print copy of his report.

Chapter 10 – Revelations

The meeting ran late – well, late by most office hour standards, but probably not so for the usual board room procedures in big corporate energy offices. Martin realized how hungry he was when they finally adjourned at seven fifteen – he hadn't taken time for lunch as he worked right through on his report, and the muffin he had on his way to the office almost twelve hours ago really didn't count as meal status. He considered in the past even he bought Jessica dinner when they worked late and laughed to himself at his thoughts of calling his new employer "cheap." He made his way back to his office and punched the quick call button to the restaurant on the main floor of the office tower and requested a delivery order.

He rested a moment, eyes closed as he lay back against the leather chair, thinking on his presentation and the obvious pleasure the group took in considering his recommendations and it pleased him. The report was well written and covered an area of vast development. The required technology was contrasted against the consideration to the delicate introduction needed with regard to public exposure. They were receptive to the schedule he provided and after some discussion regarding the actual "newness" of the nuclear concept in Alberta, they moved to initially accept the implementation plan. Discussion would take place over the next couple of months to address any changes or problems that might arise from the media awareness campaign proposed by Suzanne's company.

She presented a polished proposal, and Martin smiled, remembering her ease at being in the front of the room full of men. He knew that not one of them were concentrating one hundred per cent on her words.

He certainly wasn't. He was out of the room, somewhere discreet, tasting her lips and touching her soft skin. It was quite surprising to him when she left the room without so much as a glance in his direction once her presentation was complete. He watched her leave and wondered if he would even see her later, given the way the meeting dragged on. *First meeting and I'm already critical, wow,* he thought, and sat up, stretching his arms and neck and shoulders.

He signed on to the work station and clicked the mail icon. It was from Adam. Interoffice email was a great way to get work done without even talking to your assistant who sat just beyond the door to the office. By the time the meeting was over, Adam had left for the day, leaving a number of envelopes and correspondence stacked in the basket on the corner of Martin's desk.

"I just started here and it looks like I got too much shit in here already." He ruffled the edges of each sheet of paper and each envelope, and then drew his attention back to the high resolution screen.

"Subject: Are you joking?"

Martin scrolled back to the inbox to ensure the message was indeed from his assistant and confirming it was, continued to read the message.

"If you look out the back of the building someday – back equipment compound –   you will see a plethora of beige and grey. Your notation describes our own affiliate trucks… And I work for you?"

There was a little happy face after the comments but the words had their own barbs which stung at Martin. They were fused with meaning Martin was unsure how to take, and it wasn't just because they came from his subordinate in a less than professional manner.

"Smart ass."

Martin strolled over to the large window and strained to see down toward the back lot.

It was impossible from the location of his office no matter what position he tried to maneuver into... he would have to take a trip down there to investigate. *If what he said was true, it meant that Unified Nuclear Corporation had crews out on the corridor – but for what reason?* Transmission was not their responsibility; and with no intended nuclear plants sites even remotely close to the south corridor, it didn't make any sense at that point.

There was a knock on the door and Martin felt his growling hunger consume all other thought processes. He answered hurriedly and tipped the young delivery boy, who smiled his appreciation and was off with a 'have a good evening, sir'. Martin sat down at his desk to enjoy the hot meal and closed his eyes as he savored the first bite.

As he chewed contentedly, in his mind he formulated a careful response to the recently received information. It wouldn't be the boldly stated tell all method of the weekend when his emotions got the better of him. No, it would have to be considerate and cautious.

He grabbed the desk phone receiver and dialed his parents' number.

Chapter 11 – CEO

Rowan J. Cott was the kind of man that commanded attention from his employees and colleagues, but demanded it from his wife and the other women he bedded. Despite personality traits some would consider controlling and pervasive, he was also considered fair and quick to recognize the contributions of others when it worked well in his favor. Dedication and work compliance were rewarded with public accolades for outward accomplishments. He recognized not only business attributes but personal achievement, as well. Privately, he enjoyed submissive behavior and paid for those contributions when they worked well in his favor, too.

He was genuinely pleased with the outcome of the board meeting that afternoon and was also content in the decision he made to sign Martin Wells to their staff. He knew that Wells' input would be paramount to the approvals Alternative Energy Corporation required for the upcoming expansions.

The extensive implementation of the nuclear power interties to the grid would be seen as above board and within all regulatory requirements. He congratulated himself on the foresight to secure a future for all the associated companies he controlled. He knew it would be a delicate operation to keep things top secret, but he was also aware Martin Wells was not a stupid man.

The report Wells produced in such a short frame time for them, identified many of the problems the board and management were already aware of, but it also provided sound solutions that would address the problems. It offered a routinely succinct program and a schedule that one could not argue with, *if... they were going to do things within the legalities of the governing acts.*

Time was of the essence, however, and doing things "by the book" took more time than Rowan could see as profitable.

There were always going to be shortcuts and now he would find ways to get around them especially with someone as skilled as Wells producing the alternatives in black and white. He would go so far as to claim that the signing of Martin Wells on staff of Alternative Energy Corporate could arguably be the catalyst they needed to get the Energy Commission's approval long before any other company's application even made it before the hearings. *Time and placement* – it was what they needed to get the green light to forge ahead.

He flipped through the pages of the document Martin prepared and submitted to the board at that afternoon's meeting. He slipped them into a clear plastic folder, labeled 'confidential'. He glanced at his watch while sliding open the lower desk drawer and he pulled from the back compartment a bottle of brandy and two crystal glasses. He placed them on the desk as the door opened, both with barely a sound.

"I was beginning to wonder where you were."

Rowan stood up from the desk and took the glasses and liquor bottle over to the carved wooden coffee table. He turned to face the door and his guest.

"Lock it and come over here."

"You know I would never be late."

"You've not given me any reason to doubt you, so far."

"And I never will, my love."

Suzanne slipped her fur coat off and it slid down her body to the floor. The warmth of the fire in the closed room flushed her cheeks and she smiled, moving slowly toward him, the knit jersey dress clinging tightly to her shape.

"You are so hot, Zanne, you make me want you right now. But first, business." Rowan patted the leather cushion on the oversized loveseat next to him and as she sat down he handed her the clear plastic folder.

"Here are the documents. You should be able to get started now on the revision we spoke of earlier. You can copy his style easy enough and just use the last page where he's signed as a follow up. It would actually be fine to even use most of what he has right in there, just adjust the time lines and start dates. Say, we have it ready for early next week and I can proceed with filing it with the Energy Commission. I want to be the first to roll on this."

"Sure, Monday's fine."

"Try for Sunday, Zanne." He brushed the hair from her eyes and his hand lingered on the side of her face. "So speaking of his style... how is he?"

"A girl doesn't kiss and tell." She laughed lightly and brushed his hand away from her face.

"Sure she does... when I pay her to."

He slipped a hand under one of the straps on her dress and slowly pulled it down over her shoulder. He leaned over and kissed her skin.

"So? How is he? Worthy or lacking?" His mouth sucked at the base of her neck and his hand cupped a breast inside the slinky shimmering fabric. He could feel the nipple harden as he kissed her neck and his breath was heavy as he pulled her close to him.

"Why don't you come by later?" Suzanne said in an attempt to stall him and pushed him away slightly. She pulled at her dress to recover herself and adjusted the strap on the middle of her shoulder.

"Baby, I want to come by now. I need to come by you, right now."

"Well, it's been kind of a tiring day. Thought I'd just stop by to pick up the papers you wanted me to get and then head straight home to start work." As she stood, Rowan did, too.

"Hmmm, you're rushing away. That's not like you." He looked directly at her and laughed loudly. "I guess that answers my question. He must be very worthy. Well, then..."

Rowan grabbed Suzanne and pulled her close with one hand while the other pulled her head back exposing her neck to him. He kissed his way down to the top of her cleavage and then worked his tongue back up to her neck and then to her lips, which he pried apart. He kissed her long and hard. She was breathless when he quit and she no longer struggled to get away from him.

"Does he do that?"

"Not that well."

Rowan laughed and grabbed her hand, pulling her from the warmth of the fire into the low light of the office area where his desk shone in the night lights of the adjacent buildings. He spun her around and pushed her forward over the edge of the desk.

"Rowan, he doesn't do that either."

"Ah, but does he do this..." He hiked her dress up past her waist to expose a skimpy black thong edged with tan lace. One hand pushed on her back to keep her against the desk while the other caressed her bum and fingered the narrow lace. He slowly reached between her legs and felt her tense up as his fingers grazed her sensitive skin.

"No, Rowan... he doesn't do that, either, and definitely not that well."

"Ah, poor Zanne, such a task I set upon her. Despite the handsome bonus, she is doomed to fuck an incompetent lover who does not know what a woman wants... especially you, sweet Zanne. You... you like it hard and fast and dirty, yet you pretend to be such a lady." He smacked an open palm across one butt cheek, and then smoothed his hand over her again. He smacked the other side and followed it again with a firm caress.

"Let me up, Rowan."

"Ah, but Zanne, you like this and in any case, even if you didn't, I pay you well enough to like it just fine." His mouth touched her skin on one side, first with a soft kiss, then with a playful tongue, and then a hard bite that made her scream out.

"Damn you, Rowan, let me the fuck up. How am I supposed to keep that from someone I'm supposed to be sleeping with... so much for spontaneity? My price just went up. Now let me go!"

He released her but not before he handed her another crack across the butt. He spun her around to face him. "Oh, you are already well paid my dear and you always love the things I give you, don't you? Especially this thing..." His hand went into the loose fitting lounge pants to finger the hardness he was going to share with her.

On the couch in front of the fire, without any argument from Suzanne, he pulled aside the lace panties and entered her with a satisfying grunt. The rhythmic rocking of him on top of her squeaked the expensive leather and it was not long before he let out an enraptured moan, as he erupted into her, and he smiled.

"Your fucking cheque is in the mail, Zanne."

Martin was content once he was able to devour the meal he'd ordered and he was even pleased with the call he'd made home. Even though he only talked to his mom, she had assured him that his father was fine and would be happy to hear the incident with the strange trucks was being "looked into." There was no way he could tell him anything else until he found out more. Martin made a mental note to check the outdoor equipment compound the next morning before he headed up to the office. He glanced at his watch and stifled a yawn – nine forty five. *Time to head home,* he thought.

The building was quiet as he left the tower and stepped out onto the street. Until he was assigned his own underground spot, he parked at the pay lot kitty corner from the building. The streets were still noisy and filled with passing traffic, both vehicular and pedestrian. It was so different than his south side office where the district seemed to close down after regular office hours.

It was eerie walking to his car without a soul around. The downtown area was still alive at the late hour with as much street traffic as during the busy work day – *almost* – well, not quite the same kind of traffic as he casually glanced at the girl on the corner under the lamp post. *Cliché,* he thought, as he passed her quickly so he wouldn't get her hopes up he might stop. *Don't Stop... just proceed.*

On the green light he made his way across one street and on the red, jay walked the avenue to come into the lot almost alongside his dark blue Beamer. As he reached the car, his cell phone rang, but it quit by the time he was settled in the car with the doors locked and motor running. It wasn't that he was afraid of the area at night but there was an incident nearly every night – *he must remember to ask about that underground parking pass, tomorrow.* Perhaps, he'd even bring a shaving kit and extra shirt. That way he could always stay in his office if he decided to work late. No need making extra trips if unnecessary and no need taking chances if it could be helped. *Chicken shit,* he thought and laughed but watched closely as two vagrants sidled up to the car and moved off quickly when he honked the horn. One could never be too careful. *Yup, need that parking pass. Soon.* He checked the missed call as he pulled out of the lot onto the street and realized it was Erin's number.

"Hey, missed your call – sorry, I just got home."

"Hmmm, you're early." She teased.

"Ha. Ha. So, everything okay?"

"Oh, ya, sorry for calling so late; I forget that you might think it's about the kids and worry."

"Kid's okay?"

"Yes, they're fine."

"Okay, then... are you okay?"

"Confused and alone and managing," she paused, "but, yes, I'm fine, too. How are you?"

"Good. Tired. Confused and alone ..." he laughed when he heard her sigh, "but managing, too."

"You want to come by and have dinner with us on Friday night? The kids are asking about you."

"Wow, I really am missing out on a lot – Essie's talking?"

"Oh, shut up, you know what I mean."

"Ya, I guess I do. Forgot how much fun it was to tease you."

"You were relentless... that's not fun."

"It wasn't that bad and besides, you can dish it out, too."

"Well, I should go, Martin. So, how about Friday?"

"Let me call you..." he heard the same old story in his voice coming through loud and clear and he could imagine the same old hurt showing on her face again. He was confused and wasn't sure which way to turn, but just because he said yes it wouldn't mean it was a firm decision on anything else, like a commitment that tied his hands. It wouldn't mean he was bound to anything other than being a decent human being...

"You know what? Friday sounds great." There, he said it. And he waited for the blow to hit him, the nerves and the cloud of confusion to overcome his senses. He waited but there was nothing.

"Really? I mean... great." She tried to recover from her obvious surprise.

"Sure, it will be fun. I've put it in my calendar. I promise."

"Okay, see you about six then."

"Good night, Erin."

"Bye, Martin. See you Friday." She hung up.

And he still waited for the inevitable self-doubt and argument but it didn't come and he had to accept that perhaps it was the right decision and he swore not to miss it... no matter what. He made an entry in his Blackberry calendar, and for good measure, he put a sticky note on the coffee pot in the kitchen. Both were things he was sure to use between that moment and then. He vowed he would remember – *Friday, at Erin's.*

Chapter 12 – A Matter of Conflict

It was early the next morning while he was shaving for work that Suzanne called. He saw the number come up and even debated answering – *why,* he had no idea. There wasn't any reason not to. It was more in consideration that they hadn't hooked up as he thought they might the night after the board meeting and it was a strange feeling that hit him, seeing her number. They made plans to connect later in the week but that was before he went away for the weekend and before Erin called with a Friday invitation to spend time with her and the kids and before he had been hit with what he thought were obvious right moves. He picked the call up after the fourth ring.

"Martin Wells."

"Hey, Martin Wells – what's up?"

"Not much, Suzanne. I was just getting ready to head out the door for the office. What's up with you?"

"Oh, not much. Just wondering why I didn't hear from you is all – thought maybe you'd have called me last night."

"I meant to but I must have passed out on the sofa once I got home. I stayed at worked rather late last night. Stupid board meeting lasted until after seven and then I had to finish up a couple of things before I left."

"Hmmm, too bad. I was waiting for your call."

"Well, you know where I am."

"I didn't stick around after my presentation."

"I noticed... but, in any case, I need to at least make some kind of initial effort at this new job. Hey, great presentation yesterday. I had it pegged – you know your stuff."

"Thanks. Wasn't too over the top for you? I know you had some reservations about an all-out media blitz, not the kind of thing the public wants mixed in with their Yule log and egg nog."

He laughed. "No, I guess not. All the discussion is okay in the planning stages because we're not releasing anything until into the New Year anyway. So all is fine. Good stuff. Really, we just have to time it right."

"Yes, it's all in the timing, baby."

"Going public at the wrong time can have so many repercussions... it's critical in the timing..."

"So speaking of timing, when are we getting together? I could come by the office..."

"I'll have to put it off for a couple of days. I have some research to do and I might take a little business trip up to Peace County to check out the site for the proposed nuclear generator they are talking about."

"Oh, really? Well, let me know if you want someone to tag along. I wouldn't mind a road trip."

"This one might be better solo, after all, it is for business and I'm not even sure when and if I might head out but I'll keep that in mind. Okay?"

"Sure, babe, whatever you decide. Give me a call one way or another; perhaps, we can hook up on Friday once you're back."

"I'll have to call you. You've got my email? m wells at AEC dot com... Send me a note while you're working away at your media releases."

"Oh, it will take a little bit yet to get them complete."

"Well, when you have something written up, shoot them over for me to take a look at. I'd like that."

"I will. Thanks. Guess I'll let you go, then. Talk soon, lover."

"Bye, Suzanne."

Martin hung up the phone feeling in charge and ready to go. His normal course of his indecision would usually leave him standing there befuddled. Instead, he came away with a clear picture of what he wanted to do – at least for the next forty eight hours.

He would leave just after lunch and be in Grande Prairie by suppertime with the Beamer, or he could book a flight and be there in two... *I'd rather have my own transportation,* he thought, and the decision was made to drive – highway sixteen to forty-three and beyond... *yes, getting away in the other direction would be good for him,* he thought.

He knew that personally he could use some distance but it would also give him a chance to see first-hand what the new age generation plants might do to the surrounding environment and population. He was curious to read the findings in the studies that would have been completed in order for ground breaking to commence. He would do some checking from the hotel room and pull up any hearings and intervention documents that might have been registered on the application.

According to environmental power regulations, and laws, there had to be someone on site at all times who would be able offer him first hand insight into the potentially planned construction. At least, that is what the Ontario Energy Commission required and he was certain the reasons were sound enough to have a duplicate process there in Alberta, too.

Martin pulled into the underground parkade and paid the daily rate. He tucked the tab close to the windshield on the dash and pocketed the receipt. He would get Adam to submit it to the Human Resources officer for reimbursement, but even if they refused, he was happier with the car close by and he was able to take the stairs up one level to the back entrance by the service lot.

Peering out into the locked chain linked compound, he confirmed what Adam had so respectfully replied – light tan colored Chevy trucks, with the beige and grey United Nuclear Corporation (UNC) logo, were parked three abreast inside the secured fence. He now knew *the who* but what he didn't know was *the why.*

To him, it wouldn't matter what trucks they were because if they weren't the local electrification units' or the upstream power company or the systems operators', they had no business being on the corridor, especially on private land without permission. His dad was paid well for the inconvenience of the current transformer towers but he wasn't paid enough to entertain other trespassers. And until he could prove they had a legitimate reason for being there, they were just that – *trespassers.* Too bad they just happened to also be an affiliate of his new employer. He could see this going nowhere good.

Martin took the stairs two at a time up to the main lobby and then punched the 'up' button. He rode in relative quiet, trying to ignore the "elevator music" that he noticed played constantly, day and night. *They could at least play something upbeat,* he thought, smiling, knowing that everyone who rode elevators in every building on every street in the downtown core said the same thing. He made a mental note to mention it at the next board meeting.

They wanted to be different, why not start there.

Chapter 13 – Digging

It looked like ground-zero of an explosion. Before him, the vast blackened area was devoid of trees, plants, grass, and anything else that might define it as alive. In fact, if Martin didn't realize what should have been there it would have been very easy to mistake the scene in front of him for a desolate planet off in the great unknown where an explosion from a falling meteorite left a huge crater-like hole. Martin felt like he was a visitor, not just to another company's plant for a tour, but to another universe's planet altogether. Surrounding the vast area was a flimsy security barrier intertwined with bright yellow tape that read "danger – keep out."

Some distance from where he pulled into the electric fenced area, there rose against the skyline the beginnings of large crisscross support structures, not buildings in themselves but rather the outer braces that would be used to construct the concrete towers of a nuclear generation plant. Even though they weren't "officially" under construction, the essence of what they were and what they would become overwhelmed him. It wasn't like he didn't see the massive tubes before because he had.

As part of his master's graduate studies with the University of Alberta in his final year, the group of students registered in the class on alternate energy processes was granted the privilege of visiting the plants in their early operational stages in Ontario. He remembered the feeling then as he observed the steam rising into the grey colored sky. That morning, however, surrounded him with a totally different feeling – it overwhelmed him with the reek of potential environmental disaster. Seeing the possible implications on the Alberta landscape, and imagining the ramifications of approving such a source of energy, hit him with emotional force.

He was glad at that point he did not bring Suzanne along with him for the ride. Alone, he could not only enjoy the trip in solitude and then spend time in the hotel preparing initial reports; he could also preserve whatever manliness he might have impressed upon her by not sharing this traumatic moment. If, in fact, the construction of this single plant raped the earth of this much surrounding life, imagine what a string of units or a province full of nuclear plants would do... He shuddered at the thought.

He parked his car safely from the ravages of any wayward construction traffic and walked into the trailer marked "All Visitors MUST Check In" intending to make his presence known. *Oddly,* he thought, *he would have preferred to make his thoughts known, loudly, like one of those environmental activist protestors. This didn't appear right and in many ways it was all too wrong.*

First of all, regulatory process applied to all energy sources and he knew of no application to the Energy Commission for nuclear plant construction approval. The consultation process with the public was barely over and that, as he recalled, did not go as well as planned or hoped. He knew he had his job cut out for him to try to present enough positive information to the public to allow them to make an informed decision. For or against – he did not know, but as far as he was concerned *that* was not his goal in preparing any documentation to file with the Commission. The facts would be included from what he would report and with this first look, if he had his way, it already would not appear favorable for Alternative Energy Corporation or anyone else in the business.

"Hello. I'm here to see your site supervisor. Please let him know that Martin Wells is here from the Edmonton offices of..."

"...Alternative Energy Corporation." The young man, wearing a bright yellow hard hat, smiled at Martin's apparent surprise. "We've been expecting you. I can take you to see Grant. Here, put this on." The man handed Martin an equally bright hard hat and pointed to the construction site.

Martin was still turning the apparent expectation of his arrival over in his mind as the young gate attendant drove him to the construction site. The large crater fell meters below the carved out edge of the Earth's surface. There was a large drive down ramp encircling the interior ring of the huge dug-out where a continuous movement of earthmovers and graders worked at leveling and redistributing the dark soil. *There really wasn't much to inspect at this point,* Martin thought, as his mind played over the doubt about the value of the trip.

"Sir." Grant Russell met them as Martin stepped from the Sierra pickup truck, his hand extended in greeting. With one hand on his hat, the site supervisor leaned forward with a firm welcoming handshake in return.

"Nice to meet you, Mr. Wells." Russell's gruff exterior threw Martin off as his business manner was like one of those voices or personality traits you wouldn't expect coming from a plaid shirted, construction worker.

"Martin, please. Thanks. Nice to meet you, too, and although I am surprised I shouldn't be – that seems to be my usual state of late. I apologize as I do not appear to be up to speed on what seems to be my expected visit."

"Your name is synonymous with regulatory process and energy."

"Okay, but I wouldn't go so far as to say *synonymous*. I guess I've done my share of Commission interventions." Martin moved forward toward the barrier and scanned the vast work site and continued. "So I see it's on the move here."

"Just the initial ground preparations, of course, as you are most certainly aware, we don't have approval just yet for one hundred per cent of the construction, but we expect, with your direction at the helm, that will be something we can expect in the very near future."

"I guess in a roundabout way my work will eventually help your company, too, given the type of energy business. Alternative Energy Corporation is working through the process and I've only begun to do my research."

"We've heard that your presentations and subsequent endorsements don't take too long to sway the masses, from what I understand, and that's what we're banking on."

"Well, there's a process and I expect it will move along fairly well as we follow required protocol..." Martin stopped. Remembering his "expected" arrival, he posed the question hoping for enlightenment. "You expected me to show up?"

"Sure, why not? There's an affiliation between nuclear power companies, even when they aren't registered publicly as being associated or something... We have direct contact with Alternative Energy Corporation on a regular basis; Rowan keeps us informed."

"Couple of things..." Martin was feeling a bit uneasy as he continued, realizing the possible implications of their conversation. "Peace County Nuclear One is an associate of Alternative Energy Corporation?"

"Most definitely."

"So, by associate... I am sure you just mean in the same business and, therefore, share industry information."

"Oh sure, that and more. Same chain of command."

"How does United Nuclear Corporation fit into the picture?"

"Bad boy power threesome." Russell laughed, apparently proud of his revelation and oblivious to Martin's discomfort with the whole conversation. Although assumption were few in his mind before he started the trip, he certainly wouldn't have pegged this discovery at the top of his list of findings. Caution now filled him as reservations overcame his sense of curiosity. Martin chose his next words with careful precision so as not to raise suspicions or reveal the concerns he felt building inside.

"So what, as site supervisor, are you working towards right now? Do you have a specific date in mind or are you just waiting on my recommendation to flow through the Energy Commission?"

"Oh, most definitely. We are just anxiously awaiting your word as our green light to go and we will continue with the preliminary ground preparations while we hope for a swift, positive outcome from the inquiries and interventions."

Martin felt that perhaps his anxiety came through before he redirected his apprehension. The last response from the site supervisor Grant Russell appeared to be too contrived. It presented an answer Martin wouldn't have expected because it deviated from the revealing nature in the initial conversation. *Damn, he must have sensed my change,* Martin thought, *time to alter my direction and up the ante.*

"You want to meet up for a drink after your shift?"

"You plan on sticking around then?"

"Haven't decided. I don't really know anyone around here..." Perhaps a casual encounter might reveal more answers to questions he now almost had to choke back to keep contained. Martin hoped that he didn't spook the supervisor into avoiding him.

"You're not heading back tonight then?" Russell pushed the hard hat back as he scratched at a spot on his head revealing salt and pepper colored perspiration soaked hair.

"No, I think it might be best to stay on tonight so I can get some initial work done on some reports in a quiet hotel room with no distractions. You know what offices are like. If I return now, there will be a pile of other crap to deal with first. Want to get to it while I'm knee deep, so to speak."

"Don't I know that, sure, if that's the case we could grab a beer later."

"We could just shoot the breeze."

"Great. You at the Best or Holiday?"

"Holiday. The one on Hundredth Avenue as you pull into town from the south."

"There's a bar there just off the hotel lobby – Peace County Pub."

"Wonderful – no driving and not far to fall. Appreciate that..." Martin laughed, as he felt the tension between them break and fall away. It would create a more amicable connection and relating one on one would loosen the conversation especially with a couple of drinks and distracting topics to put him off his guard. Martin hoped Grant would share more information freely. No pointed questions of an inquisition nature to raise the warning flags. It would look and feel more like an exchange rather than a fact finding mission that would appear intrusive and too direct.

Back at the hotel, Martin set up his laptop and made some quick notations regarding his morning adventures... *more like surprise discoveries,* he thought, as he recalled word for word the revealing association the site supervisor outlined between the three big nuclear players in the province: Alternative Energy Corporation, Unified Nuclear Corporation and Peace County Nuclear ONE. *Was this a cause for concern?*

He was not sure of the present implications but all the future probabilities pointed to a nuclear monopoly which put them in the same situation as with any monopoly – price fixing and industry control in the hands of one powerful owner. Would the government actually approve such a situation given that their departments would be excluded from the future profits of a sustaining energy source? An increase in power demand could be filled with the overabundance of nuclear power, as long as Martin could discover and address all the possible threats to the consumer, the industry, and the Alberta environment.

It would have to be a heftily tipped scale in favor of safety benefits in order for him to sign his name to such a controversial process even though all over the world, including limited access in Canada, nuclear power provided a much needed energy supply. The province's need for increased power production could be met with this infusion but would it be efficient *and* safe?

The big three would have to hold onto construction starts until his discovery of public acceptance or rejection was reported and all that would have to happen before he signed any single positive intervention. Transmission upgrades had only just begun and monster towers and lines would be needed to carry the electrical influx generated from one nuclear power station.

Martin started from his thoughtful reverie with the ringing of his cell phone. His determined deliberation would have to wait but his decision to document everything from the trip was forefront as he punched open a Word document on his laptop. He clicked on the Internet Mail icon at the same time he answered the call, with a quick glance to the call display.

"Hey, Adam, how's office life treating you?" *The office calling* – he wasn't sure if that was a good thing or a bad thing.

"The Chief Exec wanted me to ensure your trip was going as you had hoped."

"Checking up on me, are you."

"No. No, of course not, Mr. Wells. We are just hoping you were able to get the pertinent information you required and bring it back for reporting. I just wanted to ensure you got this personally transmitted phone message regarding the special board meeting scheduled for Friday afternoon," Adam paused, "just in case you were too busy socializing to check your email for that special meeting notice I would be sure to have sent you." The assistant's voice included tones that resembled something Martin couldn't really pinpoint but he equated with an attitude he really didn't care to continue cultivating. *Should he call him on it now or wait until he got back to the office?* He could always send the little ass an email with "*Are you Kidding Me*" as the subject line.

"I appreciate your diligence in informing me and now I will be prepared." *Friday afternoon, huh?* Reminders returned to the previous long running meeting he'd already experienced and that prompted quick thoughts to a niggling feeling there was something else or somewhere else he promised to be. That surely wouldn't be until at least early evening. *I'll bust outta there if need be,* he thought.

"Thanks, Adam. I've got to run now, you know, so much to do in so little time. Ta. Ta." He poked the disconnect call button with an inner feeling of satisfaction and accomplishment. He hoped Adam got the point, too.

The bar, located just off the lobby in the Holiday Inn Hotel, reminded him of something out of a trapper movie with all the stuffed heads and trophies mounted about the walls. *Classy... not,* he thought to himself. He chuckled at his judgment call reminding himself that he, too, was born a country boy and at one time lived on the farm but hunting, he couldn't see the point or the need in a modernized society. He choose a table with a mounted ruffed grouse in flight feeling that at least feathers were a little less disturbing that fur and hair and big hollow looking eyes. When he chose the table, however, he failed to realize that he would actually have to look out into all those other animals and immediately changed his mind – back to bear and wolf at this time was the best case scenario. He just casually pretended the chair was not suitable and tested the new one by wobbling it back and forth, smiling, as if satisfied.

Grant Russell showed up not long after Martin ordered and almost finished his first short rye on the rocks. After that one went down so smoothly, he decided he had better stretch them out and make them last.

He wanted to be coherent and his comment earlier about not having far to fall was only said in jest to ease the tension he felt building between him and the site supervisor. He waved to the waitress.

"Hey, Grant, what would you like?" The waitress edged her way in between the tables and stood beside Martin as Grant took the seat across from him.

"Beer. Whew, what a day. Canadian, doll."

The waitress just smiled her brightest whitest smile and winked. She knew where the tips might come from on those busy evenings when work shifts let out and she played into the job with what most would figure to be an artificial act. Some wouldn't know any different but she didn't seem like the kind to care what you thought.

"Hard day at the trenches?"

Martin took the last sip of drink from his short glass and hoped the waitress was on the ball enough to at least bring him another, considering she hadn't waited for his order or even ask if he wanted another. Grant was the rough, country type – perhaps, she didn't care for the city boy look with his designer jeans and navy pullover topped with a casual jacket. He thought he looked quite good when he checked the hotel elevator mirror on his way down to the lobby. *Wow, how vain am I.*

"Same old, same old. Can't keep workers out here sometimes with them crying about hours and pay and conditions. Geez, put me back a couple of years and give me what they get when I first started working this industry and there'd be no complaints from me."

"Same everywhere, my friend. I hear ya, although I'm not in the trenches like you man, but the office world is just a bunch of whiners most of the time. And, don't get me started on the farming sector." The waitress approached the table and apparently knew how to earn her tip from him; she sat a tall rye with rocks on the table in front of him.

"Hmmm, think I best be watching my thoughts 'cuz I don't know how you knew nor do I want to know what else you know, but thanks, hun." He smiled his best city boy smile.

"You are welcome." She placed the beer in front of Grant and gave him a big smile, too. Her proximity to him roused Martin with a blast of sweet cologne he recognized from somewhere else. *Ah, yes... same fragrance Suzanne wears.* He took a quick gulp of the drink as she left the table; he watched her walk away in what he thought was a discrete voyeur over the rim of his glass.

"You married?" Grant obviously caught his glance.

"Nope. Divorced. You?"

"Na, no time up here at this point. Got a girl in Manning, though, I don't get there too much either so I expect she will be moving on soon."

"That's too easy. Not worth going after, or what?"

"Never know with this job where I might end up and she's got a kid and all, can't take her away from her family. Don't expect her to leave 'em, either."

"Well, I can relate. My job ate up any chances at my marriage. Or, rather – let's just call an ass an ass, I screwed up any chances I might have had at my marriage with my job."

"I hear ya. More common than you know around here." Grant took a long swig from his beer, looking around the room while he swallowed. "Lotsa single ladies looking for attention here if you know what I mean..."

"Well, I'm not really staying long enough to cultivate something like that... just business this time, I'm afraid."

"I'm sure you will be back up here. There's plenty of work to do with the plant and all. Be needing to have those public consultations real quick and open and close any debate up soon."

"Sure, again, just business. Besides I've got something going back home."

"Hmmm." Grant was lost in his beer while he eyed a waitress serving a table in the next section.

"So, how long you been up here?" Martin took another slow drink while he formulated the next conversation direction and sat back in his chair. He didn't want to appear too obvious in his feigned interest but certainly wanted the conversation to go the way of discovery before too long into the night. He didn't plan on hanging around too late drinking and nursing a watered down drink in case Grant had any ideas of setting them up with single ladies looking for attention...

"I've been here since the plant site cut ground. We started with the clearing and then came the dodging bullets. People don't like it when the greenery is wiped out especially those talking about green energy and then getting all environmentally conservative."

"Guess it would be something different for them, don't ya think?"

"It was agreed to and then we get all the ecological freaks out there crying and raising a stink. Mark my words; your job is going to be one hell of a show with similar uprisings at all plant sites and especially along those provincial transmission corridors when we up the line voltage and upgrade to the necessary tower requirements."

Bingo. Martin felt a sense of fear and relief, all at once.

Chapter 14 – Research

Back in his hotel room, Martin finally let out the breath he was sure he was holding from the time Grant revealed the intent of the nuclear companies until he got to the enclosed safety of his room. There was also a moment he held his breath as he felt he might just cave and take a little overnight company. The waitress was convincing but almost too convincing. He had an overwhelming sense of "being watched" and hooking up with her, despite his obvious attraction, might have been a very big mistake. He didn't need any more complications, mainly because he didn't know what else might be "expected."

Besides, as he so boldly claimed to Russell, *he had something back in the big city* but at certain points he could argue, with whom, exactly. Remembering the dinner date with Erin and the kids, he made a quick entry into his Blackberry to remind him. He knew he had something already planned when Adam announced their specially scheduled board meeting. He knew he did, it was just that the confusion over the late state of events caused a frustrating memory loss. He told himself it was short lived, if he would just get over all the stress and move on, in one direction or the other. He refused, however, to let the stress give him reason to cancel that date.

Then there was Suzanne. Just the thought of her made him hot with desire and he knew that a shower and a hand job were very shortly going to be the order of the evening. He would work on the beginning of his report first, though, at least for a little while, and then perhaps, he could call her...

He knew that just the sound of her voice would set him off and there would be no getting back to paperwork. It was only ten and a couple of hours at the key board would definitely show some production. He could pick it up again at the office when he made it back to the city. He planned to poke around the town a bit longer and scrape a bit of the nuclear site dirt off of his boots. Nothing like a walk through town with the locals to accidentally strike up a conversation with the good folks of Peace County. *Wonder what they really think of the construction going on in their back yard? So how do you like your nuclear power plants?*

Martin surfed to the provincial energy department site and pulled up the Nuclear Consultation reports completed the previous year; he would use some of the findings released to support his initial report and would build on that with some actual 'man on the street' reporting he was certain he would dig up the following day. After that, he'd hit the highway for home with a full day to prepare for the meeting and then dinner with his ex-wife and the kids.

At shortly before midnight, Martin shut off the lap top and lay back on the bed. He placed a muscular arm behind his head and closed his eyes. The other hand clutched his cell phone and his mind clutched at a decision – *who should I call?* It was a question that stalled him and confused him and although he felt a hot desire to talk to Suzanne, he also felt just as much of a desire to talk to Erin. And that diversity is what confused him considering the urge he brought back with him to the hotel. He stopped to recall the innocent night on his parents' farm and then delved farther into their past and had to admit he and Erin had had great sex and some could venture to humorously guess, at least twice. But, considering all, she was more loving and caring rather than hot and erotic.

Oh, god, stop thinking those words.

It was a dilemma many men would love to entertain but he ventured to bet that once there it would become a mind bender. Maybe he could get the best of both worlds; talk to Erin, in a quick friendly call about the kids and the dinner date and whatever else. Then, beg off tired or something equally as mundane, all the while thinking of quickly dialing Suzanne. He could jack off while thinking of her and listening to her and maybe convince her to say naughty things whispered or screamed or moaned into his ear. *Listen to me, all choosy and conniving when not too long ago I wasn`t getting any,* he thought, and with a slight smile he sat up, pulling his shirt over his head.

The vibration from his phone in his hand sent a shiver down his spine and he decided not to glance at the call display to see who might be calling and just take a chance. In fact, it was like fate calling and he, being the recipient of gratuitous joy in any form, didn't have to decide which road he was going to take.

He answered slowly, seductively, and smiled when he heard her voice.

Chapter 15 – Cooperative Spirit

Wednesday morning dawned crisp and cool and Martin wished he had packed more suitable attire for the cold wind that whipped in from the northwest. Peace County was obviously not downtown Edmonton, which could be cold but the large heat sucking buildings that made up the concrete jungle tended to keep the inner city heated even when the outlying areas suffered several degrees lower. Everyone in town was prepared for this little Arctic blast, except Martin, so his initial plan to cruise the streets looking for free information handouts was out of the question. He'd have to patronize a few of the small coffee shops instead. He could choose some dine in restaurants to not only get his fill of coffee and a warm up between each stop but hopefully he could attract the right kind of attention.

Waitresses, Martin thought, *would be a wealth of off the street knowledge, as long as they were from the local area.* He considered himself cordial with women and he saw that particular employment position as a great source of information. He banked on what he was told anyway – that he had a way with women, and he never had any problem starting or continuing intelligent conversations with them. Usually.

"Why are you asking so many questions?"

Her name tag read "Hope" but he was beginning to feel there wasn't any. Long before they even got started, he witnessed any thought of success he might have harbored upon entering the packed Fifth Street diner, escaping from his grasp, rapidly. There were numerous power company trucks parked in amongst the vehicles lining the street and Martin thought he hit the jackpot. He felt that if all else failed with his primary source, he'd chance approaching the guys, if he needed to.

If anyone had something to say about nuclear energy and large intrusive plants it would be the ones most affected; small wire owners fighting to keep what little customer base they served.

"Just trying to have a little friendly conversation with you."

"You are kidding me, right."

"No, really, I just wanted to talk..."

"– about nuclear power plants?"

"Ya, I guess it's not exactly a choice conversation starter..."

"Ya think?"

"Okay humor me? Say you were going to talk about that topic with anyone, what would you say about it here?"

"I'd say, it best stay out of my back yard."

"Why would you say that?"

"Oh, you know exactly, why. It's too out there..."

"Out there?"

"You know – futuristic – out there..."

"You do realize that nuclear power is rather safe in comparison to most things."

"Depends what you mean by most things."

"Well, you know, futuristic stuff."

"That's all well and good but if a line goes down ...those guys go out," she motioned to the power line crew at the booth in the back of the diner. "It's minor compared to a plant getting a leak or blowing up or something... like that two mile thing?"

"Three Mile Island."

"Ya, that one... I ain't had kids yet and when I do I certainly don't want 'em growing up looking like something from the apocalypse, now..."

Martin laughed, thinking it might just be best for her not to have kids anyway, but saying so would just be mean, so he laughed along with her and shook his head. *Never mind,* he thought to himself, *best leave things alone here now while he still had a chance to possibly continue this inquiry with someone a little more informed.*

He could just get himself thrown out of the cafe if he continued with this conversation and that certainly wouldn't help the cause.

Martin decided he would just have to put on his brave hat and approach the table with the local power line guys. They seemed to be happy enough, enjoying their reprieve from the cold weather over an early morning breakfast. He knew that when the call came in the outdoor work wouldn't matter because it was their job. Weather could keep them hopping if customers called and that restoring power was their main concern. On a good day, when there were no problems, it was a rather easy deal.

He knew most of the rural companies were now using radio waves to collect data from their customers so power line guys were just on call most days, awaiting instructions while ready in the field. They, too, would have their inspections to do on a regular basis but these guys didn't seem to be in too much of a hurry to step out into the sub-zero weather.

"Hey, guys. Good morning, mind if I join you?" Big assumption on his part and based on a relationship, guy to guy, he hoped they might entertain an exchange of firsthand knowledge from the big corporate world for grass roots conversation and what really mattered. That was if they cared about what happened in the power corporate. They may just take him out and hang him as talk to him. Martin readied himself for rejection and that extreme possibility dreamt up in the back of his imaginative overworked mind. His right hand inside a jacket pocket fingered the BMW keys making ready his escape.

"Not that we would mind, buddy, but ... who the hell are you?" The speaker, an older man with graying hair and a weathered creased smile, spoke up in a manner that implied he might represent the group of four men, perhaps the foreman; the others stopped eating and looked up questioningly to Martin, nodding.

"Sorry, guys. Ya my intrusion, it's kind of a weird request. Sorry, my name is Martin Wells." Martin stuck out a hand and smiled. "I'm just visiting from..."

"Hey! I've heard that name, wait. You're that regulatory power consulting guy I've heard about." The younger member of the group, sitting along the back of the booth, smiled and extended his hand to Martin. "Name's Joey. Now what would you be doing way out here, it's hardly the Energy Commission hearing room."

Joey appeared to be up on the procedures that were more than likely not of interest to most lineman, but then again, younger workers tended to be a little more diversified within the industry even though they eventually ended up doing traditional lineman jobs. That was the nature of the business and Martin would venture a guess that Joey was from the big city, too. Breaking into the business meant he needed a 'get your hands dirty application' before he could really say he was 'in the business'.

Martin remembered working for the local electrification unit when he was an early teenager. Being from a farm receiving services from the small local company, he volunteered to find out more about the local business, and once he decided farm life was not his calling, he moved away from the rural power unit, too. He was happy to have the background knowledge to take with him even if it was something he was happier to be away from, uninvolved in for the most part, and apart from the front line losing battle they often fought.

"So you are a city boy, too."

The familiarity and sharing would certainly go a long way to get him the cooperation he was hoping for and he pulled it to him and honed it.

"Yup, that's me but I'm assuming it's a good move..." He laughed, breaking the ice and he slid safely into the welcoming water.

"Have a seat, Martin, nice to meet you."

The third man to speak, a short balding fellow with a wind burned face, pulled a chair from nearby and Martin sat at the end of the table.

The waitress Martin first spoke to was quick to come by and take his order. It would be good to have a hot breakfast instead of just cup of coffee, or two. His initial gut reaction to the warm reception was now that it could just be a talk with the guys.

"So what brings you out here, Martin?" Jeffrey asked. "I'm the foreman here with this bunch and we work for..." he pointed to the logo on his jacket, "as I'm sure you can tell – Power One. What's a city government guy doing up here in Peace County?"

"Must be checking up on us."

It was said with a touch of humor but Martin knew there would be a sense of reservation and suspicion in talking to someone they perceived as "big city government" and it had nothing to do with the compassion and local camaraderie.

"Don't worry guys. I am really here on my own fact finding mission and I must admit, even I wouldn't talk to me without feeling there might be some ulterior motive. I didn't even know what I'd find coming up here, so any discussion is a surprise to me."

"He's not government," Ernie, the short balding member of the team laughed, "he's honest." This brought a regale of laughter from the rest of the crew, except for one; the one man who hadn't spoken yet, mid-forties with an attitude built on twice his years.

"He wouldn't be here without some other underlying reason. The government is full of scheming bastards at the best of times." An opinionated Ed revealed it wasn't just being cautious that offered a negative judgment of Martin and anything he represented. It revealed a prejudice that Martin or anyone else in an official capacity couldn't chip away. He also sensed something else that was almost a challenge to him because it felt that this person might know more about what it was Martin needed to dig into. Shoveling would be a problem, though. *It might be wise to treat this one easy,* Martin thought.

"You are right, Ed, and you represent feelings from most Albertans, and especially right now when there are so many proposed changes before the Commission."

"Changes? You call nuclear distribution a change? It's more like a power holocaust. It's gonna kill us and our business. This is my personal well-being. Take away the lines and what have I got? I got no experience to be involved in reactors and plants and factory generation facilities. I'm a friggin lineman, for god's sake." His original silence transformed into a soap box rant that made more sense to Martin than the speaker would ever know. He also appreciated the honesty presented and his stand on what he believed to be true. To his credit he might know just as much as the city boy Joey, although, in a much different capacity.

"You'll have to excuse our Ed here; he's a one man opposition party."

"No. No... that's exactly what I need to hear. You don't understand." Martin was pleased with his good fortune in finding someone who might just give him exactly what he was looking for... a reason to oppose the nuclear industry's requests to be made before the Energy Commission even though his own employer would be counting on his signature of support. "This is exactly what I want to hear. If it is how people in this town really feel, it must be made known. I represent regulatory process and not the government directly. If it doesn't sit right with you, it is most certainly not going to sit right with me."

The men were quiet as Martin continued. "My report will include this kind of grass root emotion. It has to." He didn't realize, perhaps, until that very moment, that a part of him still spoke out for the little guy, the underdog, the one in need of someone to stand up for them. His thoughts strayed to his father and he realized, too, that standing up for him is what he'd been doing all along, even by moving away and going off in his own direction.

"You're not going to quote me or anything, are you?" Ed was still concerned but because it appeared that Martin's convincing speech was more than just words, he seemed more at ease with its sincerity.

"We can't do that – privacy and all – but I will certainly take your comments into consideration. So, how do the rest of you feel?" He looked around the table and to draw the conversation in his direction, he threw the question out to them.

"If I were to say that nuclear power will be a big part of the province's future and your livelihood will depend upon your ability to adapt to that change, what would you say?"

Martin made a quick stop just before reaching the outskirts of Edmonton. It was late Thursday morning and he thought he'd pay a visit to the head office of one of the few self-operating electrification units that serviced rural power customers. He needed to get some firsthand information from the manager there and it had been an appreciative referral from a surprise breakfast companion. Ed.

Once they were on a level playing field, all the cards were on the table. Martin realized he held back one significant ace in the whole morning's communication – he worked for Alternative Energy Corporation and he realized that if they had wind of that, his relationship with the whole group might have taken a whole different route. Alternative Energy Corporation represented the enemy and his findings corroborated the information he received from the nuclear plant site supervisor. The big three posed a threat not only to the Alberta environment, but to the future of the Alberta power industry, as they knew it.

The manager of West Meridian Company, the rural electrification unit that bordered Morinville and stretched further north covering a small east west corridor as wide as the distance from Spruce Grove to Sherwood Park, welcomed Martin into her office.

Based on the call she must have received from Power One employee, Ed, she was more than happy to supply Martin with any information he might need in his quest for documented shortfall with regard to nuclear power.

"Martin – nice to meet you. I have had the opportunity to see you in action, so to speak, as I frequent the Energy Commission hearings. As you know, we've needed to keep on top of a few situations lately." She was businesslike, with a soft outward appearance not usually taken for a management role; Martin did not want to chance coming up against her in a debate, however, based on the knowledge she had of the industry.

"Yes, the electrification units have had their challenges," he hcsitatcd in a way that was not apparent to Marie but he knew that building a commonality worked for him in his line of business. "Dad tells me all about the issues he receives notice about from South Meridian. I'm sure many are one and the same for your organizations." *It worked,* he thought triumphantly, *this one on one thing is really working for me.* He could almost feel any guard that Marie had up as a protective barrier, fall.

"Oh, so you're a farm kid, too."

"Born and raised, although, I have to be honest; I took the first bus out as soon as I was able to. I'm just not cut out for that type of stress."

"Hmmm, so let's go into the power business and lead regulatory process…" she laughed and Martin had to forego the urge to exclaim very loudly, 'finally, someone who can relate'. "I hear you pack in just as many sixteen hour days as any farmer."

Over a late afternoon lunch, Marie told Martin more than he could ever use in ten reports. She provided him with a copy of a confidential risk assessment report that showed irrevocably the damage nuclear plant construction would impose on a fragile environment.

"It's not only the people, Martin, who will be impacted by this type of overwhelming implementation. It is the environment and the industry, as a whole."

"They claim it's safe and can generate more than enough of the power we need to meet a growing demand."

"That may be so and even if it is, is it worth the risk outlined here, to just go plowing right in?" She was passionate about power but more in a big picture way than just 'this is my home and community, so get lost.'

"I hope to keep the process reined in and within the necessary protocols."

"From what I know of you and your methods, Martin Wells, I am pleased to hear that and I think I might be able to sleep better at night now knowing that you are out there looking out for the little people."

"I always have even if I didn't realize it from the onset that that was what I was truly doing. In taking a stand, I am happy to have always been on the side of justice and good for the masses." He took a long drink from his water glass. "Listen to me; you'd think I was some kind of leader of the people." He laughed at the ludicrous comment.

"Ever thought of running?"

"Often," Martin said confidently, "but not for it, rather, from it..."

Marie almost spit the mouthful of water she just took and hastily put a cloth napkin up to her mouth. "Stop. You're too much, Martin Wells."

So he did, and he harbored guilt that although he portrayed one face, he hid the other. With a copy of a much needed support paper and an appreciative, albeit friendly hug, Martin left Marie and West Meridian Company with a promise to keep in touch, even if only by email.

He also left with his secret intact; that he essentially worked for a company that could be considered as the enemy especially by small wire owner companies such as Power One and West Meridian. Their survival was not part of the plan of the big companies who were intent on bringing plentiful alternative energy methods to the forefront of the industry. *It was true, nuclear power could supply a nation but at what cost?*

As the sleek BMW slid south bound on Highway two, Martin cranked up Cold Play in the disc changer and felt his mood and physical being shift into a more relaxed drive for the easy trip past Morinville, through St. Albert and then into Edmonton. He could slip into the office at a time when others would already be leaving and he would relish the quiet comfort of the building, alone. There, he would get caught up on some email, return the numerous phone messages he knew would be accumulated but most importantly, he'd get a head start on the report he would deliver to the directors and his boss at the special meeting on Friday afternoon.

With no pressing Thursday plans, he knew he could complete all the necessary follow up and research required to pull the findings of yesterday and today's trip into a comprehensive presentation that he was sure would impress. A foolproof work plan allowed his mind to wander to better things and he smiled, singing along to the words of the song. He thought of Erin and he thought of Friday and all its possibilities. He sang along to the words: *"Honey, all the movements you're starting to make – see me crumble and fall on my face – and I know the mistakes that I've made – See it all disappear without a trace – And they call as they beckon you on – They say start as you need to go on – Start as you need to go on...*

Chapter 16 – Erin

As the bouquet flew through the air, Erin steadied her wobbly recovery with a satin gloved hand out to Martin's shoulder. The heels were new but, then again, so was the marriage. That traditional something borrowed at this point might have been the dose of courage it took for her to finally confirm the deed as done. Saying yes was the easy part. Their incessant dating every single day of their final year of attendance at the University of Alberta cultivated a relationship she considered strong enough to weather any of life's storms. Their commitment was a bond she thought would last forever.

Erin placed the unframed photograph back into the thick satin covered album and placed it on the upper shelf of the hallway closet. It was best kept away since she didn't want to jinx any secret hopes with an outwardly display of expectation.

Martin's recent renewed interest in her had regurgitated memories she thought were stored, like the photos, but apparently, they were both easy to access and they still held some magical draw to her interest. She wasn't one to dwell on the past and had moved on happily and eventually to something that many would consider true happiness, if one were to be truly honest with one's emotions.

She no longer worried where he was or who he might be with. She used to, though, when long hours consumed what time she thought should be hers, and then after Mickey's birth, what time should be his, as well. When she became pregnant with Essie, it was no longer a driving concern to her to have him to be around because she had been on her own for so long already, and that would have been a considerable part of Mickey's first couple of years. Erin never had to worry that Martin was having an affair, at least, not with another woman. He was too committed to his one true love – his career in the power industry.

Maybe she was jealous, to some extent, because he went on and she stopped. She was not jealous of his success, however; no, she applauded and supported with all her heart his dedication and could see the reputation he built within the industry and the respect he earned from those he worked with on a daily basis.

That she envied his success would be erroneous; for if Martin was one thing, he was generous in his acknowledgements and he always attributed his achievements to the support she gave him. She would, though, admit to anyone, she wasn't pleased with her own desire to pull out of the energy business soon after their marriage.

She hadn't thought that being a mom would compare but would argue loudly that it did, at least now. Mickey and Essie became her focus and she derived such great pleasure and her greatest energy from them. She thought she'd never do more but soon realized she could do and be anything or anyone she desired. She came to be contented in her decision to be a "stay at home mom" but refused to be a "stay alone wife." They filed for divorce soon after Essie was born.

Martin loved her but conceded without a fight which was uncharacteristic for him but she knew he was hurt and, he had admitted to her, even more ashamed that he hurt the only person who always stood by him even though he wasn't always around to appreciate it. As an ex-wife and still a full time mom, Erin cultivated new interests, including a freelance writing career and a new love interest, although, it was some time for it to actually be considered as such.

Edgar Rose worked as an assistant editor for one of the magazines Erin submitted work to, and he became impressed, not only with her work, but also with her "virtual sense of humor." Once he met her in person, he fell for the Erin that once upon a time attracted Martin. Her subtle attractiveness was wrapped with a large dose of intelligence and humanity. Erin wasn't reciprocally attracted immediately but she soon warmed to his persistent advances and began to date him six months after the divorce.

She made it perfectly clear and his compliance to her rules made him even more attractive. There were to be no visits to her home when the kids were there. No men, except for Martin on those rare occasions when he managed to remember he had a family, even if only an ex-wife who no longer cared and small kids who were too young to know the difference.

Her interest in Edgar waned some time ago and would have certainly quit abruptly with the recent reconnection she felt with Martin. It took on a life of its own after their trip to his parent's farm. It was just a kiss but she felt his confusion, felt her desire and although she harbored reservations about starting up anything again, she had a curiosity that would not be cured or quieted if she didn't at least give it a chance. *Perhaps, he had changed.* She wouldn't hold her breath but it would be worth it, especially if he kissed her like *that* again. It was just a kiss and it turned her world right side up without her even realizing it was even upside down.

Friday night was closing in and Erin had hopes for her children's visit with their dad; but she had hidden desires for herself. She wouldn't go so far as to admit she expected something to happen but there was nothing wrong with feeling good about it and dressing to encourage it, *tempting fate,* she thought, as she pulled outfit after outfit from the closet and held it up, posing her sexiest enticement, pouting, throwing her head back, until she finally fell back over her bed heaped with discarded clothes, laughing hysterically.

She sat up feeling silly, yet satisfied, that whatever she chose would be fine. She never had to put that much effort into it before, *so why now... what changed...* Martin was still Martin and until he proved himself a different man, she had to be cautious.

He might not even show up on Friday, let alone, reload the guns to fire them in the direction of her target.

Chapter 17 – Guns Blazing

The Alternative Energy Corporation office building lobby bustled with Friday morning banter, workers intent on making an quick start to the day with hopes to implement an early end, with a 'thank god it's Friday' smile and attitude, most walked as if driven by some unseen force. Coffee in hand, either Starbuck's or Second Cup, depending upon the direction of approach, they entered the glass revolving doors and then awaited their turn at the elevator for the ride up to wherever their day took shape. Industrious, health conscious types headed for the stairs intent on making good on promises long before the New Year's resolutions kicked in to become verbal passions. The tower's main floor restaurant held its share of early morning meetings with talkative energy executives expelling pent up urges to get business directly underway long before heading up to the confines of the offices located somewhere in one of the twenty one floors above.

Martin entered from the parkade door way at the end of the long carpeted hallway located just past the lobby lounge and café. He paused, contemplating crowds versus coffee and coffee always won at seven thirty am – *why on earth wouldn't it?* He wasn't in an extreme hurry to start the day upstairs, having completed much of his required presentation the previous night. The afternoon meeting would prove to be quite interesting to him considering the information he managed to bring back with him from his little trip to Peace County.

His 'nuclear plant tour' went well, considering everything. It was actually more than he anticipated discovering given that nuclear power plants had not received their share of hearings before the Energy Commission yet and certainly not enough to even consider construction starts.

Standards and planning he could understand. Review and consultation, definitely, but a hole the size of a small town with building scaffolding already in place... definitely not. They were barely into the feasibility and risk assessment studies.

The acquisition of that document from a cooperative source at the West Meridian rural electrification unit virtually made his day. He also made a friend with someone who he could rely on for future reference.

Friends in the business meant a relationship that could be cultivated once reciprocated and if trust was established. *It was like an episode of survivor*, Martin thought, *establish your alliances early on, stick to your integrity, don't lie but if you do, at least don't get caught doing anything stupid because it often resulted in losing a valuable partnership...*

As Martin entered from the hallway, he thought he saw her through the glass panes lining the decorative wall. He peered through the crowd pushing up to the coffee bar as he entered the cafe, but the seat he thought she occupied, was empty. He was positive he saw Suzanne who could mistake her funky classic look with platinum blond hair, straight, shiny and falling over one side of her face in a cut that was longer on one side than the other. He thought he saw her at the very table where his boss Rowan, sat, casually continuing a conversation with a couple of Alternative Energy Corporation board members – David Burns and Nathan Price, neither whom were Martin's favorite people, if first impressions were anything upon which to base your calculations.

At his very first board meeting, they had interjected their piece of input at every opportunity on everything presented, whether legitimate or not, playing off of each other's stupidity and annoyances. It peeved Martin, no end. He had no choice but to stomach their sorry antics then, but he didn't have to now. He turned away to order his coffee, but not in time. *Wasn't he lucky enough to see Rowan signal him over to their table?*

"Martin. Bring your coffee. Sit with us for a bit. Some interesting stuff, here."

Doubt that, Martin thought, as he felt the quiet pleasantries of a solitary morning fall away. He worked his way through the chattering crowd toward the table. *He could have just ignored him,* he thought, but why piss off his boss on the very day he hoped to not only impress him in the meeting but also ditch the meeting the minute it extended past the respectable time of five pm. Although, to most here in attendance, four pm would be considered a normal end to the work day hours on a Friday, if not earlier.

He would not disappoint Erin and the kids, he determined, pleased he applied himself the previous night without distractions. He surprised himself at having to force the work on a night when he was alone, something that was a normal activity for Martin Wells.

His mind had been preoccupied with recent discoveries that baffled him, future considerations that concerned and almost scared him, and Friday night possibilities and what ifs that kept him replaying scenarios over and over again in his head in variations that continued to gain momentum. All were good in his mind, at least the ones he dreamt up...

"Martin?"

Startled from his relaxing reverie, Martin almost spilled his coffee.

"Whoa, there Marty."

The snake, David Burns, spoke and Martin cringed. *No one called him that except his mother and then only on a good day,* because it was her pet name for his father, and he couldn't quite relate to that comparison in a good way.

"It's Martin." And he sat down with a directed smile to his boss. "Good morning, Rowan. How goes the day, so far?"

"Good. How about you? How was the trip?"

"Awesome." Martin spied the half empty cup in the middle of the small cafe table directly in front of David Burns. There was a fresh set of lip prints in faint pink on the rim. "Not your shade there, Davy." Martin laughed. Rowan laughed and interjected a calming explanation before the embarrassed director could respond.

"They're so busy in this place in the morning we are lucky to get a table, never mind get a clean one."

"Ah, yes, I could see that happening. It is busy. In fact, it's so busy you could hide in this crowd and not even be noticed..." Martin reluctantly let it go before it went somewhere he couldn't get back from unscathed...

Rowan J. Cott came into the board room about one half hour later than the announced scheduled start time for the special directors meeting. Martin was advised that the required one o'clock sharp meeting launch was necessary in order to address the many agenda items accumulated over the week, and if they wanted to get out of there on time, it was a process that must be adhered to on that Friday afternoon.

Already there was an implied rumor circulating that the meeting might go longer than expected. The administrative assistants who were allowed to participate in the board room meetings passed around the neighboring pizza parlor menu flyers, talking amongst themselves about ordering and possibly meeting up for drinks later.

Complaints were whispered through the ranks about having to change previously planned clandestine rendezvous. Several of the directors texted and Blackberried their apologies to whomever would be expecting them, rescheduling appointments and dinner dates for later times of arrival.

Martin refused to follow suit.

He was not going to fall into the same old pattern, one he used to fall into quite easily. Chances were slim at best but if he even smelled a chance, however premature it might seem with Erin, he was not going to ruin it.

Their Friday dinner plans looked like a new starting point. The chance to see the kids again on a regular basis, even though it didn't seem like it was something of relative importance until lately. *What had changed?* His mother would be happy with the new developments, or rather, renewed developments as she never really accepted the end of the relationship or marriage anyway. Her interaction with his ex-wife perhaps kept the necessary contact that would be instrumental for any renewed interest.

Martin motioned to Adam, one of the assistants sitting along the side of the room, just behind his leather high back chair. He didn't quite know their role there yet, but was pleased with the fact that he was there meant he didn't have to take comprehensive notes. It was nice to be able to hand down the stenographer duties to Adam.

"Do you know what's up? What's the hold up, anyway?" Another thing he wasn't too sure of yet was the obvious controlling power the chief executive officer had in this organization which made him wonder of the presidential powers, in that case. "Where's Mr. Cott?"

"Well... he *is* the chief executive officer and nothing really gets started until he's here. Sorry, Mr. Wells. Don't know what's up... and we haven't even heard of any good gossip on any recent mergers or juicy acquisitions that I might offer you as a source of entertainment..."

"Thanks, then Adam. I am so out of here at five bells. Hope we get this show on the road real soon."

"Here, Mr. Wells, have a coffee and chill." Adam enjoyed any opportunity to pull a little attitude with Martin and any other direct supervisor he might be able to outwit. Martin knew he wasn't the kid's boss and it seemed that no one really served anyone here except Rowan J. Cott. One boss where everyone else was a puppeted employee and the strings attached came in the form of accolades and back patting in meetings such as this one.

Who knows if they were even recorded in the minutes – nothing official, nothing gained. Martin was determined to end what he saw as an awkward show and end it today.

"Thanks Adam." He took the coffee bribe. "At least you know your place..."

"Mr. Wells. I suggest you use this free time while waiting to sync your blackberry as you are missing a few updates..."

"Well, Adam, I suggest you use this time to sink your..." Martin's retort wouldn't have been the least bit professional so it was probably a good thing it was cut short by the brisk entrance of the long awaited fearless leader.

"Sorry everyone. Long lasting miserable conference calls that go on and on forever. Hate 'em but what can you do? No choice but to keep my people waiting while I listen to regulatory crap. Who needs it on a Friday afternoon, right?" Rowan took his seat at the head of the table. He was flushed like he ran several flights of stairs to get to the board room yet his office was only at the end of the hall and a walk from there would hardly qualify as a workout as it was a mere one hundred feet or so. He ran two hands quickly through his thick salt and pepper hair, like two large combs. Then he straightened a collar that was flipped up and stuck slightly askew at the back of his neck. Martin was only slightly intrigued and not amused at the late start and the further delays.

"Rowan. You okay? You look a bit flushed." Martin didn't really want to know why and he would have rather said "let's just get on with it already". He thought that perhaps his interjection might push the obviously distracted chief back into the business mode.

"Oh, just a little workout before business. You know it keeps the mind alert if your body can keep up to it..."A quickly covered snicker and a whispered 'more like just keep it up' reached Martin's ears, but nothing further was said. He hoped it wasn't just for his sake.

He didn't want to know the office gossip truth about the leather furniture grouped in his boss' office. To him it housed nothing more than just business conversations and business deals... His desire to 'hole up' in a nifty furnished niche with someone cuddly just lost all attraction. At least for the time being. Now the 'who' climbed into his mind and as tantalizing as those thoughts might be to touch upon, he didn't really want to know who...

"Okay, enough. All conjecture aside, let us get this meeting underway."

The murmur of whispered conversation at the sidebar ceased and the tap, tap, tap on laptop keys and phone pads quieted, and Martin's anxiety lessened somewhat as they forged ahead. It really didn't seem like all that special a meeting to begin with as they covered much the same kind of content that was reviewed and presented at the last meeting. Why they were reviewing some of the stuff now baffled him but he followed along on the agenda, one that was only presented to him that morning via email after he finally pulled himself away from the unofficial breakfast meeting in the downstairs lobby cafe.

All twelve directors were to give their summary presentations and most of the reports dragged on so that it became clear very quickly; they were not going to get through all of them before their scheduled break. This was beginning to be something that would drag on beyond what Martin thought he'd be able to handle. He glanced quickly at his watch.

At the announcement for a short fifteen minute break, Martin jumped up and hurried to his office across the hall, closing the door quietly behind him; he didn't need or want any company. He debated calling Erin. *No*, he thought, *if I do that I might just as well kiss any second chances good-bye, or rather, about a tenth chance.* She had been tolerant before but he knew she would not forgive his excuses and give them a second thought. He wouldn't expect her to, either.

He sat for a moment's introspection wondering where his upcoming report would leave him, that was, once they got to it. His head in hand concentrated thoughts blocked the silent opening of his office door. Thoughts of a happy evening with Mickey and Essie pulled him deeper into thought, to where he didn't hear the lock turn. A desirable place later in the evening with Erin, once the kids were in bed...

"Martin." A firm, warm hand upon his shoulder startled him and he jumped.

"What?"

"Sorry." She laughed. "You were in such thought you didn't even hear me come in, baby, were you thinking about me, perhaps?" Suzanne dragged a soft hand over Martin's chin and up the side of his face, where her fingers threaded seductively into his hair.

"No. Suzanne, sorry, not this time."

"Wow, ouch! Aren't we honest? You couldn't even humor a girl to make her feel wanted... needed..." She leaned forward and put her hands on his shoulders. Her breasts begged from a scooped neckline and her lips touched his in a kiss that was met only briefly in return. Martin entertained thoughts of pushing her aside.

"I have to get back to my meeting."

"Oh, I'm sure you have at least a moment or two to spare for me." Suzanne pushed Martin so he sat back against the leather sofa and she straddled his legs, hiking her skirt high enough that it left nothing to the imagination.

"No, I need to get back now."

"Aw, sweets." Suzanne leaned in closer and put her hand down between Martin's legs. She just about ended up on her ass on the floor as Martin jumped up suddenly.

"I really need to get back. Now!"

He left the room and was sure he heard her soft laugh followed by the words 'stupid man.'

Martin entered the board room and had to consciously slow his breathing which he realized only escalated as he sat down at the table, and it wasn't from the turn on by a hot blond but, rather, the hurried departure.

"Hmmm, you okay, Mr. Wells? You look – ah – a bit flushed." Adam's sarcasm came through in his whispered taunt from behind him.

"You can be replaced, you know." Martin gritted his teeth as he threw the empty promise over his shoulder.

"Oh, gee, I don't think so."

Adam's overconfidence stabbed back at him, reminding him that he was probably right. *Maybe Rowan was into boys, too. Rowan, ugh.* Martin's logical mind finally put two and two together – Suzanne. The abandoned cup at the table in the early morning coffee shop. The presentation and departure from the first board meeting. Here in his office on their coffee break – *coincidence* – he thought not. He'd have to remember to watch what he said around her until he knew for sure, one way or another.

Martin stood at the front of the room, the prepared flip chart beside him. As he lifted the covering sheet to reveal the first page, he picked up the bright orange felt marker and circled, repeatedly, the words 'regulatory processes'. He turned to face the group of directors who just stared back at him with their everyday meagerness as if it were valid industry promotion. Straight faced he looked along the line of bodies to see Rowan looking as if amused by the whole process, and Martin was even more determined to wipe the smugness from his boss' face. At least, that was one of his goals for the day.

"Let me begin with the obvious. I know I am new around here, but as you all know, I am not new to the energy industry in Alberta. Perhaps a little bit of my relevant history might lend credibility to the words you have presented in front of you in the form of a rather baring expose. I am hoping my efforts can prevent the ropes of undue negligence from tightening around our collective necks." Rowan's amusement did not leave his face. Martin thought his strong introduction would raise an alarm, or at the very least spike the curiosity levels, but instead, obvious disinterest left him with just a slight bit of anxiety brewing in the pit of his stomach.

"I attended the University of Calgary and then finished up my master's degree at the University of Alberta in what seems like such a long time ago, but really, in terms of this industry, it is not. Soon after my graduation, I was invited to work with the Alberta Government in my chosen field of innovation and technological design. As I continued to build expertise and experience using my business knowledge to research I decided it was preferable to become a consultant in the electrical industry. I have been called in on several occasions to review new innovations or to provide input on changes, such as deregulation."

"Today's market is so different, what relevance..." Martin would have liked to have the proverbial rope he spoke of just to strangle David Burns, instead, he cut him off verbally.

"If you keep up with industry changes and try to forecast concerns and address issues head on, relevance is always a matter of application. You need to also look at how it is going to affect the masses as opposed to the pocketbooks of a few. My reputation in this arena obviously preceded me; otherwise I suspect I wouldn't have been hired by Alternative Energy Corporation. My short time here, however, has already revealed some concerns and I am using the assumption that my expertise and consultation ability is what attracted you and your company to me in the first place."

"Oh, most definitely, Martin. Your capability is certainly something we looked at..." Rowan nodded as he spoke and then leaned back, almost too comfortable for business. Martin needed to make him squirm.

"I appreciate that Rowan, but my credentials are not my concern or a matter for discussion today..." someone snickered but covered it up with a slight cough; Martin continued... "But, rather, my concern was raised during my recent road trip to Peace County to explore the potential of nuclear plant construction. Imagine my surprise to find," he turned to point at the chart, "regulatory processes were not a concern, in fact, there didn't seem to be any process in place, at all. Construction looks like it is well under way and public consultations with the local population have only just recently been completed."

"But they are complete, right?" Nathan Price spoke up this time.

"Just. The ink the findings are written with is not even dry. There still needs to be environmental impact studies and other essential reviews that assess risk and liability. Are there really any benefits? This must be determined as well and backed with concrete evidence in order to find support among that demographic directly affected by the plant, or plants, as the case may be." Martin paused, remembering his lack of emphasis during his recent Commission presentation when he barreled full speed ahead, guns blazing, intent on getting every word out in one breath. He even took time to take a mouthful of water before he continued.

"The people in the town knew nothing of the work being prepared and done right in their own backyards. There is still a negative overview rampant among the general public. Say "nuclear" and they immediately think Chernobyl or Three Mile Island. You could even reduce their reactions to the whole process as downright fearful.

"Ignorance always breeds fear."

Rowan sat up now and drew everyone's attention in doing so. His input brought forth an attentive state from those who could smell the challenge of a battle brewing; it enticed them into paying closer attention.

"And that, Martin, is why we hired you. Educate the general population so this is no longer an obstacle. Nuclear power is the alternative wave of the future. It is the basis for Alternative Energy Corporation and its successful company future." In dramatic fashion, Rowan J. Cott pulled a half inch thick document from the leather portfolio sitting on the table in front of him. "It is the staple directive and number one objective in our new five year plan."

He tossed it to the end of the table and it slid unceremoniously towards Martin who grabbed it before it fell to the floor. He glanced down the length of the table taking in the blank stares that met him along the way, back to Rowan and then finally fixed upon the document. His gaze held on the shiny cover of the plan – *Alternative Energy Corporation – 2010 – Nuclear by 2016.* Martin read the title over and over to himself.

"That is one bold directive considering everything that's going on."

"It is the only directive you need to focus on."

"It is something that could be on track as long as the necessary processes are in place and adhered to because we all know there are steps to that end and they have to be taken one at a time. We cannot skip forward as much as we'd like to hurry any government process. I'm afraid, two at a time is not allowed in something that breeds such controversy by the mere mention of its name."

"Again, to repeat, Martin, that is precisely why we hired you and that is specifically your job here at Alternative. Enlighten those who oppose, so we can work towards lighting the way with an abundant supply of power. Make us some headway, and quickly, so we can all get to where we want to go, in a manner of speaking."

Rowan glanced around the table garnering agreement with nods of compliance from the table of directors as if controlled by simultaneous puppetry.

"I can only go as quickly as the process allows. Government protocol is in place for a reason."

Several directors grunted their disapproval but it did not dissuade Martin from continuing, with increased volume and effort.

"I am not saying it is impossible but it isn't going to happen overnight. A five year plan is ambitious and adventurous, but it is also presumptuous. It is a possibility if, and that's a big if, all things go well right from the start. The preliminary hearings are not going to be approved with just one presentation. There will be many of them and there will be many interventions from those who do not approve. They will come fast and furious to defend their stand. You know that. As everyone gets into the process and registers their intent to participate, this will increase everyone's level of participation because there will be defensive tactics and required evidence. Everyone who sees this affecting them in any small way will be involved. Then, as the banter back and forth progresses, it brings more and more as rebuttals are brought forth to counter with some new found evidence, argument or submission. Lawyers get involved and it becomes a one up man show and this is not a one man show, especially not this one man."

"We here – all of us… appreciate the process and realize the magic show it can become at times and since we are not prepared to wait we hope you are a superior magician and can make it all disappear." The statement left more than anxiety in the pit of Martin's stomach and it sent a cold shiver up his spine. He felt as if on the verge of a serious headache...

"Fortunately," Rowan continued, "we already have our supporters within the government departments and they are ready to help us in any way they can. Processes will be just a formality and I have no doubt they will listen to what Martin Wells has to say.

Rowan paused, but it wasn't to encourage interjection from Martin. It was to make his point loud and clear. "The whole reason we brought you on board, so to speak, has a lot to do with your expertise and thoroughness, yes, but it is also for the power your signature has on a document. To something, in fact, to anything involving the power industry, your written name speaks volumes.

"You are respected and your signature on a document is viewed as if it were an informed consultation founded in trust. Your mere say so confirms so much to those around the industry that it is synonymous with a comprehensive review."

Martin refrained from the normally expected 'thank you' after one of Rowan's raving back slapping achievement speeches presented during all the board meetings. Or at least, that is what he heard. He didn't have to be convinced of his status; he knew his word was respected and he worked many long years to achieve that mark in the industry. His association here might lend credibility to a concept that required thorough investigating and he intended to do his job, not for the benefit of Alternative Energy Corporation and Rowan J. Cott, chief executive officer or a profitable bottom line, but for the public, the good of the industry in general, and for his own integrity.

"Do you have any other issues or concerns that you'd like to bring forward at this time, Martin?"

Rowan perceived Martin's hesitation as indication of more and it prompted Martin to continue despite what results might come out next. *What did he have to lose?*

"A chance discovery regarding the interrelationship of Alternative Energy Corporation and the Peace County Nuclear One Company..." he paused, watching his audience for any obvious signs of surprise or interjection, "and Unified Nuclear Corporation, concerns me, to some degree."

"Ah, yes, the Big Three." Rowan smiled, pleased with himself, and not in the least bit surprised. "Read the Plan, Martin. It is an awesome relationship and one that is certain to push our collaborative directives right into the future."

"A nuclear monopoly future?"

"Exactly. The market does not need so many options for consumers to be confused with and if we can up our production levels to generate enough supplies to the grid en mass, then we are effectively contributing to the demand by meeting it with more than enough supply. Prices drop but consumption spikes – win, win, as we see it."

"Fair market – hardly?"

"Not an applicable argument when there is no other choice, Martin. We intend to take nuclear distribution to the top of the power grid and you will come along and be there with us, Martin, if you desire fame and fortune and everything else that goes along with it. I am sure you would like to provide more security for your young family and maybe even for your father if he considers getting out of farming soon. You'd be in a position to help him out and you know we will pay you very nicely for your expertise."

"Oh, there are no complaints regarding compensation so far."

Martin did not like the reference to his father and even wondered to some degree the relevance in bringing family matters to the table; whether or not his father decided to get out of the farming industry was not dependent upon the type of power supply; it only depended on there being a reliable, constant source of power. He remembered the Unified Nuclear Corporation trucks reported on the corridor. He pondered bringing up yet another issue.

"Good. If you ever have a problem, please, come and talk to us. We always extend a hand to help our Alternative family."

"Just one more thing, Rowan, speaking of family, Unified Nuclear Corporation – am I correct in ascertaining they are an associate company of Alternative Energy Corporation or are both other nuclear arms of the Big Three, separate entities?"

"Even separate, we are, of course, family due to the nature of our business. All are separate, Martin, but strive to obtain the same end." Rowan stood and approached the front of the room to stand beside Martin. He quickly checked his watch and proceeded to cut into any other objection Martin might have.

"Thank you Martin, as always we appreciate your interest in getting to the bottom of these issues and your honesty in approaching and reporting to the board confirms our decision. I am convinced I made the very best choice in signing you to this company. Let's move on then so we can all go home to whatever we have planned, or go to whatever we have planned before we all go home..." the directors all laughed. "Whatever the preferred choice may be..."

Martin took his seat again. It was already five twenty and he was growing concerned with the possibility he might not get out on time to make the planned dinner at Erin's by six o'clock.

He only needed a half hour to make his way from the downtown core to the district in the mid-south area of the city. It was already passed rush hour traffic which meant it should be smooth going by that time on Friday. *Arrgh,* he thought, *no way am I messing this up. If we are not done by five thirty, I am just excusing myself anyway.* A meeting silenced tone blipped from his Blackberry signaling a text message. He pushed 'read' as it lay in front of him alongside his note pad.

Rowan was talking at the front of the room about the upcoming reception at the Oil Rig Club in two weeks and everyone's attention was riveted to him. Martin was amused how different they were when it was social events and they all seemed captivated by the prospect.

He glanced down at the message displayed across the small phone screen:

"u mite want 2 keep a careful eye out

– the ex is hot, kids r cute

– would hate 2c something happen 2 them..."

Martin shot a quick glance around the room but no one was using their lap tops or phones. He turned to the side board where four assistants sat busily taking minutes, and shot a quick diversionary smile to Adam, pointing to his watch. It confirmed to him that none of the assistants were using their devices, either. Adam just gave Martin a "what" look as he turned back to the screen. It did not have an identification attached as the call display showed 'unknown number' and he did not recognize anything about the message that might identify who the sender might be.

Who the hell would send him what he would define as a threat?

Chapter 18 – Family Values

At five thirty five, Martin shot out of the lower entrance of the parkade, almost running over a homeless person in his haste. The old woman shook a gnarled fist at him cursing up a less than lady like storm. He just waved his apologies and continued out on to the street. A break in the oncoming avenue traffic allowed him a quick left down one hundred and sixth street and he took the hill, probably a little faster than he should but he was determined not to be late. Nothing was going to stand in the way of his date this evening. It had more desperation attached to it with the recent message although he was reluctant to think that he was the target of some scheme to threaten him into doing god knows what... *why else would they threaten a family that really only came back into his life the same time as the change in jobs occurred?*

He was not sure what to make of it but he was certain of one thing in particular, Erin would not know about this or anything else that went on at Alternative Energy Corporation. It would be for the best. He knew that the renewal in their mutual interest was due to a chemistry of some sort that probably never really died. He knew Erin, though, and if she found out about this latest development, she might think that his renewed interest was only because of a misdirected intent to 'save' her from some danger, real or imagined.

He could just hear her admonish him for getting involved in the politics of the industry again and dragging it back into his home life. She would remind him that that was the very reason she escaped from it in the first place. The corruption that could erupt from greedy demands did not appeal to her and, although it did not appeal to Martin either, it could be argued that he did like the perks of the industry job.

He subconsciously smoothed a hand over the soft dark blue interior leather of the BMW and frowned. *Hmmm, perhaps the politics is what really attracted him in the first place,* he thought, but it was not what kept him in the business or drove him into his own consulting firm. *Hmmm, why did he leave it then?* It was a question he began to ask himself over and over lately despite only being newly employed with Alternative Energy Corporation. It was something, come Monday, he'd have to really give more consideration to because if it bothered him that much already there had to be a good reason why.

Five fifty five and no sirens on his tail, Martin pulled into the driveway of his ex-wife's house and breathed a sigh of relief. *So far, he was making good on his promise;* too bad it was such a determined effort on his part to do so. With his heart racing and his blood pressure elevated, he was sure it would have his doctor more than concerned. He sat for a calming moment and closed his eyes. When he opened them, Erin was coming outside to meet him, pulling a loose knit sweater over a fitted black shirt and tan pants. *Boy, she looked good.* He put his sunglasses back into the clip on the visor and pulled his jacket from the passenger seat along with his brief case and gloves; he stepped from the car to meet her. *She must be happy to see him,* he thought, *she never came out to meet him before.*

"Hey, Erin." His smile faded as he read the troubled concern across her face. "Erin, what's wrong?"

"I just got this weird phone call. Well, actually, a very disturbing call. I am just so glad you are here and nothing happened."

"What are you talking about? Who called?"

"They didn't say and, at first, there appeared to be no one on the line. I was just about to hang up when I heard a noise and I asked again if anyone was there. Someone laughed and then they said something like your 'ex is a goner if he doesn't know how to follow orders.' What did they mean? Martin, what is going on?"

"I am not sure, Erin."

"What did they mean follow orders?"

"Let's go inside, Hun. I will try to get some answers. Where are the kids?" Martin's voice took on a worried tone.

"Mickey is watching a movie right in the den and Essie is still in her crib, napping."

Martin put a protective arm over Erin's shoulder and guided her back up the two stone steps and into the house. He quietly bolted the door. As he put his case and coat down, Mickey came tearing out of the den.

"Daddy!" He vaulted into Martin's arms as if from a spring board and Martin laughed.

"Hey buddie, whoa there. How's it going, champ? What if Daddy was so tired that he... accidentally... dropped you..." he laughingly let the little boy feel the sudden drop and catch they often played. Shortly before the floor, Martin's muscular arms brought the little boy up again.

"Daddy, Daddy. Again. Do me again." Mickey squealed with delight for more.

"You are going to tire out your old man." Martin placed him feet first on the floor beside him.

"Old man, Daddy, is an old man..." Mickey went singing into the den to watch the rest of his movie. From down the hall came another squeal and Erin turned in answer to the call from baby Essie who just awoke from her nap. Martin intervened, grabbing her arm and pulling her toward him. She smiled up to him and with that encouragement he kissed her, held her closer, and then laughed.

Mickey stood in the door way with a puckered up mouth. "Eww!"

"Oh, ya... buddie, I'll eww you." Martin left Erin, breathless and smiling, as he chased Mickey into the den. Erin continued down the hallway to pull the giggling Essie from her crib.

The sounds of the happy home brought Martin to an abrupt realization. *This was what was missing from his life and this was what he was determined to win back.*

His kids were worth every moment he worked but it was not worth missing every moment of their lives to do it. A sudden epiphany about life and learning hit him and it was Erin all along that meant more to him than any electrical innovation. His own power struggle had engulfed him over the past few years and it really had to do with losing this sense of worth, and in a way he might not have been able to retrieve. He vowed to listen to signals provided by all that was going on around him. He was being given another chance and he would have to make it all right. The sound of the phone ringing brought him back to the reality of the today.

Martin caught Erin before she lifted the receiver.

"Just let it go to voice mail, Erin. I know it's your place and all, but I'll check the messages later. It is our evening to enjoy... what do I smell? Something is positively heavenly... besides you, of course." His comments distracted her from the call, and she laughed.

"You always were a stomach man, food first and whatever, later." She patted his stomach and headed into the kitchen. Her 'whatever later' comment stuck with him and he almost forgot about the food.

"I thought you might like to have your favorite, God knows, you probably don't even cook for yourself, do you?"

"Geez, you've attempted to eat my cooking, what do you think?"

"Well, you are in for a treat then – beef stew – the kind that simmered all day long in the crock pot."

"Eww... that's not my favorite..." His teasing warranted a sharp slap on the arm and he grabbed her hand, wrapping her arms around in front of her and pulling her backwards, close against his body. His arms held her tight and he could smell the lavender and feel the softness of her hair against his face. "You know I'm just teasing, Erin..."

His conversation was interrupted by a knock on the door and he felt his back seize with knots of stress.

"I'm not expecting anyone. Who could that be?"

"Let me get it while you check on our two. It's probably just neighborhood kids canvassing for one thing or another." Martin gathered his manly confidence and strode over to the door as Erin plucked Essie from her highchair and went into the den where Mickey was thoroughly engrossed in his animated movie.

Martin pulled aside the curtain on the side light window before opening the door. His usual solid demeanor was sufficiently shaken with the weird happenings of the day and he felt that he wasn't being too cautious; after all, it was not just he who would be affected. Standing with pen in hand extended for a signature, was a uniformed UPS delivery driver.

"Good evening, sir."

"Hi. Are you sure you got the right house. We aren't really expecting anything."

"Wells? Mr. Martin Wells?"

Martin paused and frowned. It wasn't even for Erin and this was her house. *Who would be sending something addressed to him here anyway,* he thought, *and who would know to assume that he was here?* He signed for the small package, somewhat shakily.

"I guess that's me. Thanks. I think."

The driver just smiled and with a 'have a great evening' wave he made his way down the driveway back to his truck. Martin stood there, baffled, and then closed the door while turning the package over and over in his hands. The UPS protective envelope contained something he couldn't even begin to guess. With mounting curiosity, he ripped open the sealed end and pulled from inside, an envelope of substantial thickness. The branded stationery indicated it was from his new employer, Alternative Energy Corporation.

"What is it, Martin?"

Erin's voice carried from the den and he could see her sitting amongst the children's toys spread in the middle of the carpeted floor.

"Is it from Playhouse, maybe? That's it... I'm expecting something... er, you know what for you know who." She tipped her head toward Mickey who was busy building a tower of blocks for his delighted sister. Her swinging hands, however, made it a challenge and he was getting somewhat frustrated pushing her away, again and again. Essie just giggled.

"No. Erin. Not you know what for you know who, although, that would certainly make a heckuva lot more sense than this..."

"Daddy said heck..." Mickey chirped, still intent on getting his precariously leaning block tower to completion. He had Martin's determination at least when it came to getting the job done no matter what...

"Sorry, buddie. It would make a lot more sense, how's that?"

"Daddy said heckuva..." Mickey giggled and then proceeded to push the tower over before Essie could assist with the demolition. Then big brother went on to something else just as quickly.

"Martin, what is it then? I wasn't expecting anything."

"Neither was I, babe." He pointed to the label on the front panel of the packing envelope and shrugged his shoulders. "It's from work."

He saw her quizzical look turn to one of concern. He could feel the slide that occurred when something that was supposed to be private all of a sudden wasn't anymore. It felt like they'd been through it before.

"Why, Martin?"

"Erin. I really don't know how or why. Honest. You have to believe me. I would love to shout from the top of every building downtown what and how I feel lately especially in the last week or two, but I've been so afraid of jeopardizing everything that I have not told a soul, really."

She came into the foyer to stand in front of him, her back to the children playing in the den. Her stance, although it was not as confrontational as it had been in the past, was a defensive move. Martin knew his reaction would push hers one way or the other, with very little provocation.

"How on earth they knew I'd be here, I don't have a clue. And the call? Honey, I really don't have any explanation that would suit me, so there is none I could possibly give to explain it to you."

He was upset and he was trying to salvage something that barely seemed to have a chance to build a firm footing yet he could feel himself falling and she would pull away, if he let her. He led her back to the sofa in the den and sat, envelope in hand. He stared at it not knowing what or if he should even try to figure out the why. Someone was messing with him and he would have to find out why. He'd kill the bastard who messed with his family or rather ex-wife and kids because at this point he wasn't sure if he could regain any ground with the family attempt. If he could not keep his home life and his job life separate there would be no hope at all for family. They had to come first and that meant it had to be separate and apart. He hated that statement because it was the same one they declared when filing for divorce. He heaved a heavy, desperate sigh.

"Open it Martin."

Erin sat beside him, just slightly touching his arm as Essie sat at her feet on the carpet, cooing, contented to suck on the corner of her best little dress while her daddy decided the next course of action. Erin's shoulder touched against his and he could feel the safety of her closeness and the tone of her voice had changed. *Maybe she did believe him this time.* He wouldn't blame her if she didn't but he had to make an effort to try to make her see that *he* had changed, at least, in some ways.

He knew he didn't tell anyone any details about Erin and the kids and especially not where they lived. That information was only privy to his own office where Jessica wrote up his monthly support payment cheques and mailed them out, promptly and faithfully, on his behalf. Their birthdays were recorded and gifts sent. Again, Jessica took care of the timeliness of that task. Shopping was just not something he excelled in and most often it would be weeks later before he even realized that a necessary event deserving of recognition had passed. On several occasions, his assistant saved his ass by being on the ball. Erin knew it wasn't he that maintained the promptness of that chore but never let him know otherwise that it mattered. *No. No one else had access to that information.* He placed a thankful hand on hers and opened the envelope.

"It's a contract. I don't know why they would need to send it here and, besides, I already have an employment agreement with Alternative. I'm on the payroll not on call." He unfolded the wad of letter sized papers and a folded insert fell away to the floor. Mickey jumped up to retrieve it and handed it promptly to his mother.

"Thanks, sweetie."

She unfolded the paper and her mouth opened in silent comment. She sat stunned and itt was a moment before she could continue.

"Wow, Martin, you didn't say how good this job was..." She handed him the cheque with attached stub. It was made out to Martin Wells so there was no mistaking that it was for certain meant for him.

"Shit." Martin put his hand up quickly realizing a need to silence a corrective, mimicking son. "Sorry, Mickey. Shhh, don't correct me..." Mickey did not copy though a mischievous smile indicated he wanted to do so. Martin laughed and shooed him away, trying to keep it light for the sake of the kids. He did not want the concern to come out in the form of fear or anger.

"Martin." Erin leaned close as if to say the amount out loud was taboo. "That cheque is for twenty five thousand dollars." Her voice became a faint sound as she completed the statement.

"I don't know why, Erin, but this is too good to be true. There has to be some kind of catch or something. I don't make this kind of money all in one shot from a new employer. I haven't even provided that much input yet. There has to be some kind of mistake."

"Read over the contract and see what it says. I'm going to put dinner out for the kids and maybe we can both look at this later when the kids go to bed."

Erin patted his arm and picked up the giggling Essie as she stood. Martin looked up to her and their eyes met. It was there, that look he knew from years ago, it was there and he knew right then that they had more of a connection than they ever did.

Her decisive proposition with a logical solution proved it to him and the calmness with which she implemented it sealed its truth. He smiled. Relief washed over him and he put the cheque and the contract back into the package, filing them on the top of the shelf in the den. It would keep and he was happy despite the unknown.

Chapter 19 – The Backward Slide

Monday proved to be more than a simple challenge to Martin. He had to leave the happy weekend home he kept with Erin and Mickey and little Essie. The two days were pure bliss and there were no more phone calls or text messages and the contract and cheque was ignored until later that Friday night. It wasn't until after the kids were in bed, much later, that they broached the subject and opened an honest discussion on the contract and what it meant. The cheque and what it meant, too, added meat to the conversation. They both agreed the extra money would be nice but the terms of the contract contravened everything Martin worked diligently to obtain over the course of his career. Integrity was absent from the whole context of the document promising high level positions, more than fair compensation, and other end product fringe benefits *if* things went as directed under the terms of the contract. It was also accompanied by a confidentiality order that, when signed, could render large law suits if breached. It wasn't worth the payout in the long run.

"I will not sign something this exclusionary. It as much as says that my process is to overlook the regulatory steps with absolute disregard for the necessary protocols. I know they want the plan, as they call it, fast tracked but it won't be done at the expense of my reputation."

Martin was adamant he would bring it forward to the officials at the department of energy who were in a position to expose it. The chain reaction would begin with those who could shut down the nuclear 'big three.' He needed to be that voice, the one that spoke up for the safety of behalf of the whole industry.

Erin was turned on by his powerful statements. His new attitude toward taking back what was right and standing up to adversity was rewarded with loving attention from his ex-wife.

He wanted to confirm their togetherness again by not calling her 'ex' anymore. They decided as a couple that Martin would not sign the contract and would return the cheque, although, they first agreed to just pretend they kept it and played 'what would they do with it.' It soon landed on the floor, discarded and forgotten as they enjoyed playing other games – ones that involved less clothes and more body contact amongst the tangled bed sheets.

The closeness he experienced with Erin and his two children during the whole weekend was what made Monday a less than desirable day – not that it was normally a favorite for the workday audience. This time he left a warm bed and warm arms to head out into the cold street that Monday morning. The BMW started easily in the subzero weather and made good time through the light snow and heavy traffic. The commute did not like a step away considering the invitation on the table to return that evening after his job was complete. His first order of business was to arrange a meeting with his boss, even before the coffee shop stop on the main floor.

Martin glanced quickly through the crowd on his way to the stairs to ensure his intended target was not there. He debated waiting or following through with his encounter if he had been. He didn't have to worry about making a public scene, though, because Rowan was not there, anyway. The fifth floor climb tired him out as he pushed himself to do a rushed two at a time stair climb. It was almost like a self-inflicted punishment, a reminder of the task ahead. The last landing was ideal for a moment's rest and he caught his breath before opening the fifth floor entrance door. In the hallway, he paused. *His office first or directly to Rowan's.* He chose to face the demon first off, head on without chance to reconsider.

Martin entered the chief executive officer's outer waiting room and closed the door silently behind him. He motioned to Rowan's administrative assistant, Trevor, and moved to sit in one of the chairs off to one side. Trevor waved him in instead.

"Mr. Wells, go right in. Mr. Cott is expecting you." He smiled one of those smiles that hid something more and without another word to Martin he returned to the call he was in the middle of and with the phone trapped between his chin and shoulder, Trevor typed feverishly on the work station keyboard.

Martin shouldn't have felt so surprised. *In the short time of his employ there had there been anything that surprised him about this company?* Alternative Energy Corporation had opened some doors for him but it opened his eyes, too. Secrecy and corruption marched down every hall, hand in hand.

Nothing you did was safe from anyone. *Was it any wonder that someone knew where he was on the weekend?*

Martin pushed open the large oak door with its ornate brass handles, and he entered into what he thought was his chance to lay it on the line. He would give Rowan Jasper Cott and Alternative Energy Corporation a satisfying piece of his mind with a decisive ultimatum.

He should have realized there were most likely unknown things that still could have surprised him about Rowan Cott as the officer in charge of such a corporation. Martin was wise to the ways of the industry but he did not think the same manner as those connivers did.

"Good morning, Martin. How was your weekend?"

Rowan appeared cordial enough and he even had coffee ready on a silver tray sitting on the corner of his desk.

"I had no time to stop for coffee this morning. Please, go ahead fix yourself one. We all need our caffeine to keep us going around here."

Martin thought he'd take that blatant direct statement to mean that Rowan had not taken time to stop as he usually did and not that he knew Martin didn't stop for much the same reason. They both appeared to be on a direct course side by side so… *why did he feel the result would be a head on collision?*

"Thanks, Rowan. Yes, busy morning already. No time to stop, either."

Martin took the time to accept the offering and fixed himself a cup of coffee of last meal proportions. He slowly mixed in the necessary ingredients taking time to stir a bit of calmness into his soul in the same measure. He relaxed his shortened breaths as his mind got caught up in thoughts of… *what next.* He then took a chair in front of the desk, deliberately averting his gaze from the leather furniture in the meeting pit.

"So can I assume by your obvious avoidance of the question that the weekend didn't go well?" Rowan persisted as he watched Martin over the rim of his cup. He took a carefully measured mouthful of the creamer cooled coffee.

"On the contrary, Rowan, it went very well, thank you. I'd just prefer to keep my personal life private and therefore, in return keep my business life on the business at hand, too."

"Touchy subject, Martin? Defensive answers usually mean things aren't going as good as can be expected."

Martin could not ascertain what Rowan was pushing for and he was reluctant to continue the forbidden line of discussion. He meant what he said in his promise to Erin. He meant it when he declared he would keep the two major portions of his life totally and one hundred per cent separate, to the best of his ability, of course. There were times when bragging rights to cute kids or sexy wives were necessary especially when an 'I'm better than you' argument ensued, usually during conversation over drinks.

"Everything is just great, thanks. So you expected me here this morning, I gather from the warm greeting, and the hot coffee."

"Well, sure Martin. I knew probably long before you did that you'd be here first thing this morning. That is just a thoroughness you will have to get used to, Mr. Wells. Alternative Energy Corporation, *ergo me,* knows all that we need to know about all of our employees and we can certainly find out about it, if we need to."

He raised a cautioning hand. "Everything is kept confidential, of course, due to privacy laws. I never really figured out how that applies in all cases, but no worries, we only use what we know when we need to..."

Cott let his statement drift before he continued. "Now about that weekend... Are Erin and the kids doing fine?" He drew another mouthful of coffee while he watched Martin over the rim of the mug. "She has a nice little house. Does she own that one outright yet or does the Royal Bank still hold the partial mortgage?"

The crushing sensation formulated with what started as a sharp pain in the back of his neck and it soon traveled downward numbing him with fear. Martin tried to hide the urge to get up and run by helping himself to another cup of coffee. Slow and deliberate movements allowed him the necessary moments he needed to at least formulate a response that was not based purely on a reactive defensive move. He needed to keep a cool head with this so he could discover just how intertwined his personal life was going to end up being tangled with Alternative Energy Corporation. A company like this could suck him dry but they would not use Erin and the kids as pawns to force their hand.

"How is it that AEC, *ergo you,* is allowed to use information that you are not even supposed to be privy to... my family is my business, not yours, Rowan. Hmmm, can you answer me that in some manner that is acceptable to privacy laws without violating my personal rights?"

"You work in the power business, Martin. It's interchangeable with stakeholder interference and government intervention. There is no privacy in your personal life, Martin."

"Me and my information are one thing, Rowan. That of my family, my ex-wife included, is not your business and I resent the interruption and obvious intrusion into my personal life..."

Martin pulled from his jacket pocket the envelope that was delivered to Erin's house early Friday evening, and slapped it on the desk in front of him.

Rowan smiled. Martin was becoming tired of that persistent smirk; it was there whenever Rowan thought he had one up on him, like a confirmation of something sinister and pleasing to him. It was beginning to piss Martin off enough that he'd like to wipe it from his boss' face – with his fist.

"Good. You got my delivery."

"Yes, thanks. I'd appreciate keeping the business within the office. You could have given this to me on Friday afternoon."

"No, we had other business that afternoon and this is not a matter before the board; this is between you and the major players here at AEC. It is a private deal, if you will."

"Thanks, all the same, but I will not."

"You will not what, Martin? Not sign your undying devotion to the company unequivocally proving your support and dedication?"

"It is reminiscent of back room deals and under the table payments. Please, twenty five thousand dollars?"

"What? Not enough? I will give you double that Martin because you are worth it, just sign. And keep in mind – that is all you really ever have to do in the future. Just... sign... your... name..."

"The equivalent to selling my soul? Sorry, Rowan, this job seemed like it was too good to be true and here I am only a few weeks in and I find out it is... just that... too good to be true."

Martin put his cup down on the walnut finish of Rowan's desk without concern for the wood or the respect he once felt for someone in the chief executive officer's position. Over the course of his many years in business dealings, he got to know his share of management and knew many companies who were defined by the quality, or the lack thereof, in their leadership.

If Alternative Energy Corporation was to be defined by its chief officer then manipulation was the bigger part of management here. He didn't need to have that brought into his life. He'd contact Jessica just as soon as he was finished here and she'd return some recent calls and he'd be back in his own respected consulting business by morning.

"It's actually the best job you will ever have, Martin. The perks are great and benefits fringe or otherwise, will not be matched elsewhere."

"I am not interested in signing my reputation away for benefits, fringe or otherwise. It's not worth it, Rowan, even for double the blood money."

"I expected you to be a hard sell but... okay, okay. One hundred thousand dollars Martin, here and now, and not a penny more."

Rowan pulled the contract from the envelope, unfolded it, smoothed it out and set it before Martin on the table. He placed the gold inlaid ebony encased pen from the holder on the desk alongside the contract. From under the desk note pad he pulled a cheque made out to Martin Wells in the amount of one hundred thousand dollars, signed and dated with that very morning's date.

"You really are a presumptuous bastard."

"Oh, you got that right, Marty." The ensuing grin made Martin cringe and the sound of his name from his mouth made the bile in his stomach churn. Martin turned to leave.

"Martin. I think you forgot to leave your 'John Henry' first. Then you can go off to wherever it is you want to go off to... oh yes, and don't forget to deposit your well negotiated, and soon to be well earned, pay cheque."

"You cannot buy me."

"No?"

"No. Get some other flunky to sign away his life."

"Oh, but you are the flunky of choice, my dear Mr. Wells, because only you are the one everyone places their trust in, misguided or otherwise. Sign the damn contract and let's get on with the nuclear power show."

Martin moved toward the door unsure if his last steps would be the ones that took him out the door or those of going back toward the desk. He knew that if he signed the contract and took the money he could never go back.

Just the action of signing the contract ensured he would lose everything, including Erin. The thought also occurred to him that by walking away he might just lose it all anyway... his stomach churned again with the dilemma.

"Martin, don't make me beg. I hate begging unless, of course, I'm in the right mood... but we won't go there. I am sure you already know that I am fair but I can furiously go after that which I believe to be mine or can be mine for the right dollar amount."

As if on cue, the door opened and Suzanne walked in. Martin's thought processes were going to a conclusion he'd already deduced the other day. Suzanne was in Rowan's back pocket and everywhere else in those designer pants.

"Good morning, Martin. Don't you just love Mondays? Especially *this* Monday."

She walked by him and seductively dropped the shoulder of her coat to reveal bare skin. *It was friggin' December and she was parading around in who knows what or what not under that coat...* he didn't want to know anymore.

"Martin and I were just finishing up some business, Zanne, and then we can get down to some of our own..."

Martin did not want to confirm any other suspicions. He turned back and marched up to the desk; red faced he stood and stared directly at Rowan. The contract lay in front of him, the pen awaiting the pleasure of inking his signature. It would be as easy as that.

"I have no business with you. I don't even have any business being here at Alternative Energy Corporation. It appears it is not what I assumed and not what I signed up for so you can cut me my final pay cheque and I'm gone."

"Martin. Martin. This..." Rowan swept a hand over the document on the desk and then as if suggesting more, pointed at Suzanne. "It all isn't just an offer. It is a hard and fast condition of employment in exchange for no interruptions or intrusions into your 'private' life. How's that for bartering?"

"Not on my life."

"Well, then... how about on the life of your sweet little ex-wife and your two adorable little children?"

"Martin!" Suzanne feigned surprise. "Oh, my God, you are married... well, I never. Martin, honey you didn't even tell me after all we've shared..." She moved her body closer to him but he moved away.

"You leave my family out of this."

"As you wish." Rowan was determined to go for the throat. "Just sign here and take this nice peace offering and nothing – I mean nothing – will happen to your precious little family. I highly doubt there will be a happy reunion going on in that household this evening. It would be my guess that Martin will wallow in the wonder of the past weekend rendezvous and in the end you will just send a lovely cheque with lots of zeroes to your wife for her to buy a lovely little Christmas for your lovely little kids. Predictable Martin, I fear, will take the high road out of there to preserve their very well being. Am I right, Martin? Ah, you don't have to answer right now. Think on it but I don't believe you will have to think for very long."

Rowan picked up the pen and extended it toward Martin.

If his anger could have exploded into more, Martin Wells would have taken Rowan J. Cott, chief executive asshole, out right then and there, but at what cost? And besides, what good would it prove in the long run? Erin probably wouldn't get the truth and he would end up in some hole begging for daylight where no one would ever find him. He had that feeling. As he suspected, there were no surprises left to him anymore with this company and its associates. It seemed that anything was possible and he didn't doubt they could get away with murder.

He couldn't take the chance of endangering others, especially Erin, Mickey, and Essie. It tore at his heart but the decision he knew he had to make was already in front of him. He just had to accept it and make it real. Cursing under his breath, he grabbed the pen from Rowan.

The scrawl of his recognizable signature soon read permanently across the bottom of the page and then again on the confidentiality agreement that screamed death warrant. He threw the pen at Rowan, who just smiled; catching it and placing it calmly back in the holder in front of him.

Martin grabbed the cheque and briskly turned, knocking Suzanne rudely out of the way without a word of apology or explanation.

"No need to be nasty, Martin. You better rethink your actions."

The door was one of those hydraulic types that didn't even give him the satisfaction of slamming after he left in haste to close out Suzanne's overt threat. He hurriedly shut himself off from the worst decision he ever had to make.

And he had made a few. He stormed through the outer office and swiped a pile of neatly stacked papers from the corner of Trevor's desk.

"Hey, bitch!"

Martin ignored the stream of attitude that followed him and he knew that Trevor was on the interoffice line to Adam before he even got down the hallway. He took refuge in his own office where he was able to slam the door and lock it. His executive furnished, fully contained, bought and paid for office, was stained with the color of blood money. *Someone who just signed his life away deserved to hole up in a tainted office with a fucking ass hole for a boss at the one end of the hall, and a smart mouthed assistant guarding his door at the other.*

The one hundred thousand dollar bribery cheque ended up on the top of the 'in' basket and he sat, head in hands, for longer than a moment to quiet the insanity. He slammed his hands to the desk in anger. *He just signed away the happiness he left behind that very Monday morning.*

Her gentle kiss as he left that morning for work, with another more passionate to seal the promise he made to be home at a decent hour; the squealing Mickey so happy to hear his daddy would be back. Who would have guessed that the weekend would bring to an end everything he thought might be coming back together. He picked up the phone and as soon as he did, the outgoing line lit up; he slammed the phone back down. He couldn't even risk a call with all he knew about this place.

Fuck! How impersonal was that going to be... *a note and a cheque and a thank you for a great time but, geez, sorry honey, I screwed up again.*

Rowan was right and Martin hated him not because he was the snake he made himself out to be, but because he had the balls to predict what Martin knew in his heart he had to do. He couldn't risk their lives just to take the chance on calling Rowan's bluff. He also knew in his heart and even more so in his gut... if it was one of the last things he would ever do in this industry, he was going to take Rowan Jasper Cott down, and take him down good and hard.

The bottom drawer was the hiding place of executive choice for the much desired drink where one in such desperation would turn to wallow in self-pity. Martin slid open the drawer and drew from the back a stashed bottle of Jack Daniels. He originally stocked the drawer in case of celebration while tucked discreetly into the soft leather of the room's conversation pit. Today, though, right at this moment, Martin felt the lowest of low and a bleak depression overcame him with the accompanying acceptance of 'this is what it all boils down to.' He cracked the bottle open with the delight of a drug addict securing a new hit and the welcome addition to his pitiful life oozed over the mouth of the dark rimmed bottle and filled the large mug with an elixir into which he would disappear. It would become his best friend, his worst enemy and that to which he would blame all future endeavors, good or bad. Martin pulled out a paper and began to write...

"Dear Erin..."

"Regulatory processes, be damned."

Those four words would have been the best motto of choice for the nuclear power stakeholders with invested interest in the big three: Alternative Energy Corporation, Unified Nuclear ONE, and Peace County Nuclear Company. Amendments were introduced swiftly in the fall of 2011 that declared the production of nuclear energy as a critical component necessary to the survival of Alberta and the power industry. In much the same way critical transmission upgrades were declared the government's responsibility in the fall of 2009, responsibility shifted hands and a new energy future was signed. The whirlwind changes were implemented without much opposition once the newly elected government declared the necessity to take back the power control along with all other utility industry components.

The government re-regulated an industry once deregulated. The radical changes took hold of the provincial industry by once again putting into force the biggest public monopoly. The winds of change blew over a shocked land and many of the promises, made by the ousted officials to help those consumers who would face major hardship during the transition, were no more than dust. All evidence of financial assistance or demographic consideration was shredded when the new government was sworn in. Everyone would be painted with the same powerful brush and as the mandated regulations were set to print, it was either "keep up or get out."

The power generation that could be produced by the big three plants would mean Alberta would not have to worry about running short of power for a very long time. The level of production could even ensure that others would not run out of power either, if they had the money to pay for it.

It almost didn't get to that point.

Public outcry reached epidemic proportions after the reactors faulted in Fukushima aftereffects of the devastating Japanese tsunami and earthquakes. The Government's report hit the papers quickly supporting the decision to shut down nuclear production in areas sensitive to natural disasters. European countries proclaimed a reversal in progressive power sources with strong promises to dismantle current nuclear production. Alberta was not one of those areas.

Many continued to argue that the risks far outweighed the benefits but with the support of progressive politicians and with what seemed an express lane through the Energy Commission, implementation of the Alternative Energy's five year business plan was fast tracked. Their innovative objectives were introduced, met and exceeded. Martin was instrumental in convincing everyone who needed to be convinced. It was apparent that even he had a smooth ride through the usually stormy waters of debate.

Too many of the outspoken nuclear supporters who mattered found themselves succumbing to bribes while others just gave up or gave in. It soon became a running joke that there wasn't a need for a human resource department to administer payroll for Alternative Energy Corporation because everyone there was paid under the table. Over the course of five years, investors with the balls to sink their life savings into nuclear stock options saw their investments grow one hundred fold.

Year-end celebrations would go down unmatched in the power industry history books. The achievements by policy makers were of such a magnitude that there couldn't possibly be anything innovative enough to catch the market trend or profit margins for those who didn't get in on the inception of the three nuclear plants. Nothing in previous years, including the original rural electrification revolution in the late 1940s, or the mandatory Energy Plan put into effect by the end of 2012, could compare. The end of 2016 met the forecast directive in the Alternative Energy business plan and it was rumored that everyone would be getting a huge bonus that year.

The nuclear triad would begin production over the course of the next two years and when they intertied to the grid, they would immediately start producing power supplies unprecedented by newly found bio fuels, traditional coal stores, or wind turbine generation – combined. Transmission upgrades continued and would precede the nuclear interties to provide the necessary outlet for safe and efficient transfer of the large energy influx. They were making headway through the corridors and were on track to remove all remaining road blocks. The big three continued their push to the 49th parallel and beyond.

Chapter 21 – December Doldrums

December was not his favorite time of year.

Martin had vague memories of a life gone terribly wrong one December long ago. The inevitable slide into a Jack induced oblivion carried him through many lonely nights, mostly with the intended purpose of numbing and suppressing a guilt he could not face otherwise. About the time he realized how far the downward slide took him was about the same time he discovered that going back was never going to be an option. It was soon after this revelation and introspective discovery that he stopped caring and the drinking was no longer to numb but rather to feel.

December became the only time that Martin actually begged Erin for time with the kids; he, even with all good intentions, set aside other obligations and made the time to courier Erin a beautiful card and Christmas floral arrangement containing another note pleading with her to join him and take the kids away for a winter holiday. He would promise to pay for all of them to vacation 'as a family' with no strings attached other than the expectation to see his kids and be close to them when he needed them most. His request was usually refused and as she told him each year she was 'so done with his lies.' The line was usually followed by an argument fuelled by an alcohol induced rant that ended up with both of them upset, angry, and then succumbing to promises of maybe next year; that next year would be different, maybe, if he changed.

He never did and nothing different ever happened because it never occurred to either one to quit making promises and start making changes. Martin could count on both hands the number of times he was able to take the kids on an outing even though it was something Erin discouraged due to his usual state of last minute preparedness.

His disturbing unkempt appearance on a Sunday – the proposed day of his visits – put her off. This, of everything, surprised her because it was one thing she always admired about Martin – he always looked good and took care of his health. The toll of sixteen hour days, night after night of drinking, and other happenings he did not share with his ex-wife led to a less than desirable image. These events, in turn, distracted him from trying and increased his less than valiant efforts toward being a father.

Erin finally got a court order requiring the necessary solitary visits be changed to supervised visits – if – and only if – he had not been drinking and was accompanied by someone like his mother. She drew the line at allowing him to visit his kids while in the company of *the whore of the day*, despite his claims of 'being in a relationship'. During one angry encounter, Erin had commented that she didn't remember charging quite so much for their time together. In hindsight, she took the comment back and cried, remembering the cheque she received December 2010 when she was paid more than they were, or at least, she assumed so.

After that, visitation became a chore for Martin due to all the rules and he finally just sent cards and money or gifts. Or rather, Jessica sent them on his behalf. He had insisted that Adam be replaced if he was going to be happy staying with Alternative Energy Corporation. Happy, was a state of mind Martin referred to loosely when he talked about work. He knew that at least with her as his assistant he quite possibly had one 'friend' although over the following months he began to doubt that friendship, as well, and he came to another revelation. Everyone could be bought for a price and he was living proof of that fact.

The company Christmas party was more like an industry ass kissing event with all the big industry players, and even the not so big, there to show off either their latest car, house, gold or sexual acquisition. It was frequently referred to that these parties were no places for the spouse who was not in the electrical industry.

"Hooking up" meant some kind of deal was at hand because most of the hard core stuff was decided in the bedrooms, not the board rooms. Martin was not going to attend the company party if Erin had agreed to go away for the 'family' vacation, but it was the usual "not this year" so he said, *fuck it all,* and drove the BMW to the MacDonald Hotel.

Chapter 22 – All Lies

Martin left the car with the valet requesting it be parked in the secure underground parking. He booked the best room available on the company tab because... *damned if he was going to get a drunk driving charge on top of it all.* He planned to party like an animal and stumble in some unrespectable manor upstairs where he could then pass out in hotel style. The next morning would allow him the chance to decide on the rest of the day and whether he'd stay another night or not. *Who would care?*

During a brief moment of lucidity while dressing for the evening's event, Martin thought about getting out of it again, but every time he got up the courage to actually think he'd like to say it was time for him to retire, fear got the better of him and he shrunk back to the coward he had become over the past five years. He missed most of Mickey's birthdays. His little son would now be eight years old. And Essie, well he guessed she wouldn't even know who daddy was as he wasn't around for most of her early years.

It was thoughts like these that drove Martin to take another drink instead of persuading him to give it up as a crutch. The bullied threats made years ago continued each and every time he showed any sign of weakness at Alternative Energy Corporation. He couldn't do anything about it anyway with a clear conscience. Depositing huge signing bonuses, accepting and spending contract negotiation payments in the hundreds of thousands of dollars? It didn't matter what you thought or what you originally stood for, even if you accepted the blood money once it was always going to be a permanent stain on your hands or worse yet, on your record.

It was easier to just accept it for what it was and after so long he just preferred it that way because it kept his family safe. He often wondered why it had just been Erin and the kids, but perhaps their vulnerability was more obvious.

No one ever threatened his mom or dad. It was common knowledge that Martin stayed out of their lives anyway. His father would never change his attitude and Martin had no use for someone who wouldn't listen to warnings given as expert opinion of the industry. He couldn't really blame his parents if they never wanted to listen to him again especially if they got wind of what kind of man he really was; he already felt like a failure as a son.

"You are looking old, Martin, time to slow down."

He spoke to the reflection looking back at him as he shaved the stubble on his chin. His hair was greying at the temples and, despite the hollowness around his eyes that he didn't remember being there last year, he felt he didn't look all that bad for almost forty.

"You old dog, you still got it... now if you could just remember how to use it." He tried his best flirty smile and almost cut himself shaving.

The MacDonald Hotel was still the place for elegant parties with the tiered chandeliers and expensive woven tapestries throughout the lobby. The Big Three Christmas function was held in the King James Room on the second floor. Martin checked in at the front desk. Her name tag read "Marissa" and he made a mental note to remember it for later. *You never know how these events could turn out,* he thought to himself, along with other unmentioned desires. He'd been to quite a few affairs where the dogs were out and the beautiful ones, you would take to your bed with the bat of an eyelash, were few and far between.

"Here's your key pass, Mr. Wells. Would you like to book a wake-up call now or do you plan to stay with us into the late morning?" Her hand was soft and slow to move from his touch as she handed him the card for his room. "Room 405. I am sure you will enjoy your stay." He had to remind himself that it was far too early to read more into the encounter than it really was. *Flirting.* She was flirting with him and he wasn't even trying – yet. *Marty, you old dog,* he thought, *you should ask her to show you to your room.*

"Did you need a bellboy to take your luggage up – or …" she leaned forward at the counter with just enough cleavage showing to draw his eye downward. "Never mind," she smiled and straightened up slowly, "you don't have any. You must be here for the Big Three Christmas Party then?"

He was happy he didn't have to be quite so obvious and he put asking her to take him to his room on hold, at least for the time being.

"That's right, so now you have no excuse. You know where you can find me." A little suggestion couldn't hurt, just in case – *you know, a back-up plan.* Martin always found it handy to have one of those, if he remembered to put it into place long before the drinking eased into oblivion.

She smiled that 'oh, I so know what you mean' smile and he took his leave with one of his practiced flirty grins. At the top of the staircase he dared to look back and she was watching him. *Remember her, Marty,* he almost said out loud.

The tables were arranged by the social event's committee coordinators and little calligraphy handwritten place cards marked every attendee's assigned spot. Martin scoured the tables for his name on the way to the bar, just to see who he was placed with or who he might have to ditch and switch. He debated whether it would be in his best interests to stay or to change his placement when he saw that he was seated with Rowan J. Cott, chief executive ass hole and Zanne, the executive's chief hole.

On many occasions over the past few years, he had to put off invitations and visitations from Suzanne, especially when he found out she was the one who leaked confidential family information to Rowan and Alternative Energy directors. She was also the one who officially drove the wedge between him and Erin; one he could not explain away or loosen no matter what he said because it was true.

The 'conversation' in question was one he had with Suzanne one night long ago.

It all happened before he even realized things were not going to go right with her because he really wanted to be back with Erin. It was a conversation that was supposed to be private. *Who knew that the bitch was going to tape it and use it against him?* Tricks like that secured her a paid position with the company, and helped sign his 'this is no longer my life' contract.

He pulled his place setting and changed it with some unsuspecting flunky from the new government cabinet to secure his spot amongst the most corrupt of all, the Investors Syndicate Group who backed the nuclear construction projects. It was merely a front because everyone who knew anything knew it was actually government money. It didn't matter who signed the cheques when it came out of the provincial coffers.

At the bar, feeling rather pleased with his actions, he ordered a double rye on the rocks and contentedly sipped it while watching the floor. Brown nosing politics always amused him and even though he was dead centre in the midst of the corruption, in fact, so deep he couldn't find right from wrong anymore, it still entertained him.

He could usually pick out who would end up with whom and, if by some weird chance he felt that the match wasn't going to be conducive to a productive evening, just for the heck of it he pushed his way politely into the conversation, drawing the attention of the target woman. Interestingly enough, most often it was the guy who was the target and the women were the ones to be cautious of, in particular, those who might have an even higher ranking husband lurking somewhere in the background of big business.

Standing at the bar surveying the room, however, put one on display in a spot where they were most likely to be viewed by all others in the room. He didn't notice her until she was almost beside him as it had been some time since they last talked and, although they emailed as promised for a while after their encounter, his fall from grace and the industry's eventual slide into nuclear submission, put them on opposite sides of the game.

"You have a nerve standing there like you own the fucking place."

"I knew when I first met you under that soft all nice as pie exterior there was a nasty force to be reckoned with…"

"Oh, you haven't reckoned with me in any way just yet, Martin Wells."

Marie Foster fought back spitting on him; her words seethed with anger and Martin contemplated just ignoring her for the rest of the evening but decided that if he did that it could be very embarrassing if at any point he had to admit he once considered her an ally in the business.

"Marie, you know I am sorry that you lost your company but I didn't have anything to do with that, well, at least not directly. All rural electrification units took a hit when metering was made mandatory without financial aid. How was I to know the government would pull the all or nothing card?"

He brought it in with a slight, hopeful smile, one that asked to be forgiven. He was getting to be a master at the type of manipulation required to peddle his ass out of any hole sideways.

"Liar. You signed the bloody papers stating 'nuclear plants do not pose a significant risk.' What do you call wiping out all my lines and signing up my customers? I'd call that significant risk, Mr. Wells." Her voice was quiet enough that it appeared to others as if they were having just a regular conversation but he was certain that she'd rather yell her words at him.

It suddenly occurred to him that it was rather odd she was even attending a nuclear company function given her aversion to that arm of the industry.

"I don't think they meant loss of personal livelihood when they referred to significant risk, Marie." He wasn't trying to anger her further but it was true. Most cooperatives took on a slightly greedy 'me attitude' when the shit eventually hit the fan.

"I had less significant risk than some but little risk is still risk in my books." Martin was impressed that she was able to hold her anger in check so calmly.

"So, may I inquire as to why an ex-rural electrification company owner is attending this party? I'm hoping they checked your bag at the door for explosives." He poked a finger in the top of her designer purse, *much too small to be carrying more than a pocketknife,* and she slapped his hand away.

He continued. "Or I guess I should be more worried that you might just want to get close enough to hang me." He turned to the bartender and signaled for another drink and motioned to Maric as well. He could at least be cordial.

"I heard a rumor that there is supposed to be some kind of announcement made by the Big Three and because I still own a farm and produce my own wind generation in the northern corridor I needed to be here. I wouldn't put it past you to already know if I'm going to have to sell my property."

He noticed the edge creep into to her voice as she spoke and that concerned him. He remembered the connection they made way back, both being from a farm background. He knew that edge. It was the same one he heard in his father's voice and, even lately in his mother's, on the odd occasion he picked up the phone when she called him.

"Dammit, Marie. Really. I'm just here to get plastered and accept my year end 'you've kissed enough butts for another year' bonus."

Concerned, Martin glanced about the room to see if his boss had arrived yet. He caught sight of him just coming in the entrance, Zanne in tow, draped through his arm like a cheap fur coat.

"You made me believe you were a friend. Someone who claimed to be telling me the truth, so why on earth would you think I'd believe you this time?"

Martin hated being in the dark about anything unless, of course, he chose to be there, but then at that point it wouldn't matter what was going on.

The meeting of the board the past week revealed nothing of an announcement but that was not to say there were no other meetings he was not privy to; he could text Jessica. She might still tell him in private. Being there as an employee would expose her to the thing Rowan was really all about – sex with whoever would comply. Martin the remembered she was on holidays and returned his attention to Marie, pointing to his face.

"See this face, Marie? Right now along with the rugged, albeit older, rougher good looks, there lurks concern. Do you want to know why? Because now I don't know what the hell is up tonight and shit, how am I going to enjoy myself and get drunk and get laid when I have to have my wits about me to ensure I catch every fucking detail going on in this fucking company?" Martin grabbed his drink from the bar and downed it. It might be the only one he could have and he just screwed up making it last.

"Okay, so you are either a really great actor or you don't know jack and you aren't lying to me this time." She placed a calming hand on his upper arm and he looked at her, kind of squinting and kind of frowning.

"So, what? Now you're hitting on me?" He laughed.

"Well, let's just say prowess at power debates is not the only thing I've heard about you."

He guided her to his table and ceremoniously replaced the placard with the financial advisor's name on it to the next table over. *Let them fight over the chair.* At least, he'd have someone sitting beside him he could talk to, relate to, and keep an eye on.

He was still not sure why she might trust anything he had to say when, in essence, she was right. She had every right to doubt his word – that's just the way things became to be. His signature caused the closure of not only her electrification company, but several other less stable rural units, as well.

The evening made its way through the usual pre-dinner networking drinks, to the sit down waiter served four course meal, and then on to coffee and a selection of delectable desserts brought around to each table on brass carts. The service was excellent and Martin had to agree that the company knew how to put on an event worthy of report.

It just meant, in reality, the company and its representatives knew how to spend money. It was fortunate that they were in the business actually making money in the current market. Others were not so lucky, but that was of inconsequence to those attending the Big Three Christmas function that night.

After everyone had their fill of food and feast, Rowan J. Cott stepped up to the podium. It was dramatically set in a draped makeshift stage to one side of the room. As he tapped the microphone, the conversation in the room droned on for a few short minutes and then gradually faded into silence.

"The Big Three wishes everyone a very joyous holiday season and in keeping with the rumors we know start somewhere about the first of November – there is always speculation as to what bonuses might be paid. We are so incredibly fortunate to be in a business where the rumors are not 'I wonder if' but instead they are 'I wonder how much'." As Rowan spoke, company representatives made the rounds to every table and handed any Big Three employee, contractor, or temporary assistant, a brightly adorned envelope. Exclamations of delight were heard throughout the room as each person cautiously slit open the packet and peeked hesitantly inside. Marie turned a sidelong glance to Martin when the girl handing out envelopes nearby did not make a stop at their table. She suppressed a sly smile.

"Guess you've been a good boy this year."

It was a dig he knew he deserved because it was well known in the business that he was one of the highest paid consultants and was officially on the Alternative Energy Corporation payroll.

It was also common knowledge that he was blacklisted from ever representing any other power faction other than nuclear power and had been unofficially paid under the table for that dubious honor.

"Remind me to hand in my parking pass on Monday. No bloody way I do this shit for nothing."

She shrugged and he knew he might have a sympathizer on his side again. His corner was rather empty these days. Rowan began to speak again as he brought his attention back to the stage.

"We do have a special award and bonus to someone tonight without whom we could not have made this much progress in so little time. Martin Wells, come up here. We haven't forgotten about you, Marty."

Martin cringed and knew that the misuse of his name would be the main reason he would have fun strangling Rowan one day. He reluctantly stood, unsuspecting as he always seemed to be; he approached Rowan.

Instead, of the usual business handshake thank you, Martin suffered a crushing man hug from the person he'd least like to be hugged by. While pulled in close enough, yet out of pick up from the microphone, Martin heard the words repeated that were Rowan's insurance policy for keeping him on board and keeping him in line.

"Good work, Marty. Just smile and accept and play along. We all know why you do this thing you do and it's not just for the money. It's actually because you lack the balls to protect what is really important in your life." Rowan patted Martin on the back and stepped away from him, speaking into the microphone so everyone could now hear.

"I was very fortunate; rather, Alternative Energy Corporation was very fortunate to have hired this man before this all began. And Martin Wells has truly earned his keep here by being instrumental in the many directives outlined in the company business plan. He has also been involved with the Big Three now for several years and continues to impress us with his dedication. This is a small token of our thanks."

There was applause and Martin smiled lamely as he took the envelope handed to him as he had done on so many occasions before, knowing that the dollar figure written on the cheque inside was made out to him in some ungodly amount with lots of zeros in an effort to continually buy his servitude. He couldn't say he didn't like the money; however, he didn't have to publicly admit he liked the reason he received as much as he did. No one could get the industry to roll over the way he did and he guessed that their paying him to do it made it necessary. He wanted to leave the front and center now and return to his seat but he could feel Rowan's hand holding his elbow as he continued to speak.

"Another reason we are so happy to have on our staff a man with the expertise of Martin Wells, is the ability of our company to move forward on innovations that, when implemented, will improve the overall operational capacity of the Alberta power industry.

"Tonight, we'd like to announce the new deal for the upcoming year as we start 2016 with another power first. We can all argue that sustainability means survival and making that which is good even better.

"You all know that for some time now we have been in negotiations with smaller companies around the province to bring the power business under one umbrella corporation. Of course, I wouldn't be mentioning this as a proud moment, if it wasn't Alternative Energy Corporation that I speak of. We have secured regulatory approval," Rowan shifted his gaze to Martin and then back to the audience, "to assume all power company contracts, hereby, officially becoming Alberta Power ONE.

"Effective 2017, there will be no need for small company subsidiaries and the transportation utility corridor will effectively assume all adjacent farmland properties to increase the right of ways required for an expansion in transmission construction. There will be no single lines running to remote end users and those farms and ranches that do not comply with the orders will be forcibly assumed."

Rowan paused for only a moment before he brought the final blow home. "We can guarantee that if this happens, compensation will not be near what the original Assumption orders will offer."

Rowan's grip tightened on Martin's elbow and he felt the blood drain from his face. If it wasn't for the hot lights and the warm room he would have appeared deathly grey. Rowan had, in essence, delivered him a death sentence of the most powerful kind. His eyes met with Marie's, and he knew she thought him a traitor, along with whatever else she already thought about him.

Martin didn't chance a look at Rowan and made his way through the tables back to his chair. He sat down slowly beside her not sure what might happen. He put his hand on hers. She didn't move it. *That was a good sign,* but he wasn't sure.

"Marie."

"Don't talk. You can't do nothing but lie."

"For what it's worth I didn't know."

"Yes and how much were you just paid to not know?"

"Didn't look, don't care. I'll spend it just like all the rest but believe me, I don't always enjoy it."

"Martin, don't tell me you don't care. I could just scream right now but am trying to preserve my outward businesslike softness so I don't go belligerent on someone. Good thing for you that I'm trying my hardest to control it because it's you I'd like to go belligerent on."

"Marie, please. I don't know who to trust anymore and can't place trust blindly in just anyone around me. Privacy is a big issue where I work because, in fact, you have none. I am bought and paid for and am not proud of it but there's more to it than you know."

"Now *I* can say I don't care. I am in the process of losing my family farm all because it happens to stand in the way of progress – literally – the northern corridor runs right through it."

There was a catch in her voice and Martin had to figure out how to fix this or go down trying.

He put his arm around her shoulders and surprisingly she did not push him away. Instead, she picked up the full glass of wine in front of her and silently drained the golden liquid.

"You want to talk?"

Marie didn't answer right away and just poured herself another glass of wine. She drank it slowly this time, savoring it as if she was thinking of what she might say to Martin. He waited and, as he did, he noticed Suzanne watching him. He looked passed her and then away as if he didn't see her.

"Let's go somewhere and talk…" He tried again.

"Let's go to your room."

"Okay."

It was early and he wasn't even drunk yet and he didn't really know what might come of it, but she needed him and he could at least offer her that consideration. He grabbed her shawl and put it around her shoulders, leading her out of the noisy room. He didn't dare look back. He knew Suzanne would be nudging Rowan and motioning his way but he didn't care. *They could both go to hell. As if they all weren't already there.*

Martin was happy they didn't have to go down to the lobby to take the elevator to his fourth floor room. Marissa might still be at the desk and he didn't want to ruin any chance they might hit it off, later. He really didn't expect things to go too well with Marie as he was sure she'd much rather kill him than kiss him.

Inside the door to his room she made a liar out of him again. Her hands caressed the side of his face as she pulled him closer to her. She was quiet and Martin didn't think she was drunk.

Her kisses were much the same as her personality; soft lips drew him in with a vibrant passion that encouraged him to do the same. The shawl over her shoulders hit the floor and he touched her skin, running his hands down her arms. As they looped around her waist he pulled her close to him, feeling the heat of her breasts against him and the touch of her hands on his back, slowly sliding downwards.

He responded and picked her up, cupping his hands under her bottom. She responded with a sigh and that to Martin was a signed deal when it came to sexual encounters.

He put her on the bed and she grabbed his belt pulling him down beside her, unbuckling it as he lay back. He closed his eyes and felt her move over top of him. His body went rigid and he sucked in a quickened breath when he felt the length of cold metal pressing on his throat.

"Wha…"

"I wouldn't talk right now you sorry son of a bitch."

Martin held his tongue, buying his time. There was no fucking way she was going to do this now. He had been through times when he thought of doing much the same thing to himself. The suffering he caused his family and the uncertainty of his own future made living very painful, at times. But no bitch, however wronged, was going to do his dirty work.

"So how much did you get paid this time?" She held the knife steady despite her anger and her confidence, at that point, was a good thing, for Martin's sake.

"I told you I don't care. You were there, I didn't even look." He gritted his teeth and hoped he'd say the things that would keep her calm. She pulled the envelope from his pocket and tore open the end of it with her teeth. Her hand was still firm against his throat; the blade was beginning to warm up or, he was beginning to sweat – he couldn't decide.

"Half a fucking million dollars."

Martin would have jumped for joy if it weren't so dangerous to do so. *Wow,* he thought, *what I can do for Erin this year…* He felt the knife press closer to his neck. *There's no way I said that out loud.*

147

"We'll consider this my payment for being fucked."

She folded the envelope and pushed it along the strap of her dress, where it was securely hidden under the black lace. At that moment, Martin took the chance of moving quickly with a maneuver that was meant to throw her aside enough to allow him to slide out of range of the knife. A slight miscalculation and a fight back meant the knife caught him low on the shoulder with a deep slash that started to bleed, soaking quickly through his dress shirt. He pushed her back on the bed and knocked the knife hand securely against the night stand. The blade dropped to the floor. He punched the intercom and when the desk clerk answered he yelled into the speaker.

"Send the police, Marissa – Room 405 – and you might want to come up with a bandage or two, I've been stabbed. Actually, you better get an ambulance, instead." He felt the pain and quelled the urge to pass out by concentrating on the task at hand – he knew he had the right to hold on to what was his. Martin grabbed the envelope from Marie and he shoved it into his pocket.

"I don't think so, bitch. I don't get fucked for nothing, either."

Chapter 23 – Recovery

It was the first two weeks of consecutive rest Martin had in a long time, not that a private room in the Grey Nun's Hospital was comparable to the room at the MacDonald Hotel and all its possibilities. That outcome would, of course, be based on a different turn of events that fateful night. He had waved valiantly to Marissa after they wheeled him out of room 405, desperately clutching a hand to his sliced shoulder as they exited the elevator on the main level where an ambulance waited to transport him to emergency. He remembered equally important to him at the time was the apathetic panic that overcame him as he checked his pockets for the "bonus" cheque. Happy it was secure, like a junkie knowing his next hit was lined up; he laid back and almost enjoyed the stretcher ride. He wasn't even privy to the drunken stupor that usually accompanied the night of partying. There was nothing to dull the thoughts rushing around in his head. With only two drinks the whole evening, Martin's mind was clear and that scared him. He could think clearly and the harm in doing that meant there were the places his mind went without warning or wanting.

With the New Year's festivities fast approaching, he wasn't ready to think of another Alternative Energy Corporation function just yet; and he did not want to go to any more parties alone. It was almost a blessing to be laid up here because he had a legitimate excuse to miss all the celebrations – ones he was expected to participate in given the responsibilities of his job. All the government and industry networking, all the kiss ass functions were part of the deal and he was expected to attend, net and kiss at each and every one. He didn't want to think of Erin and who might be another lucky companion yet again, on another New Year's Eve. He could feel 2017 already falling to misdirected resolutions and empty promises.

Rowan played the worry card for Martin to the point that it convinced him he was genuinely concerned for his health and well-being. He even insisted that Martin take all the time he needed to recover and he was not to worry, *he'd take care of things until he was back on his feet*. Rowan even promised to ensure that his car got back to the Alternative Energy Corporation's secured parkade where it would be safe until he returned to work.

Martin, in his sober induced logic, made a mental note to check the under carriage of the beamer for explosives upon his return to work.

With a slower than usual recovery, the trial against his assailant was pushed into the New Year until Martin was well enough to go to court. He didn't even want to press charges but Rowan had insisted and Martin knew it was more to make an example of Marie than to get justice. Anyone who opposed the recently released Assumption Plan would be up against the same hard and fast rules – get with it or get on with it. Martin knew he had to talk to his dad now with more force if he hoped to convince him to get out of the business, if not for his own sake, for his mother's. It was some time since they'd spoke and he actually hoped no one from the office contacted them about the accident.

The hospital couldn't get next-of-kin contact information from Martin because he refused to give it to them. He played lone man in the world given that's how he felt most of the time anyway. *Besides,* he thought, *I don't want to upset everyone at this time of year or glean any undue attention, even though the situation might warrant it.* His mother would be upset at him for not calling; his dad might grunt an "I told you so" if he was lucky. Erin? He wasn't sure at that point whether she would even give him the time of day let alone come rushing down to see that he was okay. He expected, as always, Jessica would have sent off the necessary Christmas delivery before she left for her holidays. It was still important enough to him to ensure his kids had gifts in time for the Christmas morning opening. At least he would be there in spirit – wrapped with a bright shiny bow.

Perhaps, it was just as well. His recovery was taking longer than usual due to his agitated state of mind and his naturally run down physical condition... *he could just die here alone and would anyone even care?*

The thought surprised and alarmed Martin. There he was just lying back swaddled in hospital garb and black thoughts still swelled in his mind. His breathing accelerated to rapid cutting spurts and he began to sweat. The severe body response to the emotional upset triggered the alarms on the machines hooked up to his arm and neck. Several nurses came running into the room.

"I'm okay, really."

He took a few quick gulps of air before he continued. "Just can't stop my brain from thinking horrid thoughts that include dying..."

He let the words tumble out before he realized that black thoughts about death were better off inside his head and were not particularly something he should have shared. The nurse attending him immediately wrote furious notations on his chart and one of other young attendants left the room immediately upon her signal.

"Really, it's okay. I will be fine as long as I can rest."

"It's all right, Mr. Wells, we can give you something to calm you. You really need to sleep if you expect to heal properly. The doctor told you your recovery is taking more time than it should. You need to stay calm." She was concerned and the compassion in her voice comforted Martin; that was until he realized they meant to drug him. Worse thoughts overcame him in his drunken stupors, one's he could not control, let alone stop. He immediately feared being drugged would produce the same effects on him and he really didn't feel up to the experimentation.

"No pills, please. I'm fine, I just need to relax."

"Yes, we know Mr. Wells."

"No pills, right?"

"Right, no pills."

The young nurse returned to the room ripping open a package with a dose of medication in a small syringe. Martin barely spouted a protest when the medication hit his intravenous line and he suddenly felt an overwhelming calm wash over him.

"No pills, Mr. Wells, now sleep."

And Martin slept.

The ballroom lights were bright and they threw cascading silver beams throughout the room. They penetrated the open doors and sprinkled into the hallways, showering the dull carpet with bright flashes of blue and gold and red. Martin saw her standing alone at the bar as he entered the room. Determined to make the night a good one, almost as if to make up for the last one that went so far awry, he set his sights and mentally planned his approach.

Her back was toward him and he voraciously eyed her sequined body with a lust he knew she could be convinced to quench. He knew that one touch of her hand on his skin would set his loins afire, ready for the hardening a little bit at a time with each touch, with each look, with each thought, every word and, especially, with every deep kiss. Her lips were like crystal ice upon heated flesh, tempting and dangerous, all in one cooling taste.

Nothing stood between them as he approached slowly, watching her slight movements, thinking they were made with the thought that he was looking upon her, wanting her close, wanting her in an intimate way. He knew she would want it too, but knew her style to be slow and all consuming.

She would take her time playing her seductive game and when the time was right for her, she would take the bait and let him think that she was taken by him.

He knew it was the way in the industry. Most of the key male players were actually played by the women in the higher echelons of business. That was okay with Martin. He just played along and got his big bonus cheques and did what he had to do to keep his family safe and his lust satisfied. That was the way of his world.

Almost touching her now – he could sense that she knew he was close – he felt the heat from her body and hesitated as he moved to caress two bare, thin strapped shoulders with trembling hands. They always made him nervous though his manly exterior rarely betrayed the anxiety. They were soft with voluptuous exteriors but they sometimes held pointed, demonic secrets tucked secretly away out of sight, disguised a lace cover treats, there for the taking. But... unleashed at the most inopportune times, they could exhibit rages so unbecoming of their beauty. That was the chance he took to spend time with women; one he would risk, over and over, despite the hurt.

She sighed as his touch lingered on her shoulders and he could feel her smile, as she tilted her head to one side, resting her cheek upon his hand.

Another sigh.

And that was his invitation. Martin moved closer and his body touched hers. The low cut back of her dress invited him to places he wanted to ravage; thoughts of moving his hands down her body inflamed him and his senses responded. He kissed her exposed neck. As a shiver of expectation ran the course of his spine, he turned her toward him and he opened his eyes.

There, standing face to face with him was betrayal. It was his attacker in the flesh – Marie.

"Stop!"

Martin sat bolt upright, pulling on the cords and tubes that hooked his arm to the machine that now incessantly beeped, warning of another rapidly increased heart rate. He tried to slow his breathing as the nurses and orderlies stormed his room not wanting another shot of their fix to his problem. The little green line blipped erratically, too fast, too fast, peaking and crashing... and then, too slow.

As the machine sent its shrill piercing warning sounds out into the night of the silent hospital corridors, Martin slumped back on the bed, unconscious.

Martin would not be expected to attend the New Year's event as was customary procedure for all directors and executive officers. Although low level managers and administrative staff were invited, their attendance was optional by the terms of their employment contracts; it was the executive who made the connections and made the decisions. Mandatory 'ass kissing,' as Martin referred to it, began early on the afternoon of that holiday eve right there in the offices of Alternative Energy. Celebrations then continued long into the night until the out of tune renditions of Auld Lang Sine were long forgotten.

While the partying went on without him, doctors at one point were not sure Martin would even make it to New Year's Day. The hospital staff told him a couple of days later that they had to fight to "bring him back" and he humorously interjected "from where" to an unappreciative crowd. At that crucial point, they insisted he give them *someone's* number and he reluctantly offered his mother's when he thought that they would not leave him alone until he did. They even threatened to call the hotel to track his employer, knowing he was brought in that night from a work related celebration. He relented and, as he surmised, Faith was furious with him.

"Martin, when are you going to slow down?" Even though she hid her annoyance he knew she was truly upset. "You and your father are going to be the death of me." And he knew that fact to be true – his habits were no different from those of his father's, they were just catered to in a different setting.

"Mom, I was going very slow when this happened, believe me." He winced at the thought of actually entertaining sex with a murderous assailant. But at the time, one thought on his mind, and it seemed like the best course of action at the time.

"This industry is nothing to mess with."

He was taken aback. *Could he truly believe she knew more than he wanted her to? After all those years of trying to convince them that it wasn't something to just dismiss, could he even consider the hope that she might be able to convince his father, too?*

"Don't go getting all 'I told you so' on me, young man."

It was then he knew she was truly grateful he had called her because her eyes could not betray the truth of a mother's love for her son. Although still admonishing his stupid behavior, she gave him a careful hug to reassure him and a loving caress on the back.

"So Dad's busy with the farm?"

Was there any doubt? He didn't expect his father to come running for him when he had avoided the trip there on many occasions. But still, his father was always healthy in a physical sense and had never missed a day of farming since he took over the reins.

"Your Dad's vigilance with this herd and an early crop of Canola will be what pulls us out of this hole. The bank called the loan, Marty, but at least those vultures gave him six months to come up with the money." She was matter of fact and was calm in accepting the situation. Perhaps, she expected it or, perhaps, she saw it as the best of what was yet to come.

Martin Sr. would tend to the plumping and primping of his prize hogs for market later that year. The new crop of piglets he'd nursed over the winter promised a return investment that would go to the bank in payment to clear the loan they so unceremoniously recalled. The economy was struggling and financial institutions were cutting their risks. Ignored and overwhelmed, many clients faced a depression that led many to believe they'd be better off just cutting their throats.

"If everything goes as hoped we should be fine."

"What about your horses?" Martin tried to sit up but succumbed to a more comfortable position on the pillows as his mother propped them lower on his back.

"If everything goes as hoped..." She stopped, catching on the words and, as she looked away, Martin caught the glisten of a tear.

"Mom, this year is going to be tough – Dad needs to get what he can out of the farm and leave before he ends up with pennies on the dollar. All those years..."

Faith placed a hand on Martin's arm stopping him, calming him, and reminding him that it wasn't his worry. But there was no sympathy now for farmers and ranchers who remained in a business especially when they were given enough warning over the last few years that they would be better in the long run to make amends and move on.

Agri-manufacturing was taking over the industry with an influx of investments directed from those heavily involved in the nuclear power industry. The agri-manufacturing processing plants needed the constant assurance of a continuous and plentiful source of power. The nuclear plant proponents promised and could provide. The new energy plan was now rapidly moving through the construction phase. The northern plant was already on line ending all presumption that it might not be completed before the deadline startup date. Public outcry went viral on social media outlets but it was too little too late.

The announcement that the second of the big three plants was expected to go live by August of that year drew attention away from the first site located in Peace County. Clouds of steam exhaust billowed constantly against the northern Alberta sky. Many residents in areas immediately adjacent to the plant picked up and moved fearing the worst even though there was little indication of trouble and no identifiable issues. Ignorance did breed fear.

Martin ensured, in the application process he managed to maintain control over, that qualified nuclear engineers were mandatory on site, 24-7. He knew the chance of correcting the outcome of a malfunction was near impossible and they would not be in a position to do anything about it even if they had the highest degree of education in the world attending to its monitoring.

At least, at the very minimum, their presence presented the necessary image of experience to perform diligent compliance testing and procedural risk assessments. It gave credibility in a situation that lacked support.

The sensitivity level on the data input meters was so high that the slightest shift in ground activity or weather patterns registered the disturbances within a 100 mile radius. As long as it appeared to be safe they could convince those around them in time. The longer the plants were able to operate without an issue the less would be the concern. Nuclear Two would not go on line until the first one was running smoothly in its generation to the grid; officials would not wait long, though, six months tops.

The third leg of the big three monster was dragging behind schedule but not in construction or plant readiness. The problem lay in the fact that it still lacked the necessary transmission line upgrades to accommodate the level of voltage to be powered into the lines. It was critical for this phase to be in the advanced transmission stage to carry the surge of power on the lines to southern destinations. The corridors were not yet free and crews had been unable to access the areas to build the monstrous line towers. Several farms along the southern extension of the grid were still operational with many farmers and ranchers holding out, refusing to sell, move or do otherwise.

Martin Wells Sr. was one of them.

Chapter 25 – Martin Sr.

"Martin. It's the hospital in Edmonton... Martin Jr.'s been hurt."

"Now what?"

Martin Sr. felt a wave of emotion wash over him he was able to distinguish – it could have been panic or relief, but he was unsure which. He did, however, recognize the stab of guilt and shame all rolled into one as he posed the question to his wife. Those feelings he would never claim to feel. Without her telling him, he knew it was something serious and that it more than likely involved Martin's line of work. Despite their years of separation and disagreement, there was a natural connection unexplained by any outsider. Over the years, he could determine by his own feelings how the life of his son was going, more or less, and in the past few months he knew Martin Jr. was on a downhill slide.

Despite his son's insistence that he listen and him thinking that he wasn't, Martin Sr. heeded everything his son said. He knew what was going on in the power industry. He also knew that the Government was no picnic; combined, they were a force with which to be reckoned. Martin Sr. was proud of his son's accomplishments even though he didn't expose that fact directly to his face. The impression his son made reflected in the fact that there was always one or another of his neighbors over coffee commenting on the real important matters that the younger Martin attended to – at least, that was the case until recently. Neither father nor son would admit they were wrong for carrying on in the manner they did. Martin felt the rush of unexpected pride knowing his son really was more like him than he would wish upon anyone. Except that he never wanted to farm.

And that is where Martin Sr. thought of nothing else.

From the day he could venture out into the yards and the barns on his own, Martin knew he loved the rural life. Farming would be his future but not in the usual "when I grow up I want to be..." manner. He grew up just doing it and expecting that he would continue to farm for the rest of his life. There were no desires for other interests or thoughts about trying some other way of life. He didn't even think he could experiment and experience life and then return if he didn't find what he was looking for elsewhere. Martin never left.

What he knew in his heart was that he wanted what was beneath his feet all those years growing up and he assumed he would acquire those rights to that future without doubt. He was the only child.

He thought nothing of the early mornings, often rising long before his own father to start the chores before heading off, reluctantly, to school. There would be no dallying afterwards either as Martin ran most of the way home to be able to help his father long into the evening hours. His mother never worried or suggested he do otherwise; she simply accepted father and son as they were and kept to her own business in the house. She seemed happy enough but that was the one thing Martin vowed to himself he would never do – impose his obsessions upon another person, especially a woman, expecting them to be content.

Martin never complained openly about his father's treatment of his mother. What he did, or rather, didn't do he knew he did unintentionally, for the most part. He could describe it more like avoidance rather than an intrusive abuse – his father never hit his mother, he was certain of that, because he never touched her. She merely existed as his mother and a cook and a housewife, with no life or recognition of her own. Martin helped his mother as much as he could without interfering in what he thought was the natural order of things. As a teenager, he learned to realize more and he identified her longing.

Attention.

That was what she craved and all she lacked.

When she died, Martin felt like she just finally faded away. Life continued as it did for the father and son on the farm. At that point, he silently made a promise to himself to respect and love a woman should she ever have an interest in him. That was when he met Faith.

"Martin? Are you going to come with me to see your son?" Faith's voice interrupted Martin's thoughts and although she knew the answer she would receive she gave him the benefit of the doubt, as she always did. Faith was already gathering her wallet and keys as he rose to accompany her outside.

"Chores to do."

It was matter-of-fact and unnecessary but what she expected. Martin kissed the top of Faith's head as he gave her a quick hug before she climbed into the Escalade and drove off. He lingered a moment watching the exhaust settle in the frosty air, his thoughts lost in the crisp winter morning. His eye followed the line of fencing and power poles to the west as the SUV disappeared over the rise in the west from their ranch. Down the road he could see work crews off on the neighbor's right-of-way and he wondered what they could possibly be doing on a cold, snowy January day.

He turned toward his own work. Entering the warmth of the barn to tend to the needs of his animals, he left his own worries at the door.

Chapter 26 – Back into the Foray

Martin Jr. hesitated outside Rowan's office.

It was going to be a confrontation that had been a long time coming but Martin just did not realize it until today. It should have been the decision he made all those years before when given the choice. Confined to a hospital bed for six weeks on the slow track to recovery not only weighed heavily upon his spirit but it weighed heavily upon his mind. He came to surmise that he really didn't deserve to live given all that he had a hand in. Yet, he was spared even though he, in essence, indirectly signed many death warrants over the last couple of years by effectively cutting off life lines to farmers and ranchers throughout the province. The good of the power industry was forefront with the future of the province held out for compensatory explanation. He was well paid for his endeavors and his actions he just grew to accept as part of his job description under his employment contract with Alternative Energy Corporation.

Lying there, he had time to think even if he didn't want to; there was no choice. His mind would go to places he couldn't control and he was at liberty to review and scrutinize every known action his signature pushed to approval. No one held a gun to his head forcing him to do what he did although there were the threats. *Threats.* He decided he wasn't sure enough of the situation or himself to know if they were empty threats or if there might have been a chance someone would make good on them just to keep him in line. He would never have taken any chance to test it, though. With his signature on those industry documents, he signed away any chance he ever had with Erin but he kept her safe. His kids were growing up without his involvement but they were unharmed at least in the way he perceived a threat might possibly be carried out.

His parents' future was in question but there was never any mention of their safety. *How could he just keep on doing what he was doing given all that was going on around him?* He knew.

Lying there, he had plenty of time to rationalize over the reasons why he just did what he was told and he finally had to admit to himself that he just didn't have the balls to stand up for what was right despite all of his good intentions. He gave up on the little guy when he accepted that first cheque. He gave up on himself when he accepted the second one.

Standing in the hallway he felt the heated rush of nerves which forced him to open the door to the office in a sudden panic. If he didn't do it then he might have taken the easy way out again and walked back to the safety of his office.

"Mr. Wells, good to see you back. Was Mr. Cott expecting you in today?" Niceties out of the way, Cott's assistant picked up the call line to the office and then nodded to Martin. "He'll see you now."

Like he has a choice, Martin thought, as he entered the executive's office, still mulling over in his mind the best way to lay out his decision, *direct or work up to it?* He felt submissiveness cloak him with doubt and he stopped half way to Rowan's desk. He steadied his nerves with a touch to the forehead and he took a deep breath.

"Martin? Come, have a chair. You still look white as a sheet."

Martin looked up to the man who signed all those cheques that effectively bought his compliance. He watched as the man sat there casually drinking his coffee in engraved designer mugs as if nothing in the world had an effect on him. He watched as the man just sat there oozing confidence while Martin felt like he was teetering on the brink of destruction. He moved toward the desk with growing determination and in the process decided upon the best way to lay out his decision.

"I quit." *Direct was always the best way.*

"Have a coffee – sit down, Martin, and let's talk."

Martin poured himself a coffee but this time he wasn't messing around with the pleasures of a casual conversation or giving into further delays to try calm his nerves. He took a sip of the dark liquid and sat across from Rowan.

"There really isn't anything to talk about Rowan. I need to get my shit together and I can't do it here."

"You've been through a lot and I don't want you to make any hasty decisions."

"It might appear hasty to you but my decision is made; I need some time."

"Take all the time you need, we understand. But that doesn't necessarily mean you're quitting. I can grant an extended leave..."

"Then extend it forever, Rowan, because I still quit. I quit, permanent, that's it, final."

Rowan shook his head and gave a soft chuckle. He slowly raised his coffee to his lips exhibiting all the actions that agitated his subordinates. Given the right amount of time and the calm of leadership, his confidence displayed that he knew what they wanted before they did and everyone eventually came around to agreeing.

Martin held his gaze even though he felt the sticky wetness of perspiration building under his collar and at his hairline. He took a mouthful of coffee and sat back in his chair trying to maintain his composure despite the knot in the pit of his stomach. He wasn't a fearful person but the unknown consequences of what could happen as a result of his decision scared him. *How could he protect those around him when he wasn't even man enough to protect himself?*

"Martin. Martin. Martin..." Rowan gave in and Martin almost sighed with relief, albeit premature. "You are not quitting. You belong here and we made that clear, remember?"

"You are not going to continue to threaten me. I don't have a family anymore; all this..." Martin stretched his arms to encompass the room and ended by pointing at Rowan, "...and you, made sure of that, so don't threaten me, Rowan. I have nothing more to lose."

"Ah, poor Martin. All alone and now proposing to be the martyr by going out into the big world on his own. It won't work; there's too much already in motion to matter, Martin."

"I don't plan to be a martyr. I just don't want to be a pawn anymore."

"Well, we played you well enough and managed a few check mates, dear Martin. With nuclear power well underway it's a step to the future success of the industry and in particular, for Alternative Energy Corporation. Now that a majority of the land is clear and ready, the transmission construction can continue to the borders and beyond. And we have you to thank for all that. You should be proud of your accomplishment, Martin."

"You can keep your accolades, Rowan. I am not proud of those achievements and I have come to realize that I did this province a great disservice by working here, by signing all those regulatory papers, and merely accepting there was nothing else I could do. But I was wrong, Rowan, very wrong."

"And just what do you think you can do about it now?"

"I quit. That's my first step and I know there will be a long road to recovery and redemption before me, but I plan to do it."

"We have a contract, Martin." Rowan proceeded to pull the infamous papers from his top desk drawer. Martin slammed his cup on the desk.

"Don't! Don't even start with the threats. I told you, I have nothing to lose and I am not going to continue succumbing to your every whim on those threats. You killed the man I was and who I could have been – there is nothing more to take."

"Okay, okay. The ex and the kids provided us with wonderful collateral and you don't have to worry about them – we don't want to hurt kids. Come on, Martin, we are not monsters. We never would have hurt the kids."

Martin extended his hand toward the papers Rowan held.

"You want our assurances? No problem." Rowan ripped the contract down the centre and tossed the pieces in the garbage can alongside the desk.

It was a simple act that seemed almost too easy to achieve but Martin accepted it as Rowan's answer to his demands. As he left the office, he knew it would be the last time he would ever be in that room but he was also aware it probably wouldn't be the last time he saw Rowan J. Cott.

In his office behind locked doors, Martin collected his personal belongings; not that there were many mementos of his own life on display. *What life,* he questioned, shoving lap top and cell phone into his leather brief case, discarding the Blackberry into the "in" basket on the corner of his desk. Nothing around him reminded him that he had a life other than the one in that very room and the quality of which one was highly debatable.

Now what? With the naïve assumption that Alternative Energy Corporation would be a thing of the past for him, he contemplated his options. Sitting there reflecting on his executive surroundings he had a sudden feeling of uncertainty. All his education and training did not prepare him for this moment. He could take a position and write a compelling paper on it; propose workable business plans and implement necessary steps to market compliance, but he couldn't for the life of him think of his next step.

Bridges had been burned. *What? Was he thinking everyone was just going to say 'yes, Martin, we believe you'?* He stepped on a crowd of toes and countered some high profile dignitaries in his crusade through the Commission. He had even been black listed from industry meetings because of his association with Alternative Energy Corporation when it was revealed that the Big Three were not associates but subsidiaries owned by the giant conglomerate. They truly believed in a power monopoly.

At one time he stood for truth and his integrity won him the recognition of leaders within many departments of the government and with stakeholders in the industry. *How on earth, in this lifetime, could he rebuild that kind of trust?*

Martin's eye came to rest in its inventory of the room upon the very first paper he wrote for AEC, newly hired and eager to prove his competency. That report was flagged as the one that officially got the ball rolling – downhill. He flipped through the pages remembering the hours he put into the document and as he reread some of the passages he stopped and sat up. Opening his briefcase he pulled another copy – the original he used for his boardroom presentation – and placed it on the desk next to the first one. With increased anxiousness, he compared the papers, realizing that changes had been made to the original paper and they were alterations not made by him.

In fact, with further comparison he found they deviated so far from what he would have written, it was hard to believe it was the same paper. The last page held its deception to be what everyone grew to accept – his signature.

He knew then what he needed to do.

The light flashed on the jump drive as he opened the file on the desktop of his office monitor. Quickly and precisely, he dumped the computer's files onto the storage device and waited impatiently as they copied to the receiving folder. He ran a nervous hand through his hair and grabbed the paper copies of the reports and shoved them back into his briefcase. He spied the connecting sync wire for the Blackberry and hurriedly connected the unit to the computer and copied its contact content and files, too.

The buzzer on his desk from reception startled him and he jumped.

"Mr. Wells?"

"Yes?"

"Security is here to see you to your car."

"Okay. I'm just getting my personal things together. I'll be right there."

He felt cold despite the heated rush of action. He knew he would never get physical files or papers past security for he knew Rowan would insist upon the thorough inspection of his brief case and pockets. He pulled the reports from hiding and unclipped them. He shoved them in the fax machine and dialed his own number, pushing send. It would have been more convenient to email them to his personal account but he didn't have the time to sign in and they might have already blocked his internal email.

As the pages slowly made their way through the machine, he returned to the desk and pulled the jump drive from the dock. He closed all the open files and cleared the recent documents listing. He signed off and grabbed the Blackberry. He would hand it to Jessica as he left – then maybe they wouldn't think to check his desk before he had a chance to leave the building.

As a knock sounded on the door, he gathered his jacket and case. He opened it quickly without emotion and was surprised to see only one guard as his send off. *Perhaps, Rowan didn't perceive him to be as much of a threat as he assumed he might.*

"Can you open your briefcase for me, Mr. Wells?" Martin nodded, somewhat reluctantly, so he didn't seem so willing to comply having predicted the expectation. He handed the Blackberry to the guard who just handed it off to Jessica.

"May I?" The guard reached for Martin's jacket without waiting for a reply and swiftly searched all pockets, inside and out. Confident of the results, he handed it back and Martin slipped it on.

"Follow me." Martin just smiled briefly to Jessica and left without a word. He didn't know the level of her involvement with Rowan and the company, and he didn't want to.

Perhaps, at some time in the future he would pursue their relationship but there would have to be many checks and balances to ensure trust. He was certain it would never be what it once was.

In the parkade, security left him with a warning from management that he was not to return to the building under any circumstances. In his car, the engine running, he let out a long breath and pulled the jump drive from under the securely held position of his watch strap. It had remained undetected under cover by his shirt sleeve even though he feared its discovery during the check-out process. He proceeded down the ramp and out onto the street, making it through the parking gate arm just before it closed.

His mother's voice was firm but filled with a hidden emotion that Martin recognized as her own personal agony as she related the latest developments on the ranch to him. Since the hospital visit, they had renewed contact with one another, something that had faded from the forefront of their relationship since his final separation from Erin. He learned that Faith had remained close to his ex-wife through frequent visits with her grandchildren.

"I have to sell the horses."

"Mom? No."

"The bank wants part payment or they will take the whole thing in whatever manner they please."

"But why do you have to suffer for the cause?"

"Martin, really."

"I mean it, Mom. Why doesn't Dad sell the equipment or something?"

"He needs that to finish out the fall."

"Finish out?"

"The flooding just may have pushed him a little closer to realization, son, and just maybe, now we can move on. I think he might entertain an offer."

"Wow, Mom. That would be great. You don't know how that makes me feel – I just want it to be easy for you." He stopped, realizing that the sound of what he said what not exactly as he meant it to come out. "You know, what I mean..."

"The farm has been the only thing your father worked hard for all his life – it's just not that easy to give it up."

"I know, Mom. I understand that, really. But, this..." Martin stopped, exasperated with his father's need to control everything his mother ever did. "Your horses, they mean everything to you, too. Why should you have to give in again?"

"It's okay, son – the sale will appease the bank and give your father time to bring the hogs to maturity and get a good market price. With the flooding, he's counting on that now..." She paused and Martin could hear her talking to his dad in the background.

"Your father just came in for lunch. I have to run but I'll call you later. The buyer should be in this afternoon for the herd."

"Okay, Mom. If there is anything I can do – I know, it's an offer made a bit late, but hey, I plan to make good."

"You always were a good son."

"I'm sorry Mom – for everything. But, I promise, I'll make it up to you."

"Make it up to yourself first, Marty."

She hung up leaving him to realize that he had a lot of recovery ahead of him if he was going to make amends in every area of his life. It was then the debated initiating another call, one that he regretted doing each and every time it came to fruition. He could at least claim this time to be clear headed and not under the influence. He hadn't seen his kids since before Christmas and he, at that point, was almost willing to give up all of his parental rights when Erin refused to go away for the holidays, again. It was just too much effort every year to try and convince her to go along with his plans.

He failed to realize that it was he who needed to take a good look at his efforts. A once a year dad was not something the kids needed and poking into their lives when it was convenient for him to do so was selfish.

"Erin?"

"Martin. What a surprise. What do you want?"

It wasn't said with anger or hatred. Erin's voice was void of emotion and with that reception Martin felt all chances of reconciliation were mute. He would concede any attempts for the sake of his kids in hopes that he could at least give them a better person as a dad at some point down the road.

"I just wanted to call to let you know I might not be around for a while."

"Like you were all the times before…"

"I also just wanted to call..." he let the sting of her comment settle in before he continued for another attempt, "…to let you know I am deeply sorry for everything I put you through."

"Like you were before..."

"Okay. I deserve that and everything else you can throw at me but… please. I know you don't have any reason to believe me, but it's true."

"Martin, what's up?" She always could read him.

"What do you mean?"

"It sounds like you actually think I might believe you this time. How am I supposed to distinguish this truth from all the other bull shit you've handed me?"

"I don't know. I was just hoping you might understand."

"I did understand. Don't you remember, you asshole?"

"Erin, I'm sorry."

"You cannot just waltz back in here and expect that 'I'm sorry' is going to cut it."

"I didn't expect anything."

"I'm not just one of your deals you can sign and stamp and approve. You don't get to buy your family back that easily." There was anger now building but Martin knew it was a tearful anger that hit an emotional spot in her. He could always read her, too.

"I quit my job, Erin."

"Oh, too bad... no big bonus cheques this year..." She was crying now.

"Erin. I'm so sorry. If you only knew..."

"So tell me and quit jerking around. I can't take this anymore."

"I want to come by and see the kids."

She didn't answer right away and for the first time he couldn't determine how to take her silence. He continued, floundering in his attempt to hold on.

"And, just so you know – I haven't been drinking, either."

"I know."

"How do you know?"

"Martin, I know more about you than you know about yourself. That's why I couldn't believe some of the things I was hearing about you."

"I tried to keep you and the kids out of my business."

"You did and we managed but I still heard about you and the company and everything that went on. Your mom knew, too. We stayed close, you know, and she made sure I realized you wouldn't do those things if there wasn't a real good reason. I had to believe it for the sake of our kids; she just believed because she loves you so much."

Now Martin was crying. He held the phone to his chest as he sobbed, thinking of how wrong he had been and that together they possibly could have battled any threat. He mourned the years lost with her even though at the time he knew he did what he had to. He wasn't selfish, *then*; at that moment of decision, their safety had been the most important thing to him.

"Martin?

"Yes?"

"Are you okay?"

"I've been better."

"You really quit?"

"Yes."

"What do you plan to do?"

"Redeem myself."

At that moment, Martin was certain the situation would be better between them but he didn't hold hope for anything more than friendship. He needed to be there for her and contribute more than just financial support toward the raising of their children.

"It's your daughter's fifth birthday this weekend."

"I knew that..." Martin said, with slight embarrassment.

"Come and visit the kids then and stay for cake and coffee."

"Are you sure?"

"I wouldn't offer, Martin, if I wasn't sure. Come by whenever you like. Your Mom will probably be here, too."

"Thank you, Erin."

"We'll see you Saturday."

"Erin..."A sharp pain in his shoulder radiated down his arm. "I'll make it up to you."

"Make it up to us, Martin, by making it up to yourself, first."

He hung up the phone, absentmindedly massaging his arm, with the echo of her words reminding him of his mother's advice. He was determined to win back the respect he worked so hard to earn, once upon a time.

Chapter 28 – An Official Apology

The boardroom chairs were filled with the directors from the board of the Energy Commission as Martin sat waiting in the hallway for his turn to be called to address their meeting. It took some convincing and thorough documentation to get his presentation added to their agenda. They were not remiss in advising him 'they would not take his word' solely upon his say so. They obviously found evidence to support the claims he outlined in his report to them, as the Commission did not usually entertain evidentiary process as a matter for their monthly private meetings.

He took their finding of evidence with a positive outlook despite the fact that an escort comprised of two security guards waited for him at the main doors and then accompanied him to the area where they sat waiting.

They still believed him to be a threat and how could he blame them? Although forgiveness from his mother and Erin was easier to acquire, but of no less importance to him, the proof before the Commission would have to be exceptional for them to forgive him in an official capacity. He could still be charged; he could still end up in prison for his deceit and he was willing to take that chance as a consequence of taking back control of his life.

He did not have much more than a few file documents and his own verbal input to the operations and management of Alternative Energy Corporation. He hoped it would at least be enough to bring them before the Commission to force them to do their own explaining. At least, if he introduced a little doubt through hearsay, it might be just what was needed to expose them to other leaders in the industry. It was also his hope that not all the leaders in the industry were in the pockets of Alternative Energy Corporation.

Or the beds.

There was a murmur of discussion throughout the boardroom as the recording secretary called Martin in to address to the directors. He found a spot along the side of the large table and took the liberty of pouring himself a glass of water and taking a drink before the chairman addressed him.

"Mr. Wells."

"Thank you, Mr. Chairman for allowing me to come before this meeting today."

"We do not have a lot of time for frivolity, Mr. Wells, so please proceed with your presentation. We will give you ten minutes, tops." Long time Chair of the Commission, Raymond Knorr, sat back relinquishing the floor to Martin.

"Thank you. I assure you it is not with frivolity that I address your esteemed Board but rather with a request for leniency when considering my past actions through the Commission. I admit I was acting on behalf of my former employer and, although I appeared to use my influence within the industry for the good of one company, I must explain that the initial deception was not of my doing and my continued actions were based on the acceptance of that first filing. I would further like to file my official apology to the Commission for my part in the process and leave it up to the discretion of the Board regarding my continued license and practice as a power industry consultant within the province of Alberta."

Martin handed his life to them in one short speech. No signature of guarantee or even a shadow of expectation. He meant to make amends and, simply put, their decision would determine whether or not he would be allowed to work within the industry, in any capacity. He felt that his involvement with Alternative Energy Corporation wasn't total deception in that they were acting as a private company and even as a publicly owned one, he was certain that given time, nuclear power proposals would have made their way through the process – his influence and expertise merely expedited their growth.

His later recommendations, in response to harsh government regulations, offered to affected businesses, farmers, and ranchers included, advice that they took too lightly in the aftermath or, perhaps, he just wasn't as forceful as he should have been in getting his point across. He got tired of talking and trying to explain. Yet, with all his shortcomings, he refused to claim one hundred percent of the blame as the Commission signed his filings with their blessing and, after all, it was their job to ensure that the projects proposed were researched and found to be 'for the good of the whole.'

"If the legality of this company's filing process were to be questioned, Mr. Wells, would you be prepared to stand in court against Alternative Energy Corporation?"

"I have already submitted all the evidence I have in my possession."

"Would you, Mr. Wells, swear in court to that evidence?"

Knorr was insistent with his questioning and Martin could not reason either way to its benefit. If he refused, it would leave him to shoulder all responsibility if any wrong doing were to surface; if he agreed, it would be a game of 'he said, she said' for the most part. The two faxed documents at least proved the initial fraudulent attempt as long as they believed he wrote the document one way and it was altered to the other before filing. He thought briefly of a private law suit regarding misappropriation of his signature on doctored documents and then visions of the large payouts came to mind and he quickly dismissed that avenue for consideration. If he was going to take complete control of his life Martin had to quit procrastinating.

"Yes."

"We have had a chance to review your submission of apology to the Board and the Commission has determined that, although you might have been coerced into submitting filings that were against your nature originally, we would only take that argument into the consideration for the first little while, Mr. Wells.

"Your activity spanned a number of years and in its wake we now have nuclear construction through the corridors running the length of our province." Raymond Knorr held up his hand to silence any protest Martin may have entertained. "The Commission also realizes its part in this advanced procedure and any unfortunate manipulation, perceived or otherwise, should have been halted as our responsibility. Taking that into consideration, we are proposing you operate with limited industry involvement, for the time being. At least until the situation – if there is to be one – with Alternative Energy cools off."

"Limited industry involvement?"

"Take a break. Have some rest. Set up your office. Resume private practice in a consulting capacity. Let's just say, that although we are willing to grant the industry pardon, we don't want to see you around the Commission for a few months."

Martin felt like he had just been released from prison – not that he knew what that completely felt like – but he was confident he could guess it was somewhat the same. His freedom had come with a price and he was willing to accept the consequences of his long running actions. It was well worth the effort; yet, in his heart he was certain the battle had just begun despite any recent victories.

Later that evening, after he showered the stench of the ordeal from him, he contemplated calling Erin to share the good news. Why he needed to share now he couldn't decide but it was possible he was just feeling the positive effects of the day and, given the encouraging reception he had recently received from her, it was an overwhelming combination of good feelings. He would not go so far as to assume all to be just fine. *At least, not yet.* There were so many more puzzle pieces to fit back into place. Martin's struggle still stretched in front of him as he discovered his way back and it was nowhere near completion. He could identify some progress and that encouraged him. He jumped with surprised as the phone rang, interrupting his thought; he was even more surprised to see Erin's number on the call display.

"Hi – I was just thinking of calling you."

"Martin. You have to come over right away. Can you?"

"I can be there in a few minutes, Erin. What's wrong?"

"Just hurry."

Martin's overactive mind went to every explanation he could imagine on the short trip over to Erin's house. He just wished she would have given him some kind of explanation because he hated imagining the bad ones. A person couldn't help but to go to the worst case scenario despite their attempts to avoid it. The cover of night allowed for a hurried drive the four short blocks from his apartment – his anxiety returned.

She opened the door before he had a chance to knock; he entered quietly, knowing the kids were asleep and she wanted them to stay that way. Her concern showed as she closed the door, peeking out to the driveway through the sidelight window sheers. She shut off the front light, inside and out.

"Erin? What's wrong?"

"There's been someone driving by the house all evening."

"Did they stop?"

"I'd just catch them slowing down and then they'd speed up and disappear. I'd hear noises; I go check and see no one. Yet, I know there's someone watching the house."

In the dim entry way he could feel the nerves rising to the surface as she spoke and he knew there was substance to her fears because Erin did not call him out of the blue for nothing. He pulled her to him in a consoling manner to hold her close and protect her, something he had always promised to do.

"It's okay. I'm here now."

"Martin."

"I know, Erin. Don't worry."

Down the hall Essie called out for her mother and Martin let Erin go to her. He moved through the house, checking doors and windows, scanning the walks and the yard as he went.

He didn't see anything out of the ordinary until he got back to the living room with its large front window. From behind the drawn curtains, he was able to peer out onto the front street. He saw a car slow down to a crawl as it came to the house, stopping at the end of the driveway, its lights off as if in stealth mode. He could see the driver get out of the car and move a few steps closer to the BMW, stooped over as if to read the license plate. Martin determined at that moment, staying there would not be such a good idea. Once the car moved on, he moved away from the window and met Erin as she came from Essie's bedroom.

"I think we should take the kids to my place."

"Why? Oh, my God, what's going on, Martin?"

"Okay, no need to panic but I'd just like to do something out of character that it might take a bit longer to discover."

"Why – there is someone out there, isn't there?"

"A car stopped but he noticed my car in the driveway. I'm not sure if that's a good thing or a bad thing at this moment."

"Is someone following you?"

"I don't know, Erin. I just don't know."

"You could stay here with us."

"It's a bit too open for my liking and besides if someone is watching, they expect I might be here. There's nowhere else I would go."

"So do something out of character?"

"Yes, you and the kids don't spend time at my place. And I feel so much more fortified in an enclosed apartment with a security door." His comment wasn't meant to scare her but it did. He hugged her close and kissed the top of her head in a motion he didn't feel out of place offering. They bundled the kids into the BMW and made their way to his apartment for a 'camp out at Daddy's house.'

The sleeping bag sojourn in the middle of Martin's carpet turned out to be one of the best times they had shared as a family. There was no purpose in the move other than to keep the kids entertained and with no distractions they could also keep their minds off the world outside. No one called; no one came to the door except for the pizza delivery boy and even then Martin met him at the lobby door paying for his delivery without letting him into the building.

There were no expectations but by the end of the two day camp out Martin felt that Erin was closer to trying again, without any coercion or suggestion on his part. She agreed – slowly, she would let Martin back into her life. He didn't push for more all the while hoping for it. He still admonished himself for years of bad behavior while thoughtfully reminding himself, *he was lucky to have been given yet another chance.*

When the nerves calmed and Martin finally drove his family back to their home, he was saddened to leave them but felt it was a necessary part of the recovery process. He'd have to earn his way back in and it certainly didn't come after two nights of chivalry and popcorn. That didn't stop him from parking down the street for the next two nights that followed.

On the third, convinced no one was out to get them, he went home exhausted but relieved.

Chapter 29 – You Can Never Go Back

The security detail Martin hired watched Erin's house and followed her to the kid's school and home again without incident over the next couple of weeks. Thinking it was a ruse to scare him into pulling his report from the Commission, Martin decided the best thing to do was to get back to routine and back to business. The old office was dusty from being closed up without a day to day tenant. He was happy no one showed interest in renting it over the time he had offered it as a sub-lease. The building needed to be refurbished but in its current state, Martin found it relaxing and just the right match for his aging, changing temperament. It was time to settle down and get serious about many things. He couldn't determine which aspect of his new to-do-list was more important, so he decided he would work slowly on each component of his life and bring them along to where they were supposed to be, if they were to be moved forward, at all.

Although, he hoped to be back in business sooner than later, he hadn't expected the phones to ring off the hook the very first day he had them reconnected. There were calls from both sides of the fence; surprising yet heartfelt "welcome backs" and, the ones he half expected to fill his answering machine day and night – threatening. *That was* the only concern he had with hanging his shingle on the old office door – many would know where to find him even if he hadn't been there for some time.

The call that caused him the most grief, however, was from someone he'd hoped to never hear from again. Unable to identify the numbers on the call display and without a receptionist to screen them, he just picked up every line and was taken aback when he heard the voice on the other end.

"Hello, Martin."

"Rowan? And how could I possibly help you today?"

"Oh, just wanted to see how things are going? Everything's fine with the family, I presume." Martin could see him sitting back sipping on his imported coffee, grinning with feigned innocence, sweating arrogance.

"I told you before my family are none of your business."

"Touchy, touchy. Just exchanging pleasantries, no need to bite my head off."

"I have nothing to exchange with you, Rowan, least of all pleasantries."

"Oh, I think you do, Marty – perhaps, you'd like to return the files that were taken from your office the day you left."

"You had security all over me the day I left. I wouldn't have been able to get them past the door even if I wanted to. I'm sure you checked my outgoing email, too, so you know damn well I didn't send anything to me or anyone else."

"Well, that surprises me considering the recent turn of events"

"And, pray tell, what evens might that be?"

"It seems I've been called before the Commission to answer to a few information requests." Rowan paused, and Martin realized he was right in assuming that the battle had only just begun. "Now where would they get the idea that our project filings were not up to par, considering Mr. Wells signed the applications?"

"I haven't a clue what you're talking about, Rowan, and I really don't care."

"Oh, but you should care, Martin."

"Try explaining yourself out of if you can but I will have nothing to do with you or Alternative Energy Corporation, ever again."

"Need I remind you that you walked out on a contract and I could very easily pull you down with me?"

"I don't think so."

"Oh, Marty, I'm sure you'll see it my way. I expect the Commission was fed a line of shit from you in an effort to buy back your credibility. You've been on the market for a price, for some time now, Martin, and the Commission won't turn its back on that fact. It's going to take a lot more than a written apology and some bogus reports to push us into the background without a fight."

"You do what you need to do."

"I will, you can bet on that."

"Just be a man – do what you have to do but stay the fuck out of my personal life."

"Hmmm, you've grown some balls since you left. I like that. It will make the fight a little more interesting."

"If you want a fight, you'll get a fight..." Martin was losing all patience but he didn't want to lose the control he'd managed to regain, especially to a low life like Rowan. He had catered to the man's whims and listened to his idle threats for too long. Martin was doing now what he should have done years ago.

"It will never be a fair fight, but at least it will be closer..."

"I would hardly expect you to fight fair."

"What's not fair is that you assume you are entitled to regain everything, and I mean everything... without having to put up any kind of fight at all. Now how fair is that?"

"Leave my wife and kids alone!"

"Ex-wife, right..." Rowan let out a low wolf whistle.

"You're a son of a bitch."

"Calm down, Martin. I have no interest in your sweet ass ex and, as I told before, I certainly don't hurt kids, so... I guess you win." Rowan hung up the phone before Martin could reply.

He wasn't quite sure what he won.

In the late spring of 2017, private industries realized the futility in fighting against the government and accepted the conditions of the Provincial Energy Plan without further consideration. It was also the year that the turbulent political climate was as hard to predict as the weather. The extreme Smart Party took over the power reins with showy campaign promises of fast tracking slow moving initiatives including the lumbering movement to bring nuclear power the length of the entire province. Nuclear One was operating without incident or concern. Proponents who rallied for plant construction now turned their attention to the hectares of land appropriated for transmission upgrades in an effort to speed up production.

The outgoing conservative officials had held their cards close to their chest, fearful of playing the whole nuclear hand. Protests that followed the nuclear disaster of 2011, in Japan, pushed the closure of plants worldwide and social precautions replaced economic expansion. Despite the fact that the global industry was forced to take another look at technological advances, Alternative Energy Corporation led the Big Three as if there were no worthy opponents in the Alberta ring. Foreign governments scrambled to reevaluate the effects of nuclear industrialization within their communities and came to the same decision worldwide – the convenience today wasn't worth the long lasting effects on future generations. Pillars of sustainability crumbled. The highly touted smart grid would operate using wind and bio mass generation given that the proposals out there in the community supporting nuclear production of power came back stamped as failures.

With the backing of a power supportive government, the Big Three renewed their public campaign to complete phase two and three of their operations.

They contended that if their counterparts in Ontario, who had operated for a significant period of time without concern, were able to provide their utility customers with reduced rates, and more importantly, one hundred percent reliability, so could they. Alberta power consumers deserved a break. The Smart Party moved in to make good on campaign promises and it was assumed they had the financial backing of big corporate sponsors.

The Utility Commission cancelled its review of Alternative Energy Corporation's procedural filings upon the suggestion of the newly sworn in energy department minister.

Farms still in operation did so under the radar providing local communities with produce, crops and livestock. It was only a matter of time before government agents knocked on the door but for some, until that happened, they were standing firm in doing what they had done for generations. Alberta farmers had a tenacity that could not be matched by any other grassroots worker; *come hell or high water* they worked to provide a living for their families. However, sometimes that very statement was a useless mantra against the fury of nature.

Spring 2017, not only brought forth a flood of political change but nature's watery deluge. Flood waters wiped out early crops and with them the chance of recovery for most farmers. Financial institutions, even those who were historically inclined to service farm accounts, called in loans – small and large. Insurance companies, taking millions of dollars in claims, pulled policy provisions for high risk clients, namely, farmers. It was just another nail in the coffin with the drowned crops taking many casualties.

It was also a time that rolling black outs began to plague the province. Although they were 'planned', there was no way to know where and when they would hit. Industry and government representatives claimed it was because the transmission could no longer carry the large voltage requirements of a growing province.

They pushed the appropriation deals to secure the necessary land for massive tower expansion.

The word on the street was that input into the system from the one nuclear plant caused such a tremendous surge of generation that the lines throughout Alberta felt the effects. Those producers who relied on a steady source of power found themselves installing the outlawed substitute generation equipment because there was no way to insure you would have a reliable power source. An outage would mean sure death.

Martin felt all those events were warning signals to all who would not comply. If one did not take precautions, the losses would be severe. No matter the reason for the shut downs, it was as if the planned attacks solidified the progression to the agricultural Assumption Plan.

Farms were too few and far between that it made the continued service of power to singular lines unproductive and uneconomical. Areas abandoned by the agricultural sector were to be better utilized for the mainstay of the province as a whole. The nuclear power industry promised a bright future for the residents of Alberta.

The new government rushed Bill-2017 through an early legislature sitting with a proclamation that, in essence, stated the redirection of power transmission was to be a priority, and the construction of the necessary upgrades were to be for the betterment of the province and its future economy, not just one dead end consumption outlet. Farms at the end of single phase lines, one by one, lost utility services from the power grid forcing them to shut down. At that point, the message was clear – options were exhausted and any previous offers were withdrawn; if the lights went out, it meant there was no deal.

The proclamation and the results made news headlines around the world. The mandated Assumption also outlawed the ownership and use of private generators; discovery of same on any property intertied to the main grid would trigger an immediate seizure and other undetermined consequences.

It was signed and sealed with the legislative assembly's official stamp of ascent on the last day of spring – June 2017.

"Son, Martin – please come home. Your father needs you."

His mother's voice pleaded with him and he did not have to ask why. He could hear the urgency in her voice and recognized something else he never expected to hear – fear.

"Mom – I'm on my way – I'm right in town. So, you know forty minutes tops once I get past the traffic." Martin paid for his meal with a few bills thrown on the table and left the main street coffee shop. Leaving now to go to his parent's ranch would just bring his planned encounter sooner rather than later. He had made his way to High River leaving the main highway to go through neighboring small towns, on a back country road, taking his time to arrive. He had intention of confronting his dad about the direction the government was taking with transmission and nuclear plant construction. The Wells' ranch had always been considered prime appropriation property with its expansive size running north and south along the current transmission corridor.

At least that was his intent as he left Edmonton and drove south on the Queen E; as he got closer to his target he was less sure of the reason he was attempting to open old wounds. *His father never listened to him before, what made him think he would now?* If his mother was right about her hunch, the senior Wells' plan was to cash in on a profitable herd of hogs, pay out the bank, and then take the best deal they could from the Assumption Plan administrators. He wasn't convinced his father would give in that easy but Faith knew her husband, so Martin had to believe his mother.

"Careful, Martin, the lights are out."

"I know, Mom, they're out all over."

The rolling blackouts reached as far north as Red Deer and seemed to be localized to the central and south central regions of the province.

"Martin – hurry..."

Martin accelerated through the streets beyond what would be considered safe without the guidance of traffic lights. Thankfully, the traffic was light and the delay at intersections, transformed to four way stops, was minimal. His mother began to sob as he held the phone against one shoulder and he maneuvered carefully over the last bridge leading to the road out of town in the direction of this parents' farm.

"Your father needs you, now."

She had hung up the phone leaving him to wonder. He went to that imaginary place he often found himself going. It was a place where he invented scenes he'd play over and over again in his mind. They were not always good scenes, either. He recently acquired the pleasure of happier times and the visits into his dark imagination were less frequent.

The opportunity to reconnect with his kids played a big role in helping him to recover. He was better able to deal with his own struggle and make sense of recent happenings. A renewed interest in his own business kept him busy but it wasn't what he studied all those years to do – the Commission refused to let him back in to pursue the necessary regulatory avenues with all his clients so it wasn't feasible to take on small power consumer issues.

He was relieved, too, that no more threats had been made against his family; in fact, it was almost too good to be true. Erin had insisted on a casual relationship to keep it simple, for the time being, but had allowed him the courtesy of claiming they were unofficially 'dating'. It didn't matter to him. He just needed to get it together – *all together – and now this?*

As he drew closer to the ranch, he was unsure what he would find. Martin hoped his mother would watch for his car on the road and come out to meet him when he arrived.

As he turned over, in his mind, more possible scenarios when he crested the rise overlooking the Wells' ranch. He felt the blood drain from his face and his hands gripped the wheel tighter as he pushed the car to its limit on the dark road.

Orange flames licked at the side of the barn and traveled the length of the roof as Martin Jr. brought the BMW to a screeching halt in the barn yard. He could not hear his own screams over the roar of the raging fire as he pushed open the large door. The pressure of contained heat forced him back and the explosion that followed threw him even further.

Nothing or no one would have survived within the walls of that fiery building.

Martin checked his notes, reading and rereading the information he recorded from what he remembered from that fateful August night. The technical stuff was easy to record and that was what he remembered the most. The emotional stuff – he kept that locked up, safe and away from the permanency of ink on paper. He justified keeping it to himself, unspoken and unheard, therefore not really existing. *Existing.* That was the only thing he managed to do over the past three months and was continuing to do at that time while sitting alone in a sweltering hot apartment.

December. He hated December and just when he needed the connection of his family the most, it was the one December Erin decided to take the kids away on vacation. He had his suspicions that his mom had master minded the whole trip but he couldn't argue since he'd been the one to insist every year for the past half dozen that they do it. It wasn't her fault he refused to leave the city and at times in the grip of despair, refused to even leave his apartment. *He couldn't just move forward and forget. Not yet. Not before he formalized what it was he needed to do to make amends; that was, if there was anything he could do.*

Self-analysis of the dreams told him that they were the key to the answer he was searching for but he couldn't for the life of him figure out what or why. The only thing he knew for sure... *frickin' 4:00 am was way too early to rise on a cold December day.*

The forced black out had continued well into the night that night and, as Martin discovered, all the farms and ranches bordering the corridor that ran through his dad's property, experienced a tragedy of one kind or another.

There were no other human deaths but livestock died, or had to be put down, and buildings burned. The spring floods, the threat of assumption, and finally the heat wave, was way too much.

The push gave most still in the area the incentive to bail, with the alternatives suddenly very real and frightening – and limited. Most speculated that the black out that August night was deliberate but no one could prove it.

Martin stared at the clock. He did not want to rise like a farmer or be continually reminded of the tragic loss of one. That day was supposed to force change either in him or in his dad. He remembered sitting there in the High River diner, stalling, eating slowly, not wanting to impose, and all the while knowing he needed to. He felt it was his duty as a son to at least try because he had made many changes in his life up to that point. *Some felt he didn't deserve the chance he received but he would argue; he paid his dues and made his peace with everyone but his father.*

The answer to the struggle that pursued Martin lay in the content of the dreams and the horror he had to endure in reliving them on each and every night they occurred. It was a constant reminder he had unresolved business that must be brought to a culpable resolution. He knew the real reason behind the dream was the conscience of his guilt. He also knew that he was alone in this battle and he needed to make things right before it was too late.

Sitting on the edge of the bed, sweating and shivering all at once, Martin felt drained of life; physically he was really in little better position than the same time the previous year. He had kept his distance from drinking to extreme even though he maintained a fully stocked bar – the dreams forced him to take action to sleep. Without sleep, he couldn't function and if he couldn't get his rest then there would be no chance of thinking clear enough to devise any plan worth carrying out.

His brain ached. His heart ached. He lay back on the bed his feet still touching the cool hardwood floor. It would be easy to just give up. *What did he have to prove at this point?*

For as long as he could remember he always stood for something. He always had a plan or a way. He picked up the notebook and held it up over his head, reading and rereading the entries he'd made. Lying there, he tried to make sense of the senseless; it was like trying to determine if that little voice you heard way down deep inside your soul screaming out for help was your own. *If I just let things be what would happen? Who would care? No one depended on his expertise now, so why should he care?*

Martin never shied away from a challenge before and that, perhaps, was not only his best quality but his worst, as well.

Chapter 32 – Redemption

When the sirens sounded in northern Alberta, Martin knew what it was he was supposed to do. The resolution hit him in the gut. It was through his actions, whether coerced or voluntary that the processes for approval of the menace was expedited. Without his track record of industry success or his field of expertise, Alternative Energy Corporation would not have had the outlet by which to serve their directives. Martin realized too late that he should have stood for more than just progress. He should have stood his ground that day he visited the construction site in Peace County – it was then that red flags went up, waving brightly in his face, yet he ignored them.

But one man could not take down a whole industry especially when that industry was backed by a cutting edge government hell bent on taking Alberta to the forefront of industry innovation. The apparent stall in smart grid mandated implementation in 2011, kept the province on the reactive end of global advancements. New technology was being integrated into the system by several power divisions but they weren't being legislated as mandatory. Nuclear power over stepped what would seem to some to be a backward step and went forward with action.

Having ventured out into the brutal cold, Martin sat alone in the quiet solitude of his office, scribbling on some paper in distracted fashion. He had the Internet open to the local news just to keep an eye on the weather; he didn't fancy getting stranded in the office when getting stranded at home would do just fine.

The 'breaking news' logo appeared and the headlines read, "Nuclear One Sounds the Alarm." Martin sat up, his pen poised motionless over the inked notebook.

Now what?

His thoughts, his words had a déjà vu feeling to them and he remembered that a similar not too long ago exclamation proved to be that worst case scenario one always goes to yet hopes with all their heart for it to be untrue.

In this case, the worst case would be too extreme to imagine. He watched the reporter talk, unwilling to turn up the sound to hear his deepest fears repeated. A problem with a nuclear plant was not just a line or a pole going down in a snowstorm.

To date, considering the infiltration of nuclear plants throughout the world, there were not many examples of the process going bad but the ones that did were catastrophic. The results were far reaching and irreversible. He sat back and closed his eyes, thinking, not thinking, ignoring, and wishing it would just go away.

The buzz from his cell phone called him from his reverie and he cautiously checked the caller display, answering quickly when he realized it was Erin.

"Erin. What's up?"

"We just got back into the airport – Martin, the news..."

"Don't worry – and tell Mom not to worry, either..." he paused long enough to hear her start to struggle with a question. "It's okay, Erin, I just had a feeling she was with you and that's fine. I'm fine with it. I just needed my time."

"Martin – the news, is it true?"

"Sweetie, the whole system is set to signal at the slightest hint of irregularity. It could be something in the wind, that's how sensitive those gauges are – it was made like that for a reason. I didn't really listen to the news report but you know how they always jump the gun just a little bit."

"I just want to get home, Martin, and this weather is horrible. Mom's got the Escalade in the Park-n-Fly so we should be able to navigate our way into the city. Are you at the office?"

"Yes."

"Are you going to meet us at the house?"

"In a bit, as long as I don't get snowed in here," he stopped, and continued quickly, recovering before she could voice the anticipated disappointment, "...no, I won't stay too long." It was automatic now to correct his choices whenever he fell into the habit of just letting things go. He knew their relationship would take work and he was committed to making a true effort this time. He wouldn't deny that the temptation to just sell out remained with him and he had to wrestle with his decisions on more than one occasion.

"Okay, you promise, don't stay too late?"

"I won't, Erin. I'm just finishing up and reading through a paper I'm working on and I'll be along shortly. Erin?"

"Yes, Martin?"

"Tell the kids I love them."

He hung up wishing he had said more but knowing his containment was directed toward preserving the good in the whole situation. His emotions checked meant actions could be truly invested when the time came. He felt he could stretch it out until such time things were improved. *Considering the news that might never happened,* he thought, as he pulled a file folder from the lower desk drawer. His hand slid along a smooth familiar surface nestled against the back corner of the compartment. The familiarity with its contents returned to him as he pulled the bottle from its hiding place and sat it on the desk in front of him. He eyed the emptied afternoon coffee mug as a convenient receptacle. Martin poured a generous amount of the amber liquid and brought it to his lips. Just the smell enticed him and he had visions of relishing the taste of it as a large gulp burned the back of his throat then continued on to nestle into his very being with radiating warmth. *To go this route would be so easy – maybe just one drink, just one before I go, just one to get me through this hell I've created and don't really know how to escape.*

Faith pulled into the driveway of Erin's south side home plowing easily through the day's accumulation of snow. The kids piled out of the vehicle and ran to the entry way door playfully tossing small bits of snow at each other while they waited for their mother and grandmother. Erin smiled as she watched them together. Their happiness encouraged her to think about the evening ahead surrounded by family and warmth – *what could be better on a cold December evening a day away from the last night of the year?* It would be a great precursor to a memorable New Year's celebration if all went as she hoped. Martin was joining them for the evening and she would make the invitation permanent. She heard his hesitancy earlier on the phone and wondered, hoped, yet understood that he was still being cautious. There was no doubt he loved the kids and as a couple they had always shared a common bond even when they were apart; but it was more than just about being parents and sharing in the lives of their two children. She truly believed they were soul mates and, if the past half dozen years didn't prove that wrong, then it had to be the truth for which they were searching.

As Faith locked the vehicle, both women loaded with bags and blankets, a large dark car pulled into the driveway stopping within inches of their sport utility. Two heavy garmented occupants got out and herded the women to the house with whispered threats.

"We don't hurt children... so we won't do anything to change that if you both just cooperate."

The cup sat just off to one side of the paperwork Martin intended to review, still filled to the original line of initial temptation. He wasn't sure why he poured the drink except that it proved to him he didn't need it if he didn't take that first mouthful.

He sat staring at the web site with the latest news flashing away on his open lap top, ignored for the most part, but monumental in contributing to the depression that would hit if Martin let his guilt get the better of him. He had to keep reminding himself he was not the singular cause of what could be the worst disaster in the Alberta power history.

The core of the nuclear reactor, even on the coldest winter day, could accelerate quickly to an astronomical temperature that was far from just an 'overheated' unit. The advanced cooling system, installed to counteract any such increase within the core, had a tendency to just delay a breach, not prevent it. From all accounts, it looked as if the reactor was prematurely ignited without consideration to where all that wonderful nuclear power was going to go.

Martin could do something, as if anything would matter at that point, or he could numb the pain that was embedded within.

The ringing phone stalled his immediate decision and he glanced at the caller ID to determine if it could take a back seat for the time being.

The Power Commission.

Now why on earth would they be calling me? They made it clear my opinion and my expertise and my presence was not welcome.

He let the phone ring and it went to voice mail. He brought the mug to his lips and the phone rang again.

For God's sake, he thought, almost salivating at the thought of the rye coursing the lining of his throat – *just let me go.*

The Power Commission, again. He shook his head and put the mug down, picking up the phone without an answer.

"Mr. Wells?"

He just listened, wondering what the hell Raymond Knorr, Commission Chair wanted with him at this late hour at this late date in the worst year of his life.

"Martin? Sorry for being so informal but this call is an emergency. If you are listening to me, if you are there, please answer."

The longtime leader of the Commission never, in all his thirty years dealing with top industry business and bull shit, lost his cool. Martin sensed a difference in his voice having been around the man for many of his incumbent terms.

"Yes, I'm here."

"We called for an urgent meeting this afternoon and we had a very unpleasant encounter with someone you know."

"And this concerns me how? You haven't called on my opinion for six months or requested my expertise in any inquiry, why on earth would I care to hear about something unpleasant at this late hour?"

"Rowan Cott was before the Commission today to answer to the allegations dropped earlier in the year. Given the seriousness of the situation developing with Nuclear One we felt it was prudent to do so at this time."

"And if you would have found it fucking prudent back then, perhaps none of this would be happening now!"

Martin discovered in that moment the source of his lasting irritation. If they had taken him seriously earlier in the year and stuck to their decision, even when the new government took over, perhaps…

"Martin – he considers you a traitor to the industry and as much as pointed the sole responsibility in your direction, in an effort to absolve himself and Alternative Energy Corporation of any wrong doing."

"I knew he was a bastard."

"There's more, Martin. He made threats… and he suggested to me that I'd better call you to tell you. That you'd know what threats he was talking about."

Martin blanched and he felt his stomach churn with nausea – there he was sitting contemplating drinking himself into oblivion to escape and his family was in danger. The contents of the mug scattered across his desk as he grabbed his keys and cell phone. He pulled his coat on as he ran out the door to the underground parking garage, taking the stairs, two at a time

The blue machine slid into the curb at the end of the driveway and Martin was out of the car before it barely came to a stop. He ran past the pile of luggage sitting where it was dropped in the driveway and up the stairs opening the door as he ran.

Inside, he stopped.

Martin kept his mind focused on the situation – something he hadn't been able to do for a very long time. During long years of study and university preparation in his chosen career field; during presentations at the many commission hearings and inquiries; during his rise to infamy with AEC and then the backward slide to the acceptable position of private consultant; his frustrations, his losses, his rocky road to recovery – nowhere and in no situation had he been so focused and determined to remain in control.

Rowan was intent on exacting revenge.

The problems affecting the whole province were interfering in the one thing Rowan worshipped most, other than sex – money. Alternative Energy Corporation took the hit from the backlash related to the recent project issues. The question of the safety in nuclear power generation made headlines and he didn't like the negative attention. Contractors from the site were authorized only to reiterate that the "issue was a minor operational problem involving software interfaces and was in no way contributory to malfunctions which would affect the safe operations of the plant." That afternoon, the Power Commission pulled the previously filed regulatory approval for further nuclear development until the issue with Nuclear One was clarified and rectified to the satisfaction of the Commission. *If it could be rectified at all.*

Martin deduced from his follow up to the reports that the constant power surge to the grid was of such force that the partially upgraded transmission lines could only accept an influx to a certain point. A single plant operating at top capacity generated thousands megawatts of power to the grid in a matter of minutes. With nowhere to effectively go through a maintained continuous flow, there was an increased back powering to the core unit transformers.

It was a situation not initially anticipated. Power storage and containment was unavailable; the only recourse outlined in the initial standards was the push of electricity through extended transmission lines running through the utility corridor of Alberta directly into and through the United States and into Mexico and beyond. High voltage lines were required the entire length of the system and that was where Alternative Energy Corporation met its roadblock – the southern leg of the Alberta portion of the transmission upgrades were not yet constructed to par and had, in fact, fallen behind their allotted construction time schedule. The main impediment to AEC's project landed right in the vicinity of High River, Alberta, and its surrounding rural communities. One of the most prominent blocks to the innovative flow was the delay in the land acquisition that was comprised of the sprawling Wells' ranch.

And the main impediment to Rowan's scheduled rise to industry power was Martin Wells.

Martin quickly caught his breath while he surveyed the situation. There were two: Rowan and another hooded figure who remained off to one side of the entryway when he came in.

Faith and Erin sat side by side on the loveseat inside the den. He could see their fear and he tried to convey courage to calm them. His kids were not in sight and he hoped Rowan was at least true to his words about not hurting them and in that case he'd expect they were asleep in their own rooms a safe distance from whatever might happen.

"Lives are at stake, Rowan, or does that not matter at all to you?"

"The plant is safe. There is no threat in that community. Nuclear One is providing something we all need as Albertans... a guaranteed, low cost power source."

"No, it's proving that nuclear power doesn't belong here and it may be too late to decide whether or not we made a mistake by igniting that beast too soon."

"It was ready to go online and the benefits will be evident once this little glitch is fixed. That's all it is... a glitch."

He placed a patronizing hand on Faith's knee and patted it. "Don't worry, the benefits out weight the costs."

Faith pushed his hand away and slid closer to Erin, putting her arm around the younger woman's shoulder.

"There is no guarantee to any benefit at this point."

Martin's irritation with the man was growing and he would not back down to him again. It was obvious he was not going to admit there was a serious issue in northern Alberta and that to be concerned about the money aspect was irrelevant if there was a nuclear meltdown in the plant core. He was not going to continue this line of argument in front of his mother and his wife... his eyes met hers and he could see the tears.

"Well, it's too late for backing out now – the deals are signed and we extend power to the North American grid in a matter of months..."

"You don't have the authority and, besides, I hear the Commission already pulled your approvals."

"They gave me the authority when you signed those regulatory filings and they were approved through the Commission. They signed them! The government is just slow to keep up their end of the process with transmission upgrades. Stupid farmers are still hanging in there causing me grief. What? Do they need more collateral damage to get the picture?"

Rowan's face was red, his words seethed with anger; there was a hint of reference in his tirade that stabbed at Martin like a knife. He cringed, unable to ask directly, glancing quickly in his mother's direction.

"All that suffering just to line your pocketbook, Rowan, for personal gain. Where will it end?"

"It doesn't end until I'm well south of the border and..." he paused, with an intentional direct look to Martin, "more will suffer and more will die... if – they – refuse – to – comply."

The deliberate direction of Rowan's words twisted the knife. He now knew there was no accident that fateful August night. He knew his father would have stood up for what he believed to be true and right, despite all the legislation and scare tactics. If the Assumption Plan proponents arrived on his father's door he would have told them where to go. The livestock was his first priority in order to make amends and meet his obligations before he would have considered settling for his own consideration. He wouldn't have told them so in nice words – and that was what would have sealed his fate.

Martin lunged at Rowan. He wanted to strangle the man who caused so much strife, not only in his own life, but in the lives of others. Sure, he didn't do it alone but Martin was only one man and as such, he could take out a single match. His hands gripped the AEC officer's neck with a power he mustered from inside as they hit the floor with a deafening thud. Thoughts fuelled his determination as he was reminded of the lost time with his wife and kids, ruination of his reputation, erosion of his integrity, and finally the image of the fire that consumed his father. It was a painful realization to him that the voice he heard from deep within that burning building that night was his father's anguished cries for help.

One of the women screamed and there was a shot into the ceiling. Martin relaxed his gripped and Rowan pushed him to one side as he calmly rose to his feet.

Martin moved to do the same but remained sitting on the floor staring into the barrel of a 38. The shooter pulled the hood and mask from their face and he wasn't really surprised to see her.

"Stay there, Martin, or you will be very sorry."

"He'll be sorry enough in good time, Zanne. Why don't you go get the kids up? They need to say good-bye to their daddy."

Suzanne laughed and turned toward the hallway at the same instance Erin's eyes met Martin's desperate gaze. It was as if she knew what he was thinking and he knew what she would do.

"You will not touch my kids!"

Erin was small but fast and caught Suzanne by surprise knocking her to the floor and, in the process, dislodging the gun from her hand. Martin knew Erin wouldn't match her one on one without the element of surprise but knew that she would defend their children to the end if she had to; Martin needed to get to her before she was hurt or worse.

Martin, however, underestimated Rowan's anticipated reaction to his movement and he felt the sudden kick of the man's boot to the back of his head. As he fell forward, he heard another shot. He would be able to rise this time, and Rowan would stay on the floor. Faith held the gun firmly as if she had been handling one all her life. She moved her aim to the other target and Suzanne froze.

"Mom?"

"Martin. He killed my Martin."

"He can't hurt anyone else now."

"Erin, I hear Essie."

"Mom. Let me take that and you call 9-11. Erin, honey, please check on the kids and keep them in their rooms."

Martin took charge despite the pain in his neck and the reopened wound on his shoulder. Suzanne, covered with a large winter coat, her hair all askew, looked hardly the temptress she might have once been to him. Looking down on her at that moment he felt anger and betrayal, yet was relieved in some small way to have this part of the worry, over for good.

"Aw, Martin. You and me, we were good." She drew out the line in a sultry voice her intended target arriving back in the room.

"Martin told me all about you," Erin smiled, "yes, everything, bitch. So you're little attempt to cross him and I won't work because we are a team. It just took a lot of players to show us that..." She grasped Faith's hand, trying to comfort the woman who had become one of her best friends. "We are all a team and that, 'Zanne', is something you will never know."

The sound of sirens moving closer to the neighborhood brought a wash of relief to Martin. Suzanne went with the police without further comment to the Wells family.

As the scene was inspected and evidence tagged, Martin pushed the thoughts of all else from his mind. Attending officers took their statements; EMTs made quick routine assessments finding, to their disbelief, no other injuries needing attention; the Medical Examiner's officer removed the body of Rowan Jasper Cott. It was only then that Martin felt the true sensation of freedom, knowing this time, he would never see that manipulative asshole again.

A quiet evening enjoyed as a family ensured a special New Year's Eve celebration. Faith had actually laughed out loud at their invitation to 'camp out' in the middle of Martin's apartment living room. With sleeping bags spread over the carpet and snuggly blankets tucked up under their chins, the children giggled themselves to an early sleep without obvious repercussions of the night before.

"Goodnight, you two."

Faith decided to leave Martin and Erin alone to talk and shushed a dual protest with a quick hug to both.

"I'll take your bed, Martin. See you in the morning."

She left them to the glow of low lit lamps and quietly closed the bedroom door at the end of the hallway.

"Erin?"

"Martin?"

"There's something I want you to know. I meant to say it earlier but I was afraid and fearful and all those less than bravely men things…" She put a finger to his lips to silence him and touched the side of his face.

"I know… I love you, too."

Their impassioned kiss matched and exceeded the one they shared so long ago; the one that made them realize there was still something there despite the turmoil and confusion it caused; despite the separation they endured and the anxiety that resulted. In the end, soul mates find each other because they are destined to do so no matter what happens in the world around them.

Erin and Martin held each other close in an embrace that would solidify the vows they once made, and promised hope for the future they knew they deserved if only they worked together.

The lamps flickered and all went dark.

Content in one another's arms, they fell asleep, unaware that all the lights in all the houses on all the streets in this city to the next, went black.

About the author:

Born and raised in Edmonton and Sherwood Park AB, Linda found a place to feel right at home with her writing passion - the Writers Circle and the Writers Foundation of Strathcona County (WFSC). Both are important components of her writing life. Although poetry is her first love and was the mainstay of her writing for many years, screenplays, novels, short stories, non-fiction articles, and blogs have made their way into her writing repertoire.

For this author, dedication to the craft involves a constant learning – sharing – creating triad:

- always **learn** new things to improve your skills
- **share** time and expertise with others to promote their work and achievements
- actively **create** your own new work

The balance shifts from one to another, but the triad is always there in one way or another. With focus and forward momentum, fulfillment of a writer's dream is only a process away.

One key piece of advice this author offers and lives:

"Be true to your creative spirit."

Her mantra:

"Learn the rules like a pro,
so you can break them like an artist. "   ~ Pablo Picasso

… break all the rules... and be your own artist.

Linda is a published author with ebooks available on Smashwords and Amazon Kindle. She has written several electrical industry papers for her job as Business Management Coordinator with the AFREA in Sherwood Park. She is a contributing writer for the online news magazine Strathcona Connect. To read blog posts inspired by her writing life and to link with fellow writers, visit Linda's blog:

http://www.wildhorse33.wordpress.com

Follow her on Facebook
@wildhorse33 on Twitter

Other works by this author:

A Journey of Brothers – Novella I (2012)
A Writer's Life ~ My Ode to the Bard (2013)

Contributions to:
Writing Prompt Journey ~ The Road to Your Creativity (2010)
From a Solitary Drop ~ History of the Strathcona County
        Writers Circle (2001 – 2011)
Your Lifetime of Stories ~ WFSC Writing Series Workbook (2013)

Watch for her upcoming novel:
An Elizabethan Affair
 and
Novella II and III – the continuation to *A Journey of Brothers*